T0005557

PRIMARY STORM

BRENDAN DUBOIS

SEVERN RIVER PUBLISHING

Severn River Publishing
www.SevernRiverBooks.com

This is a work of fiction. Names, characters, businesses, places, events and incidents are either the products of the author's imagination or used in a fictitious manner. Any resemblance to actual persons, living or dead, or actual events is purely coincidental.

ISBN: 978-1-64875-443-2 (Paperback)

ALSO BY BRENDAN DUBOIS

The Lewis Cole Series

Dead Sand

Black Tide

Shattered Shell

Killer Waves

Buried Dreams

Primary Storm

Deadly Cove

Fatal Harbor

Blood Foam

Storm Cell

Hard Aground

Terminal Surf

To find out more about Brendan DuBois and his books, visit

severnriverbooks.com

To Jeannette Pinette, Paul Pinette, and the memory of Roland Pinette.

Qui habitent dans les montages et dans mon coeur.

FOREWORD

Welcome to this, my sixth novel in my Lewis Cole mystery series, and in some way, the most personal. Often, I'm asked what I have to do in terms of research to write a book, and while I've done considerable research in my other works, such is not the case here. For having lived in New Hampshire all my life, the research for PRIMARY STORM was just living here every four years, when the New Hampshire primary kicks in. The mention of the campaign signs, rallies, endless phone calls and mailboxes stuffed with campaign literature is not exaggerated one bit in this novel.

It may not be fair, and may not make real sense, but I and so many others in my quirky home state take pride in hosting the first in the nation's presidential primary. True, we're not typical when it comes to demographics or income, but we take our responsibility very, very seriously. We listen to the candidates, we attend campaign rallies, and unlike the bigger states, we force them to answer our questions. There's an old joke that says something to the effect of a reporter asking a resident if he intended to vote for a certain candidate. The answer: "I don't know. I've only met him three or four times."

True, we're spoiled. And we know it. And when I was a newspaper reporter during the 1984 primary, I knew just how spoiled we journalists were. Senator Alan Cranston is in town. Would you like a one-on-one conversation with him? Sure. Senator Gary Hart will be in town tomorrow morning. Would you like to have breakfast with him? Absolutely. Governor Reuben Askew would like to share some conversation time with you. Why not?

In fact, the only candidate who didn't approach me and my little newspaper at the time was Vice President Walter Mondale, who later got stomped hard when the votes were finally cast in the primary, being defeated by Senator Hart.

Guess you should have stopped by, eh, Walter?

1

Two days before I was arrested for attempted murder, I was driving down the snow-covered collection of ruts that mark my driveway when I spotted the man standing outside my home on Tyler Beach, New Hampshire. To get to my driveway, one has to pass through the parking lot of the Lafayette House, a huge Victorian style hotel set on the opposite side of Atlantic Avenue, and past the odd collection of SUVs and luxury vehicles that belong to guests at the hotel. The past month or so had seen a rash of break-ins among the guests' parked vehicles, but I didn't see any broken glass as I drove through the lot, so maybe the forces of light were winning over the forces of darkness, or at least, the forces of vandalism.

What I did eventually see was my unanticipated visitor. The man standing at the doorway did not seem to be a hotel guest; there was no apparent luggage in sight. He was in his early thirties, slim, wearing a dark gray heavy coat that reached mid-thigh, dark pants, and some sort of sensible winter shoe. He looked at me and I looked at him as I pulled into the unattached shed that served as a garage, right next to my home.

I gathered up my mail—retrieved a while ago from my PO box at the Tyler post office—and got out of my Ford Explorer, knowing I would probably have to go back to town later in the day to take care of a forgotten errand at my local bank. Outside, the cold salt air felt refreshing, but I didn't like the look of the guy as I approached him. He had sharp hunter's eyes, and his black hair was cut close and trim and looked perfect, like it had been trimmed by someone who charged three figures for a haircut. Up close, I could see that he was wearing a blue striped shirt and a red necktie underneath the long coat. There was a light snow falling from the gray sky.

"Lewis Cole?" he asked.

"That's right," I said. "What can I do for you?"

He said, "I'd like to ask you a few questions, if you don't mind."

Being the middle of January, it was cold, and I wondered how long my visitor had been waiting for me outside. "Sorry, I do mind."

"Excuse me?"

"I said, I'm sorry, I do mind. I don't know you, and I don't know why I should answer your questions."

He nodded. "A good point. My apologies."

He reached into his coat pocket, took out a thin leather wallet, and flipped it open. As I looked at his photo and the cardboard identification slip and the nice shiny badge, the man decided to be redundant and announce himself.

"Mr. Cole, the name is Spenser Harris. And I'm an agent with the Secret Service, from the Boston office."

I looked up to his sharp face. "All right," I said. "I guess I don't mind after all. Let's get inside."

"Thanks."

I unlocked the door, kicked the snow off my boots, and went inside. Before me was a closet and closed door that led to a small cellar, flanked by a stairway that aimed up to the second floor. To the left was the small living room and sliding glass doors for the rear deck. Next to the sliding glass doors was a tiny kitchen that had a nice view of the Atlantic Ocean. Most every room in my house was described as being small, which happens when one's house is more than a hundred years old and once was a lifeboat station that rescued mariners on their way in and out of Porter Harbor, just up the coast.

I tossed the mail on the couch and followed it up with my coat, and then I looked over at my guest, standing there, slim and polite. I said, "Curious to know why the Secret Service is visiting here today."

"Strictly routine," he said, offering me a smile that said the visit was anything but. He started unbuttoning his clean coat and said, "Mind if I sit down?"

"Go right ahead."

Any other guest I would have offered tea or coffee or some other liquid refreshment, but I didn't like the look of Agent Harris, and I didn't like the way he had barged in on my day, standing out there like that. He could have easily called me to make an appointment, away from my house, like at a coffee shop or something. Instead, he had stood outside in the cold January weather, knowing I'd be back soon. Which meant some sort of surveillance, which meant some sort of effort on the Secret Service's part, which meant this visit wasn't routine, no matter his cheery nature.

From his coat he took out a small notebook, flipped it open with an experienced toss of the wrist, and said, "Mr. Cole, in just over a week, the New Hampshire primary will take place."

"As a resident of New Hampshire, I don't think I need the reminder."

"I'm sure," he said. "And part of our duties within the Secret Service is to do a threat assessment of the area whenever prominent candidates come by to make an appearance. For example, tomorrow Senator Jackson Hale will be stopping by the Tyler Conference Center."

"So I've heard."

"And my job is to interview those people who appear on our list of...well, people we're interested in."

This was becoming fascinating. I eyed him and said, "Are you telling me that the Secret Service considers me a threat?"

"Not at all," he said, protesting just a bit too much. "It's just that we have a list of people who have come to our attention over the years. Most of the time, it's just cranks. Guys who tend to hate anything and everything. Guys who've been overheard at bars making threats against prominent candidates. There are also a couple of high school students on the list as well, who've written e-mails threatening to kill the president. Unfortunately for them, they're going to get visited every few years if they come within a certain distance of the president or a presidential candidate."

"And how did I come to appear on your little list?"

"Something about your background, Mr. Cole."

"I'm sure," I said. "But I've been a resident of New Hampshire for a number of years. Why now?"

He shrugged. "I gather that we've been tasked to be more wide-ranging and thorough in our reviews. Now, from the records I've reviewed, I see that you used to be with the Department of Defense. Correct?"

"Yes."

"You were a research analyst with a little-known intelligence interpretation group within the department."

"Also correct."

"Now," he said, shifting his weight on my couch, "this is where it gets a bit interesting. According to the records we've been able to review, you left this group under...under questionable circumstances. And being with the Department of the Treasury, we were also able to ascertain that you receive a monthly compensation payment from a certain disbursement fund within the Department of Defense. It appears that for a number of years, even with your position as a columnist for *Shoreline* magazine, that you have received a healthy payment from the government."

I looked at Agent Harris and wondered if I should boost the thermostat up a notch, for there was a wicked wind coming off the Atlantic, finding its way through some odd nooks and crannies by the sliding glass doors.

I kept on looking at him.

"Well?" he asked.

"Yes?"

"I'm sorry, I didn't hear your reply."

"Oh," I said. "I'm equally sorry. I didn't hear a question."

There was a tiny bit of a struggle on that composed face, and I wasn't sure if I had angered him or humored him, but he pressed on and said, "I guess I'm just asking you to confirm what I've just said."

Well, there you go. Aloud I said, "I'm sorry, when I left the employ of the Department of Defense, I signed a standard nondisclosure form. I have nothing to say."

"Can you tell me why you left the Department of Defense, Mr. Cole?"

"No, I cannot."

"Can you tell me if your departure had anything to do with your mental state or capacity?"

I was going to say something rude and sarcastic about that question but thought better of it. Open that door, just a tiny bit, and Agent Harris could slip in and raise merry hell for the rest of the day, poking and probing. I was going to have none of that. So I said, "I'm sorry, I can't say anything more than what I just said."

"Can you tell me if your experiences in the Department of Defense have left you angry? Bitter? Holding a grudge?"

"Yes, yes, no," I said. "Clear enough for you?"

"Not really."

"But it'll have to do. I'm sorry."

A flip of the page. "Do you have any opinions about Senator Hale?"

I shrugged. "Last I checked, he's one of four candidates for his party's nomination. Having won the Iowa caucuses, he might be unbeatable if he were to win in New Hampshire."

"Excuse me, Mr. Cole, but that's not an opinion. That's a news report."

"Maybe so, but my opinions I keep to myself."

A tiny bit of a smile. "Good for you then."

"Are we almost done?"

"Almost."

"I believe that you are...let's say romantically involved with a member of Senator Hale's campaign staff. Correct?"

"Partially correct," I said. "She's a volunteer. She's not a member of his paid staff. That I know of."

"But you and a...Miss Annie Wynn have been together now for a few months. True?"

"Also true, and none of your damn business."

"Have you attended any of Senator Hale's political functions in the past?"

"Nope."

"Do you plan to attend the rally tomorrow?"

"Depends," I said.

"And what might that depend on?"

I looked him squarely in the eye. "It depends on whether my attendance there will improve my chances of later wining, dining, and bedding his fair campaign aide."

That brought a smile. He closed the notebook. "Very good, Mr. Cole."

I walked him outside and, by then, he had transformed himself from Chilly Secret Service Agent to Tired Guy with Lots of Work to Do. He said, "Sorry about being so inquisitive and such, but in these times, it's better to look at things more closely than have something slip by. There's a list and each name on that list has to be checked off by an agent who's juggling lots of cases. For every ninety-nine interviews like yours, we'll get one where a guy is sitting in his living room with a dozen dogs in the house, piles of pizza boxes on the floor, pictures of the candidate plastered on the walls, and an AK-47 across his lap."

"Seen any AK-47s lately?"

"It certainly isn't for lack of trying," he said. Outside he rebuttoned his coat, shivered. It was now dark. It got dark early in New Hampshire in January, a law of nature, but it didn't mean it was a law I particularly liked. The falling snow had stopped but no doubt it would return the next day, next week, and next month.

Agent Harris said, "In these particular times, you really have to make the extra effort to nail everything down. One missed appointment, one follow-up you don't make...well, if that guy shows up with a bow and arrow at a campaign appearance, and it could have been prevented by you, it's a hell of a thing."

"I can imagine."

"Sure. The news coverage alone would send you to a field office in Nome...but on days like this, Nome seems a hell of a lot warmer."

"Been here before?"

"Sure. Primary season, four years ago. When all the candidates, news media, and assorted hangers-on and campaign staff bustle around your fair state, the Secret Service follows."

"Sounds like the guy whose job at the circus is to follow the elephants with a broom and big shovel."

That got a laugh from him as he turned to me and said, "Thanks again for your cooperation."

"Not a problem. Are we done?"

Even in the poor light coming from my house, I could make out the smile on his otherwise serious face. "Sure we're done. Just don't write any threatening letters with crayon and grocery bag paper, and we won't ever see you again."

"It's a deal."

One brief handshake later, he trudged up the hill to the parking lot, and I watched him until he was out of sight. I shivered from the cold, walked into the house, stamped off snow from my boots, and went inside, shaking my head at what had just happened. Poorly run job, if this was what passed as Secret Service agents nowadays.

For I had a connection to the fair senator, a rather intimate connection, and I was surprised that the Secret Service agent hadn't called me on it.

But surprises and the thought of surprises could wait. It was time for dinner, and a special guest. My planned trip to the bank would have to wait. I turned on the outside lights for my guest and went to work.

I went to the stove and began with the basic bachelor cooking technique, i.e., boiling water, and started two pots, one large, the other small. When they had boiled long enough and hard enough, I went into the refrigerator and took out a small paper bag, nestled within a plastic bag, secured earlier this day on a shopping expedition. I opened the bag and carefully reached in twice, pulling out two pound-and-a-half lobsters.

Saying, "Sorry about that, guys," I tossed them into the water and put the cover on the larger pot. There was a faint clatter and then silence.

With the other, smaller pot boiling merrily along, I threw in some fettuccine noodles and set the timer. About ten minutes to go, which gave me time to microwave an Alfredo sauce I had made that morning, and to wash and tear some chunks of romaine lettuce. When the simple salads were complete, the lobsters were done, and I pulled them out of the pot with a set of metal tongs.

There was a sound at the door. I turned, one steaming red lobster held in my hand, water dripping on my kitchen floor.

A redheaded woman came into the kitchen, wearing black slacks, small winter boots, and a heavy red cloth jacket, which she was shrugging out of as she came up to me. She dropped a leather purse and a soft black leather overnight bag on the floor. A quick kiss and Annie Wynn said, "Honey, I'm home."

"That you are," I said. "Thanks for coming back on time."

"You're welcome."

"Hungry?" I asked.

"Starved."

"Good. Earn your keep, why don't you, and set the table." That earned me a swat on the rump, and she grabbed some silverware and dishware as I cracked open the lobster, washed the meat in the sink, and cut it up in small pieces. The fettuccine was done, which meant a trip to the strainer, and in a minute or two, we were at the bar side of the kitchen countertop, sharing the dinner, and a bottle of Australian pinot noir as well.

"How's things with you?" I asked.

"Great."

"Really?"

She shrugged. "Most of the people at Hale headquarters are eating two-day-old pizza. I, on the other hand, told my coworkers that I had a man waiting for me, a man waiting to cook me dinner. Be thankful I got out of Manchester in time."

"Thankful I am. How goes the campaign?"

"It goes," she said. "It goes. I've been doing a lot of phone work, trying to winnow out a list of campaign contributors here in the state that have yet to pull out their checkbooks or bank account for the good of the party."

"Are you good at taking money away from citizens?"

She smiled. "Quite good. Which will no doubt serve me well when I get my law degree, also known as a license to make money."

"Just what the world needs. A good-looking redhead lawyer who likes money."

"And likes magazine writers as well."

I smiled back. "Lucky me."

"Damn straight," she said, and we ate for a while longer, and she said, "So, what's new with you?"

"Well," I said. "When I came back from the post office today, like you, there was a man waiting for me at the house. But he wasn't here to make dinner."

"Really? A campaign volunteer?"

"Not really," I said. "A Secret Service agent. From their Boston office.

Seems he's in the area, doing prep work for tomorrow's rally for Senator Hale."

"What kind of prep work?"

If I do say so, the fettuccine and lobster dish was delicious, and I hurried in another bite before replying. "The Secret Service maintains a list of what they call 'persons of interest' that they interview before a campaign appearance by a presidential candidate. Guys who write threatening letters to the UN. Guys who're known to be stalkers. Guys with interesting criminal records."

"You've got any of those things in your background?"

"Nope."

She pursed her fine lips. "Then you must be interesting indeed. Did he take you down to headquarters? Pull out the rubber hoses? The folded-over phone books?"

"None of the above, counselor. We had a nice little chat in the living room, he determined that I'm not watching for black helicopters to come kidnap me, and then he left. End of visit."

Another forkful of dinner went into her mouth. "So why the interest in you?"

"Because of my years at the Department of Defense, I imagine."

She shook her head. "No, I don't think so. I think it's because of what happened to you at the DoD, and the circumstances of your departure. That's why."

I didn't reply. She was skating into an area I really didn't want to visit, and I think she sensed it, for she smiled and said, "I guess they were looking for a disgruntled nut and came up empty."

I returned the smile. "I may be a nut, but I'm not disgruntled. If anything, I'm very gruntled."

That made her laugh, and she tossed her napkin at me, and in a matter of minutes, dinner was complete.

In the living room I started a fire in the fireplace, and Annie took the couch and watched one of the early evening cable network shows as I did cleanup in the kitchen. Before I started, I gave her a kiss and she said, "Lacey, one of the communications people back in Manchester, she said if she had a man waiting to make her dinner and clean up afterward, she'd jump him on the kitchen table when he was done."

"Sounds like marvelous campaign advice."

She touched my cheek and said, "Kitchen tables can be so uncomfortable."

I nodded in agreement. "Sure. Crumbs. Butter dishes. Odd pieces of silverware."

"But your bed is nice and wide and warm."

"Sure is."

"Hurry up in the kitchen then, sport."

I walked back. "Free advice from a lawyer-to-be. Better not let the Massachusetts Bar Association hear about that."

I thought she'd say something sharp in reply, but by then, she was curled up on the couch, remote control in her red-painted fingernails. I kept an occasional eye on her as I scrubbed out the pots and washed the dishes and silverware and glassware. There were no leftovers—thankfully, for usually leftovers in my refrigerator transmute themselves into science experiments within a week or so—but there was entertainment as I worked. Annie takes her work and her politics quite seriously, and from the kitchen I heard her shout back at the television, "Moron! Idiot! No, you're behind in the polls because your candidate can only debate the issues when a script is written for him!"

I kept on cleaning and then wiped down the kitchen countertop, and when things were dried and put away and the lobster shells were put into the trash, I went out into the living room.

The television was still on, another cable news show was broadcasting a couple of campaign operatives screaming at each other, the fire had died down, and Annie Wynn, my Annie Wynn, was lightly snoring on the couch, the remote still in her fingers.

I gingerly pried the remote from her hand, set the television timer to shut down in fifteen minutes so the sudden quiet wouldn't wake her, and I gently picked her up. She started murmuring and through a quiet yet forceful touch, I got her off the couch and upstairs in my bed in just a manner of minutes, holding on to her tight as we maneuvered up the stairway. There were two highlights of bringing her into my bedroom: undressing her and seeing what manner of undergarments she had chosen that day, and the sweet wine-tasted kiss I got from her as I slid her under the sheets, and the way she murmured, "Thank you so much for taking care of me."

I pulled the sheet and blankets up. Taking care of someone.

It had been a very long time since I had taken care of anyone, and though I was seriously out of practice, I found that, to my surprise, I was liking it.

I checked the clock. It was not even 9:00 P.M. I wasn't tired but I didn't want to go downstairs and watch television by myself, so I got undressed and slipped inside the cool bedding and switched on a reading lamp. By now I was learning about Annie and her habits and foibles, and one thing I knew was that once she had fallen asleep, it would take something on the order of a tidal wave to wake her up.

So I read for a long while, a biography of Winston Churchill, and I enjoyed the sensation of being warm and safe and having a woman slumbering in bed with me. I read until the book seemed to gain weight in my hands and fall on my chest, and soon enough, the reading lamp was out and I was asleep. The touch woke me up, and I was startled for just a moment, wondering where I was, wondering where my weapons were. Then I felt the touch again, the light scraping of fingernails against my back. I kept still and silent, just liking the touch of her hand upon me, and then her lips were at my ear, whispering, "Are you awake?"

"I am now."

The scratches were wider on my back. She kissed and licked and nibbled at my ear, and then her hand moved about, so it was now scratching at my chest. She snuggled up against me, her warm skin upon my back and rear and legs, and she said, her voice still quiet, "I meant to tell you something earlier, but I forgot."

"You did, did you. What is it?"

Another kiss, a flick of her tongue against my ear. "You're a secretive man, Lewis, but I have secrets of my own."

"Keep on talking."

She giggled. "I'm part of a confidential organization, providing technical support to the Secret Service. And I've been tasked to subject you to a severe interrogation."

I rolled over and she was in my arms, and I kissed her and she kissed me back, and I looked up at her in the faint moonlight and said, "I surrender."

She moved about, so that she was gently straddling me, and the bed suddenly got warmer. She bent down, her red hair tickling my nose. "Have you now, or have you ever been, a member of the Communist party?"

"No."

She started moving on top of me. I held her tight, with my hands against her side, her flesh smooth and warm. "Have you now, or have you ever been, a member of a group advocating the violent overthrow of the government of the United States?"

"No...ma'am."

I kissed her and she lightly moaned, and said, "Have you now, or have you ever been, a male with extensive lovemaking fantasies?"

"Guilty as charged," I managed to say.

"Good," she said, holding on to me with her strong hands. "Interrogation over."

"Best news I've heard all night."

"Oh, stop talking already," she said. "You started it."

And she didn't say anything for a while after that, and neither did I.

2

Sometime in the morning the shower was running, and I suppose a male who subscribed to *Playboy* magazine and worked out and was in top shape and form would have leapt out of bed to jump in the shower and wash Annie's back and see what else happened. However, since I'm one of those few who do buy *Playboy* occasionally for the articles and its fine fiction, I confess that I looked at the time and rolled over and went back to sleep. She's a dear but she can thrive and flourish on four or five hours of sleep, which I still didn't understand. I suppose I could give it a try, but I doubted I would live that long.

So when I eventually woke up, got dressed, and went downstairs, she was finishing an English muffin and a glass of orange juice and she had gotten changed into the contents of her overnight bag, which was now slung over her shoulder. For some reason my stomach felt queasy, and the sight of the food and drink made me just a bit nauseous. Probably the after-effects of not enough sack time and a too-rich dinner.

Annie said, "I would have made you breakfast, except you were still snoring and sleeping."

"Only half true, counselor. I was sleeping. I wasn't snoring."

"Says you. Give me a kiss good-bye."

"Sure," I said. "But not here. Up at the parking lot."

"Oh, you romantic, you."

I took the overnight bag from her shoulder and grabbed a coat from the downstairs closet. We both went outside into the early January morning. It was overcast. It seemed like every day this past week had been overcast.

Annie said, "Brrr. Damn cold. Sick of it, I really do get sick of it."

"Part of the grand plan," I said.

"What's that?"

"To make us appreciate summer more," I said.

"Bah," she said. "Sounds like crap our Puritan ancestors made up to justify the lousy weather, and for settling their poor butts in this part of the world. Come along, sport, let's go."

She slipped her arm into mine as we maneuvered our way up my frozen driveway. To our left were a mess of boulders and rocks that marked this part of the eighteen-mile New Hampshire coastline, and to our right was a sharp rise of land and more rocks, hiding Route 1-A, also known as Atlantic Avenue, from my house, and vice versa. Before us was the Lafayette House's parking lot and Annie's BMW—leased from a Boston law firm that she did work for as a paralegal—and I said, "Still can't believe the firm lets you drive that Beemer, seeing how you took a leave of absence and all."

She squeezed her arm against mine. "They see it as an investment, Lewis. All those potentially juicy contacts I can make during the campaign might pay off down the road. You know what the three biggest pastimes in Boston are, don't you?"

"Sports, politics, and revenge."

A quick laugh. "You've learned well."

At her BMW she turned, and I gave her a quick kiss, and she said, "See you at the rally today?"

"I don't see why not. What time is it again?"

"Two p.m. At the Tyler Conference Center."

I had my hands on her hips. "Will I see you?"

"Probably from a distance, Lewis. But I'd like to know you were there."

"Then I will be."

She touched my cheek. "Two o'clock. Don't be late."

"I won't. Maybe I'll see my Secret Service agent friend."

"Maybe you will. Maybe he'll show you his gun and everything."

"Sounds like something you'd like."

That got a big smile and she got into her BMW, started it right up, and then left the parking lot, and I got a *toot-toot* from the horn as she turned onto Atlantic Avenue, and that's how this day started, a day before I was to be arrested for attempted murder. About halfway down the driveway, there came another blare of a horn, and I turned, half hoping and half expecting to see that Annie had come back, perhaps having forgotten something, perhaps deciding that crawling back into bed with me and seeing what Turner Classic Movies had to offer for the day on television sounded more appealing than a campaign rally, but no, I wasn't that lucky.

A blue Mercedes-Benz convertible had stopped at the parking lot, and a man came out, clad in a long gray winter coat, gray slacks, and wearing black leather gloves. He waved and I waved back. I stopped, putting my hands in my coat pocket, as the man quickly made his way down my driveway. Any other guy wearing those kind of dress winter shoes would have taken his time walking down the slippery driveway, but Felix Tinios isn't what one would call any other kind of guy. He came down to me, nimble as a mountain goat, and gently slapped me on the shoulder as he came up to me.

"Lewis, good to see you," he said.

"And the same. Did you give anybody a wave back there?"

That confused him. "From the parking lot? Why?"

"Dumb joke, that's all. The Lafayette House has seen a number of its guests lose radios and other stuff from parked cars over the past several weeks. Rumor has it they now have the lot under surveillance."

"Then I would have dropped trou, if I knew that."

"A lovely sight to some, I'm sure. What brings you by?"

Felix said, "Was heading down to Boston and gave you a call. No answer on your end, so I thought I'd swing by and see what's up."

"I was seeing somebody off. Didn't hear the phone."

Felix grinned, cocked his head. "The lovely and talented Annie Wynn?"

"The same."

"Good for you. C'mon, it's too cold out here. I need a quick chat."

"What for?"

"Need your advice, that's what."

I looked at the smooth-shaven face, the thick mat of black hair, the cocky confidence in his brown and happy eyes. Felix was originally from the North End of Boston and told people he didn't know that well that his occupation was security consultant, but I knew him well and I knew him better. I folded my arms and I said, "You feel that?"

"Feel what?"

"Felt like the Earth was spinning off its axis. Because I thought I heard you say you needed my advice."

Felix grabbed my upper arm with a firm grasp and said, "Come on. Maybe this will be a day full of surprises."

In my house I made us both a cup of tea, and though I should have been hungry, I wasn't. We sat at the kitchen counter and Felix had his coat off, revealing a black turtleneck sweater and the usual bulk of his shoulders. He clasped the hot mug with both of his hands, and I said, "Advice. What in hell kind of advice can I give you? Spelling? Grammar? How to get an agent?"

He looked hurt by my comments. "I'll have you know that when I was in seventh grade, at St. Mary's Academy, I won a rosary in a spelling bee."

"A rosary? Do you still have it?"

"Of course."

"And do you say your rosary?"

He lifted up the mug, smiled. "Every goddamn night. Look, here's the deal. I've got a job lined up for the next couple of weeks, and I want to make sure that it won't cause any difficulties with you and yours."

"What kind of job?"

He took a slurp. "Working for one of the presidential candidates."

"Which one?"

"Senator Nash Pomeroy. From our fair sister state to the south."

I took a sip from my own tea, grimaced. The nausea down there was perking right along. Two thoughts: I hoped I didn't have food poisoning, because it sure as hell would mean Annie would have the same problem. And I sure as hell hoped it wouldn't keep me from this afternoon's rally.

"I knew the senator was in trouble when he lost the Iowa caucuses, but now his campaign must be really collapsing."

"Why's that?"

I resisted an urge to burst out laughing, because Felix had such a serious look on his face. "My God, Felix, your background...I mean, no offense, but how many times have you been arrested?"

"No offense taken, and trust me, I don't particularly care about the number of arrests. It's the number of convictions that matter. And that number is quite, quite low. Just so you know."

"Maybe in your world arrests don't matter, Felix, but this is politics. Any hint of scandal with the campaign and...well, hell, it can't matter to them, because you've said you've been hired."

"That I have."

"Doing what? Security? Driving around the candidate?"

"Nope." Another sip of tea. "Oppo man."

"What?"

"Oppo. Opposition research. You've heard of that, I'm sure."

"Sure. Digging up dirt on the other guys. Sounds beneath you, Felix."

"Maybe so, but it's good money...and can I tell you a secret?"

"Sure."

He made a point of looking around, and again, I was going to laugh, but that look on his face...It was a different look, a hesitant one. "Here's my secret. Tell anybody and...well, I know you. You won't tell anyone. Thing is, Lewis, I don't know why, but this winter is slowing me down. Get up in the morning, the usual aches and pains I got, they don't disappear like they used to. Working out...the thought of starting up a cold car and driving out to the gym in the morning, when it's so goddamn dark...I don't know, maybe I'm getting old. More often than not, I stay home instead."

I tried to keep my voice innocent. "Getting old is the secret I should be keeping?"

"No," he said, his eyes flashing at me. "Slowing down is the secret you should be keeping. And a lawyer acquaintance of mine, we were talking a couple of weeks ago, said that the Pomeroy campaign needed some help. Wondered if I could do it, and he mentioned the money, and it's good money for work that mostly involves talking. This winter, talking I can handle. The other stuff...well, there's always spring."

"Yeah, you can count on that. So. What's the advice you're seeking?"

He put the mug down on the counter. "Okay. Maybe it isn't advice. Maybe it's just reassurance. I like Annie. I like you and Annie together. It's a good thing, something good you've needed for a while. But I don't want her pissed at me—and through me, you—because she's working for the Hale campaign and I'm working for the Pomeroy campaign."

I nodded. "A sweet attitude, but I don't think it'll make a difference...except, well, there's two other candidates besides Hale and Pomeroy. Congressman Wallace and General Grayson. Who will you be doing the opposition research on? If it's Wallace or Grayson, I doubt she'd care. If it's Hale, she might be pissed no matter what I say."

That made Felix smile again. "I'm doing oppo research on Senator Pomeroy."

"Hold on. The campaign that's hiring you, they want you to dig dirt up on their own guy?"

"Sure," he said.

Despite my nausea, I had to smile. "Come on, you've got to tell me more. It doesn't make sense."

"On the contrary, it makes a lot of sense. Nobody—especially a guy running for president—wants to come forward and expose his warts and imperfections. They hide, they shade, they ignore. Just ask what happened to McGovern back in 1972 when he went shopping for a vice presidential candidate, and his first selection turned out to be a guy who went through electroshock therapy treatment for depression. And people who back candidates—the guys with money, the guys with power—they don't want surprises. When you're this close to getting nominated for the most powerful office on the planet, they want to make sure everything is vetted. They don't want something to blow up in their faces at the very last minute, ensuring that their investment has gone for nothing. That's what I'll be doing, working as if I were one of Pomeroy's opponents, instead of coming from his own campaign."

"You've been reading up on political theory?"

"Theories I learned came from the streets, my friend." He finished off his tea and said, "So. We okay?"

"Yeah, we're fine. Go ahead and do your oppo research. And by the by, here's one bit of advice."

"All right. I'm in a good mood, I'll take it."

I raised my tea mug in his honor. "Make sure you get paid in advance, or at least on a regular basis. In politics, bills sometimes get lost, sometimes get ignored, and more often than not, never get paid when the campaign is over. There's lots of horror stories about car rental agencies and photocopying centers and other small businesses still looking to get their bills paid years later. Make sure you get paid first, Felix."

"Thanks for looking out for me."

"Nice to be on the other end for a change."

Felix declined my offer to walk him back up to his car, which pleased me, because by the time he left my home, I wasn't feeling so hot. My face felt warm and the tea seemed to slosh around in my stomach, and even though I had skipped breakfast and didn't feel like lunch, I still wasn't hungry at all. Instead I was achy, and I took a couple of aspirin, chased them down with a swallow of orange juice, and went back to the living room. I started up the fire from last night and stretched out on the couch, a thin comforter across my legs. I picked up a copy of *Smithsonian* magazine and started to read, and when my eyes felt thick, I decided to rest them.

For only a while, I thought. For only a while. I slowly came to later, feeling groggy, feeling out of place. When I saw the living room ceiling, I realized what had happened and sat up, and then held on to the couch cushions for support. My head was spinning and then it calmed down. Well.

I stood up, checked the time. It was 1:40 P.M.

The campaign rally for Senator Hale was at two. If I was lucky, it would be a fifteen-minute drive to the Tyler Conference Center and I wouldn't be late. If I was lucky. It felt like a mighty big hope. I coughed, headed out to the closet to get my coat. I supposed I should have stayed home, but I promised Annie that I'd be there, and my plan was to drive out to the rally, slide in and stand in the rear, applaud at the proper places, wave to Annie if possible, and get home and get to bed.

Some plan. The Tyler Conference Center is on the west side of Tyler, almost right up to the border with Exonia, home to Phillips Exonia Academy. It's a small hotel with conference rooms, within a five-minute drive from Interstate 95, and it serves as a convenient meeting place for businesspeople out of Porter and Boston and Nashua who need to meet without fighting a lot of traffic jams and traffic lights.

But the fight seemed to be here today. Once I got within a half mile of the center, traffic had slowed, bumper to bumper, and I felt like I was suddenly transported into downtown Boston on a Monday morning commute. I couldn't remember the last time I had been stuck in traffic in Tyler, except during the middle of summer at the beach. But not at this end of town. There were plowed mounds of snow on each side of the road, and I checked the dashboard clock and saw I had exactly five minutes to go before the official start of the campaign rally.

Some cars in front of me were pulling off to the side, and I decided to give up, too. I managed to squeeze into a spot and got out, locking the Explorer behind me. The cloud cover was still there, there was a sharp bite to the air, and my throat and chest hurt. Just slide in and slide out, I thought. Enough to make an appearance, and then time to go home. And then let my bed and sleep work their magic.

I slogged my way to the conference center, a four-story hotel with a low-slung building off to the right, a banner saying WELCOME SENATOR JACKSON HALE AND SUPPORTERS flapping in the breeze above the main entrance.

And the supporters were there. Scores of them. The parking lot was full of people holding up campaign signs, most of them for Senator Hale, but there were a few brave others working for his three opponents. These folks were getting jeered at by some Hale supporters, but in a relatively good-natured way. Three large buses were by the rear entrance of the building, diesel engines grumbling, Senator Hale signs hanging off their sides. I moved through the crowds, working my way to the entrance, and I stopped. The crowd was just too damn thick. Some people were chanting, "Go, Hale, go! Go, Hale, go! Go, Hale, go!" Their voices were loud in the cold air. I moved away from the crowds by the entrance, about ready to give up, when there was a tug at my arm.

"Looking for something, Mr. Cole?"

I turned, smiled. The voice and face were a welcome sight. It was a woman about my age from the Tyler Police Department, wearing green uniform pants, a knee-length tan winter coat with sergeant's stripes on the sleeves, and the typical officer's cap, which looked very out of place upon her head.

"Detective Sergeant Diane Woods," I said, raising my voice.

"How very nice to see you."

"The same."

"Out of uniform today?" I asked, making a sly joke, since I hardly ever saw her in her official dress uniform.

"In uniform, on detail, making a nice piece of pay per hour. What's up?"

"Trying to get into the rally and not having much success."

She smiled. "Didn't know you had such a burning interest in politics."

"Well... "

The smile remained. "Perhaps you have a burning interest in someone involved in politics."

"Perhaps," I replied. "But right now, I have a burning interest in getting inside to the rally. But that crowd isn't moving."

"That's right. But why go through the main entrance?"

"Excuse me?"

She reached up and gently tapped me on the cheek with a gloved hand. "Silly man. Lovemaking on a regular schedule is screwing up your mind. You're obviously not used to all that attention and it's scrambling your thinking process."

"Meaning?"

"Meaning you're a magazine columnist. You have a press ID issued by the New Hampshire Department of Safety. Go through the press entrance."

"Oh."

"Come with me."

I followed Diane as she maneuvered her way through the crowd and went to a side door that was offset by a set of orange traffic cones and yellow tape. There was an older, beefy man with a red beard at the door, holding a clipboard, and when I turned to say thanks to Diane, she was gone. From my wallet I took out my press identification badge, which has my vital stats and a not-so-bad photo of me taken a couple of years ago by the same people in the state who do driver's license photos.

The bearded man, who had the nervous energy of being part of a process that might make his boss the most powerful man in the world, looked at my identification and me and then the list. For just a moment, there seemed to be a flash of understanding on his face, but I was mistaken. He shook his head.

"You're not on the list."

"I'm sure I'm not. But why can't I go in?"

"Because you're not on the list."

I took a breath. For Annie, only for Annie. I said, "This is the press entrance, right?"

"Yes."

"And I'm a member of the press, aren't I?"

"Yes, yes, of course."

"Then," I said brightly, "it's all coming together, right?"

I pushed by him, he squawked some things at me, and after a brief walk through a narrow hallway, I was into the large conference room and into—

Chaos. Absolute and unfettered chaos. I moved so that I was standing against a wall. Near me was a raised wooden stand. There, almost a dozen cameramen with their cameras on tripods were aiming at the stage at the far side of the room. If the gatekeeper had followed me in, I had lost him in the crowd in a matter of seconds. And the crowd inside made the crowd outside look like a meeting of surviving World War I veterans. People were jammed up tight against one another; the room was hot and loud, the sound coming from rock music over a sound system and hundreds of people trying to be heard over the din. Balloons and bunting hung from the ceiling and walls. The stage was nearly empty save for a large JACKSON HALE FOR ALL OF AMERICA'S TOMORROWS sign hanging at the rear. A lectern was in the middle of the stage, along with a number of empty chairs on each side.

I wiped at my face and my eyes. My heart was racing, and my throat hurt, and nausea was sloshing around in my stomach. A woman's voice, close to my ear: "Hey, Lewis. What brings you here?"

I turned. A young woman was standing next to me, wearing a thin down tan winter coat and a bright smile. Despite how lousy I felt, it was good to see her. Her ears stuck through her blond hair, and Paula Quinn, reporter for the *Tyler Chronicle*, one-time lover and now friend, and second-best writer in Tyler, stood there with a reporter's notebook in her small hands.

"Just getting a piece of the political world," I said.

"Yeah," she said, smiling knowingly, "A piece of something, I'm sure. How's it going?"

"Not too bad."

"Really? Don't take offense, but you look like crap. You coming down with something?"

"Sure feels like it."

She gently nudged me with her shoulder. "My, she sure is something, to get you here today."

"That she is. How's your day?"

She laughed. "Campaign rally here, another rally this afternoon, and another rally tonight. Rah rah, sis boom bah. The joys of primary season. Look, I'm going to get closer to the stage. If you feel better, let's do lunch later this week, all right?"

I nodded and tried to say something, but she had moved by then and the noise seemed to have gotten louder. I looked around the crowd, trying to spot Annie, and gave up after a few minutes. It was impossible. There were just too many people, too many signs, too many conversations, and as I stood against the wall, as the crowd flowed and ebbed around me, I could only make out quick snippets of the give-and-take.

"—latest polls show it's tightening up—"

"—can't believe we'd lose to somebody like Pomeroy, even if the moron is from Massachusetts—"

"—budget deficit as a campaign issue is a loser—"

"—so I told her, if I don't get five minutes with the candidate, then—"

"—God, guns, and gays, how often have you heard that--"

The crowd was a mix of journalists, young, enthusiastic volunteers, and in one comer, a knot of well-dressed older men and women who talked among themselves like veteran campaign observers who had Already Seen It All. One woman with brown hair, wearing a dark blue wool dress, seemed to be the center of attention, and I found it amusing that a few of her companions were busy trying to hear what she was saying, instead of paying attention to what was going on elsewhere in the room.

I closed my eyes, my stomach rolling along. The music went to some sort of crescendo, and there was a burst of applause as people started filing across the stage, waving at the crowd. There were four men and two women, and I didn't recognize any of them. Was something odd going on?

I took a breath as one of the women—older and wearing a sensible pantsuit, bright pink—came out and adjusted the microphone on the lectern. Something went wrong and the squealing feedback felt like an ice pick stuck in my ear.

No, nothing odd, as the feedback went away. Just politics. The woman started speaking in a loud, breathy voice, and I quickly learned that she was the head of the county party organization, and that the people sitting behind her were candidates for local state representative openings, the governor's council, and county attorney.

As she started introducing each of these people, it quickly became apparent that the crowd was not in the mood to listen to the candidates for state representative, the governor's council, or county attorney. The respectful silence moved rapidly to low mutters and murmurs, but the head of the county organization kept plugging away, talking about the challenge facing the local towns and the county, and how all must work together. As she gamely went through her fifteen-plus minutes of fame, I wondered if the crowd would eventually revolt and charge the stage.

I leaned against the wall. Closed my eyes. Kept my eyes closed. It was so loud, so hot.

And then—

"...my honor and privilege to introduce the next president of the United States, Senator Jackson Hale!"

The crowd erupted with cheers and applause, long bouts of applause, which grew even louder as the senator came up on the stage, waving and laughing, pointing to people in the crowd. I had seen him, of course, on television and in the newspapers, but in the flesh, he seemed more fit, more tan. He was about six foot tall, with a thick thatch of gray black hair, and an easy, engaging smile that seemed to make everyone in the room think they were his very best friend. He waved and waved, and then motioned, and a slim woman joined him up on the stage, Mrs. Senator Jackson Hale herself, also known as Barbara S. Hale, and known to a few others, years earlier, as Barbara Scott, a name I knew her by back when I had dated her in college, so many years and lifetimes ago.

3

The applause went on and on. Hale held up both of his arms like a prizefighter, finally getting to a place he belonged, a place that was soon to be his destiny, and then he went to the lectern, where he adjusted the microphone with practiced ease. Near me the cameras on the raised platform moved as one, scanning to one side as he made his way to the lectern. The applause began to ease and he bent forward, saying, "Thank you, thank you, thank you..."

I noticed that I was being watched by some of the people about me, staring at me with hostility, and I started applauding, too. No reason to upset the true believers in my immediate vicinity.

Senator Hale said, "Thank you so much for this lovely reception. I'm honored to be with you here today, among the good people and voters of New Hampshire, and I'd like to take a few minutes to..."

I looked around the room again, trying to find Annie, but gave up. It was impossible.

So I looked at the senator's wife instead.

Barbara.

She stood next to him, smiling widely, and something inside of me tingled just a bit. It had been a very long time since I had seen that particular smile in person. Her blond hair was different, of course, for in college she had worn it long and straight. Now it was cut more fashionably about the shoulder, and Barbara, whose idea of fashion in college had been tight jeans and a T-shirt, was wearing some sort of skirt and jacket combo that was probably worth more than my home computer.

Her husband said, "This election is about more than just me and my opponents, it's about the direction we plan to take, the direction that all of us in this fine country will choose in the next several months as we determine what kind of people we plan to be, what kind of nation we intend to be..."

Barbara stood there and smiled and applauded at all the right points, and I wondered what was going on behind that bright smile of hers, that smile that years ago I had found so relaxing and inviting. When I had known her in college, we were both majoring in journalism, both of us planned to be investigative reporters, and both of us planned to change the world. Corny, I know, but when you're that young and that intelligent and that fueled with righteousness, well, it was easy to make fun, years later.

But it didn't mean I sometimes didn't miss that clarity.

So, years later, and here we were, together again, separated by a few dozen feet and so many years of experience and relationships and moves on both our parts. I had never changed the world and had long ago given it up as a goal. I wondered if Barbara still thought about doing it, and if so, if she planned to do it with her husband's help. That would make some sort of sense, though when I had known her, the thought of her trying to achieve some sort of goal on the basis of one's marriage to a powerful man would have gained me a hefty punch in the arm and a sharp and to-the-point comment.

The senator said, "... Just last week, we made an important start in this process, with our victory in Iowa..."

The news of his unexpected victory in that Midwestern state caused the room to erupt again. More cheers, more applause. Barbara applauded right along with the crowd, laughing and smiling, even though she probably knew the speech and the applause lines by heart. And as she applauded her husband's words, she kept on looking at the people in the crowd, looking at all of the supporters, looking—

At me. She looked right at me. And I looked back.

Her face froze, just for a moment, and for a quick flash, she was no longer the senator's wife, the possible next first lady of the nation, but a woman with whom I had spent some lovely months, years and years ago, arguing about writing and style and poetry and Faulkner and Orwell and—

My stomach rolled. The heat was just too much. The noise was too much. It was all too much.

She quickly recovered, going back to her role as supporter and possible first lady. She was no longer looking at me, which was fine, since I was no longer looking at her but for the exit. I elbowed my way through the crowd, through my fellow members of the press, through the true believers, through the short hallway and outside into the crisp, cold, and clean air.

I took about five or six steps, leaned over, and vomited in the parking lot. The usual cramps and coughing and drooling followed, but in a manner of moments, I was sitting on the rear bumper of a Honda Accord, wiping my face with a handkerchief, feeling my arms and legs tremble. I looked around the lot for a moment, embarrassed that somebody might have seen my discomfort, but this part of the lot was blessedly empty, save for the parked vehicles and nearby news vans.

And being on that car bumper, wiping my face with a soiled handkerchief, is how I came to miss the attempted assassination of Jackson Hale, senator from Georgia and probable next president of the United States. The first sign that something was wrong was when a low "oooh" or "aaahh" came from the crowd inside the conference room, audible even out in my part of the parking lot, followed by loud yells and screams, which I could make out from the open door that I had just exited. More yells. More screams. I looked over and people were running out of the main entrance and the side entrance, holding on to one another, tripping, falling, and picking themselves up and running some more. Their faces were white with fear or anger or terror, and many glanced behind them, as if they were being chased by some evil force.

There were a couple of camera crews already out in the parking lot, and the crew members started shooting footage, no doubt not knowing what the hell they were recording, just knowing it was something important, something to be kept and interpreted later. I stood up, tried to get a better look at what was happening. Then the sounds of sirens cut through the cold air, and from the rear of the hotel a New Hampshire State Police cruiser roared out, followed by a black limousine with tinted windows and two dark blue Chevrolet Suburbans with flashing blue lights in their radiator grilles.

When the second Suburban hit the road, I saw that the rear hatchback window was wide open, and two Secret Service agents were sitting back there, leaning out, both holding Uzi submachine guns in their hands. War wagon, a memory came to me, that's what the heavily armed Suburbans were called. War wagons. Full of weapons, from sub machine guns to Stinger antiaircraft missiles and everything in between, all to protect a president or would-be president.

A weeping young woman came by, and I said to her, "What happened in there? What's going on?"

"Somebody...somebody shot the senator. The fucker. They killed him! They killed him!"

Jesus, I thought, not here, not now.

I thought of Dallas, I thought of Memphis, I thought of Los Angeles, I thought of all the places marked by so much history and death and shootings and assassinations and broken dreams and not here, not in my hometown, and I thought of Annie and Barbara and—

More people came out, and somebody was yelling, "He's okay! I just got a text message from one of his aides! Nobody got hurt! They missed! They missed!"

I wiped at my face again, legs quivering. More and more people were streaming out. They were now being intercepted by members of the fourth estate, whipping into action, and I suppose if I were a better magazine writer, I would have been doing the same thing. But I wasn't. I got up and started going through the crowd, looking for Annie, to see her and hold her hand and find out if she knew anything else.

But after long minutes when I thought I might get sick again at any moment on the feet or legs of the people near me, I still couldn't find her. I wanted to go back into the conference center, but the doors were blocked by state police officers, backed by serious-looking men and women in suits with half-hidden earpieces, and I gave up. I slowly walked back to my Explorer, dodging some of the traffic streaming out of the parking lot, and

got in and started the engine and put my head down on the steering wheel
for a moment.

I raised my head, saw that there was finally a break in the traffic
trundling by. I got out onto the road and drove home. Along the way, from
some of the homes on this stretch of road leading out from the conference
center, residents were standing in their driveways, looking out at the traffic,
no doubt knowing they were viewing some sort of historical event, and no
doubt not knowing what in hell it was. Well, it wasn't my place to tell them,
and like the rest of the world, they would learn what had happened back
there soon enough. Halfway back to Tyler Beach, I caught a bulletin on
WBZ-AM radio out of Boston, which announced that the Secret Service
and New Hampshire State Police were investigating the attempted assassination of Senator Jackson Hale, who was fine and was being protected at an
undisclosed location somewhere in New Hampshire. After the bulletin was
a series of live reports from shaky-voiced reporters at the scene in Tyler and
at Hale campaign headquarters in Manchester and down south in Atlanta.
What followed were several minutes of prediction, analysis, and the ever-
sorrowful   what-does-this-attempted-assassination-mean-for-us-as-a-
people.

By then I was home at my very disclosed location, probably feeling no
better or no worse than poor Senator Hale. I parked in my shed and
trudged through the snow to my front door, and before going inside,
doubled over again in another bout of vomiting, this time just bringing up
some harsh bile. I kicked some snow over the mess I made and went inside,
straight to my telephone. I placed a call to Annie Wynn. Her cell phone
dumped me into her voice mail, and I said, "Hi, it's me. I was there at the
rally...couldn't find you...hope you're okay...call me or come back here I'm
coming down with something and I'm going to lie down."

Which is what I did, stretching out on the couch and resisting the urge
to turn on the television, knowing that everything I saw now would be
repeated later, and so I just stayed there, comforter up to my neck.

And despite everything that had just happened, I was feeling so lousy
that I did fall asleep. I woke to the sound of the door being unlocked, and I
sat up as Annie came in, face red, eyes red. She dropped her bag and came
right at me. I sat up on the couch and she sat there, now in my arms, and I

held her tight as she choked and cried some and then cried some more. She then pulled back and rubbed at her eyes, and I said, "Get you something? Drink? Something to eat?"

She opened her purse, took out a tissue, blew her nose. "How about a new day? Can you do that for me?"

"If I could, I would."

She managed a wan smile, crumpled up the tissue in her hand. "Oh, Lewis, I never want to go through anything like that ever again."

"Tell me where you were. Tell me what you saw."

She took a deep breath, clasped her hands around her purse so tightly I could see her knuckles whiten. "I...I was backstage, with some of the campaign people. You see, most of us, the volunteers, what little compensation we get is the ability to be behind the scenes, to say hi to the senator and his people. A couple of times, though, I snuck a peek out to the crowd, tried to spot you."

I said, "I was near the press section. I couldn't see you. And I guess I'm lucky...I mean, I didn't see what happened. I got sick, had to get out of the building. Went out to the parking lot, dumped my guts on the ground, and then people started running out."

She closed her eyes for a moment, like she was trying to see again what had happened back at the conference center. "He came in...right on time...Hale time, you know? He's always on time. But he had to wait backstage. That dimwit county chair, she had to go on and on, practically introducing candidates for dogcatcher...but then he went out with his wife, and started his talk..."

"Yes," I said, now holding my hand over her two hands on the purse. "I was there for that."

She said, "You know, I've read his damn stump speech, and I've seen bits of it on TV, so it wasn't any surprise...but you know, seeing him in person, it was wonderful. It's a damn cliché and all, but he held me. He's a great speaker, Lewis, he really is...and about halfway through it there was a gunshot, and then another."

"Just two, then?"

"Yeah. Two too fucking many, if you'll excuse my language. The first time, I think we all froze, thinking maybe it was a balloon, but the Secret

Service jumped ugly real quick, heading to the senator and his wife, and there was another shot, and people started screaming and running."

"Did anybody see who did it?"

"Nope. You saw how crowded that place was...Jesus, what a mess. There were two shots and then people started running, and the senator and his missus were practically carried out the rear...and that was that."

"Annie, I'm sorry it happened. Even more sorry you were there to see it."

She smiled, squeezed my hand back. "Sounds crazy, but there's no place I'd rather be...I had to be there, Lewis, and I'm damn glad I was."

"Any idea who or why?"

"Why? Take your pick...every position the senator holds, there's sure to be some sort of nut who opposes him. And who...no idea who the shooter was, but I heard a rumor that the cops and the Secret Service caught themselves a break."

"How so?"

"After most everybody bailed out, they found a gun on the floor of the conference center. There you go. Some of the cops tried to keep people from running away after the shooting, so they could be interviewed, but you saw what the crowd was like. Lucky nobody was trampled to death."

I squeezed her hand again. "That's a big break. It could mean a lot in tracing who in hell was involved. Look. You must be tired, must be hungry, why don't you—"

She shook her head. "No. Sorry. You're being a dear and all that, and any other day, I'd love to sit here in front of the fire and veg out, but not today, not after what happened."

"You're going back to Manchester."

"Yes," she said, a bit of steel showing in her voice. "I've talked to others in the campaign. I'm going back to Manchester and make the phone calls and stuff the envelopes and crunch the numbers, and I and the rest of the crew are going to work twice as hard, after some asshole tried to take our candidate away. Our next president, Lewis. He can make it, he really can, and I'm not going to sit on my butt and be intimidated."

"And such a lovely butt it is."

On any other occasion, that would have brought a smile, but this wasn't any other occasion. She stood up, put her coat back on, and bent down and kissed me quickly on the forehead. "I'll call you, okay? Don't worry about me. I'll be fine."

"All right. Be safe."

And in a few seconds, she was out the door, and I was alone.

I coughed some more and rolled myself up in the comforter, and thought again about turning on the television, but decided I needed sleep more than news. So sleep is what I got.

The phone ringing got me up, and I sat up, nose runny, throat raspy, my stomach still doing slow rolls. I answered the phone and there was nobody on the other end, and then there was a click and a bored female voice said, "Sir, good day, I'm conducting a survey of the presidential candidates, and I want to ask you a few questions if I may."

"I don't—"

"Sir, would your vote in the New Hampshire primary be different if you knew that Senator Nash Pomeroy accepted PAC money from gun manufacturers, even though he comes from a state that saw two of its favorite sons cut down by assassin's bullets?"

"Good try," I said.

"Excuse me?" came the female voice.

"I said, good try. This isn't a survey. It's a push poll. You're trying to drive up the negative poll numbers for Senator Pomeroy by asking crap questions like this. Who's paying the freight? Which campaign or PAC?"

Click. The mystery caller had hung up.

The constant joys of living in the first-in-the-nation primary state. Annoying phone call after annoying phone call.

I stumbled into the kitchen, washed my face, took a big swallow of orange juice that almost made me cough as the acidy juice slid down my throat, and then I started the stove to make a cup of tea.

Another ring of the phone. Another brief delay as the automated computer connected me to a live person, a woman again.

"Sir, I'm calling from Alliance Opinion Surveys, gauging the mood of the electorate. On a scale of one to ten, with one being strongly disagree and ten being strongly agree, how would you rate orbital space-based weapons as a campaign issue this year?"

"Orbital space-based weapons?" I asked, looking for a clean tea mug and accompanying tea bag.

"Yes, sir," she said. "On a scale of one to ten, with one being—"

"How long?"

"Excuse me?"

"How long is this survey?"

"Sir, it's only fifty questions, and we find that most callers complete the survey in—"

Click. Now it was my time to hang up.

I usually find these types of surveys oddly amusing, but I guess that's just me. Being from Massachusetts, my dear Annie never receives such phone calls, and Diane Woods of the Tyler Police Department says she hardly gets any at all, since she has an unlisted number. Paula Quinn of the *Chronicle* follows the three-second rule, meaning that if nobody on the other end speaks up in three seconds, she hangs up before the computer can switch her over to a live operator.

All of us in this state have different strategies, but I guess I like Felix's best. He politely listens to the opening remarks, and then says he has one question of his own: Does the caller have any suggestions for cleaning fresh bloodstains out of clothing? "Usually, they hang right up," he told me once. "And it really has cut down on the follow-up calls."

Now the water was boiling, and I was about to pour it in my tea mug, when the phone rang again, and by now I was tired of all the attention. I picked up the phone and said, "I swear to God, if this is another survey, I'm going to trace this number and hunt you down and rip your phone out of the wall."

The woman on the other end laughed. "Can't do that, Lewis. I'm on my cell phone, right in downtown Manchester."

"Oh."

Annie said, "I feel bad about something, and I need to tell you that."

"Okay, go ahead." I poured the water into the mug, liking the sensation of the steam rising up to my face. "Still upset about the shooting, I'm sure."

"No, it's not that."

"It's not?"

"No, and if you let me talk, I'll tell you all about it. Look I came in and dumped all over you, and you gave me a shoulder and a few hugs and all that good stuff. But you told me you were sick, that you threw up in the conference center's parking lot, and I found you all wrapped up on the couch when I came to see you. I should have asked you how you were doing. I should have offered to help you. But I didn't. I'm sorry."

"No apologies necessary," I said. "You've had a tough day. Don't worry about it."

"Well, I did worry about it, and I wanted to let you know. Okay?"

"Okay."

"Good. I'm in front of the campaign headquarters now. I'll call you tomorrow. Hope you feel better. Bye."

"Bye right back," I said, and sure enough, even before I had the cup of tea, I was feeling better.

Dinner was a couple of scrambled eggs and toast, and maybe my aggressive nap schedule was working in my favor, for I felt more human as the day dragged on. I caught a bit of the news at six-thirty and saw some of the shooting coverage, but missed the actual first footage of the shooting and what it looked like from inside the building. Still, most of the coverage was similar, with all channels showing a graphic of the interior of the Tyler Conference Center—I'm sure the management couldn't buy advertising like this, and I wasn't sure what they thought of this particular good fortune —-and there were interviews with a cheerful Senator Hale, who did his best to shrug off the attempt on his life. Plus the usual and customary interviews with a variety of eyewitnesses, none of whom actually saw a damn thing, but heard plenty, or thought they did. This was followed by the typical stories of our violent society, and how we were all to blame for what had happened in Tyler this day.

When that coverage was over, I decided that I'd had my fill of politics for the day, so I channel-surfed for a while, and almost cheered my luck when I saw a two-hour documentary on one of the cable channels on the history of U-boat operations in the North Atlantic. I settled back on the couch, fire in the fireplace, comforter wrapped around me, and cherished a time when the conflicts were so clear, so finely drawn. The next morning when the phone rang, I was washing my breakfast dishes, feeling much better, and I was surprised at the woman's voice on the other end of the phone: not my Annie Wynn, but my good friend Detective Sergeant Diane Woods. It sounded like she was on a cell phone.

"Hey," she said. "How are you doing?"

"Doing all right," I said. "How are you?"

'Well, got my fingers in a bit on this Senator Hale incident," she said.

"You do, do you? I thought the state police and the Secret Service would be all over this and pushing poor little you aside."

"I'm not poor, and I'm not little."

"All right. Point noted. And what part of the investigation has your fingers in it?"

She sighed. "You."

I folded up the dish towel I had been using. "Mind saying that again? I had the oddest idea that you just said 'you.' Meaning me."

"That's right."

"Why?"

Another big sigh. "I don't know, Lewis. All I know is that the Secret Service wants to talk to you about the shooting. They came to me, asked me if I knew you. When I said yes...well, here's the deal..."

I took the folded towel, wiped down an already clean kitchen counter. "They asked you to bring me in. Right?"

"Right."

"All right. What's the deal? You want me to meet you at the police station?"

"Um, no..."

Then I got it. "Where are you? Up the hill, at the parking lot?"

"Yeah."

"Okay. I'll be up there in a minute."

I hung up the phone, thought about making a phone call, but to whom? Annie? Her law firm? Felix?

No, nobody, not now.

I went out of the kitchen to the entranceway and grabbed a coat, and then went out the door and trudged my way up to the Lafayette House's parking lot.

There Diane was waiting for me, standing next to an unmarked Tyler police cruiser, a dark blue Ford LTD with a whip antenna, engine burbling in the cold morning air. She was bundled up in a short leather coat with a cloth collar and dark slacks. I stood there and she said, "Sorry."

"No, it's okay. If I'm being brought in, would rather it be done by a friend."

She got in the front seat, and I walked around and joined her.

As in all cop cars, the upholstery was heavy-duty plastic and there was a police radio slung under the dashboard. She picked up the microphone and said, "Dispatch, D-one, coming in."

"All right, D-one."

She tossed the microphone back in its cradle, shifted the cruiser into drive, and in a matter of seconds, we were on Atlantic Avenue, heading south. Six months earlier or six months from now, the roadway would be packed, each parking space would be filled, and the sands of Tyler Beach would be packed with almost as many people who were set to vote here the following week.

But this was January. The road was nearly empty, and the temperature inside the car seemed to match the temperature outside.

After a few minutes I said, "Anything else you want to say?"

She looked troubled. "No, I'm afraid not."

"You know why the Secret Service wants to talk to me?"

"No," she said.

I stayed quiet for a little bit, and said, "Well, didn't you ask them?"

She turned to me for a quick second, exasperated. "Hell, yes, Lewis. I asked them. Over and over again. And all I got was polite and federal push back. The attempt on the senator's life is a matter for the Secret Service, and the state police are assisting. I've been told by my own chief to cooperate, and that's what I'm doing. Getting your cheerful butt from your house to the station with a minimum of fuss. All right?"

I thought for a moment and said, "The Secret Service has already talked to me. Two days ago."

"Really?"

"Truly," I said. "Came by on what he called a routine check. Thing is, I seem to be on a list of 'persons of interest,' to be interviewed before the arrival of a president or presidential candidate. He came by, made sure I didn't have a bomb factory in the cellar, and left. Ten, fifteen-minute visit, tops."

Diane said, "Might be a routine visit then. Just to check your name off a list."

"Sure," I said. "Routine."

"Routine," she repeated, and as we pulled into the police station's parking lot, I was sure that neither of us believed that at all.

4

At the Tyler police station, she parked in the rear of the fenced-in parking lot reserved for police and other official vehicles, and she led me through the back door, where the on-duty dispatcher buzzed open the rear inner door after seeing Diane through a closed-circuit television. The building was the usual one-story concrete style of decades earlier, and one of these days, if the chief could convince three-fifths of the eligible voters in Tyler, he would get a new station built nearby.

Sure. One of these days.

We went through the booking room, past the empty holding cells, and through an open door marked INTERVIEW. A tired looking man with wavy black hair in a fine dark gray suit was sitting there. He stood up when Diane and I entered. There was a battered conference room table and four chairs, and the usual one-way glass mirror on the near wall. Diane reached over, squeezed my hand. "See you later, Lewis."

"Sure, Diane."

"Thank you, Detective," the man said in a quiet and firm voice. "Please close the door on your way out, will you?"

She said nothing but did as she was requested. I sat down. The man said, "Mr. Cole, I'm Glen Reynolds, Secret Service."

"Nice to meet you."

"Sure," he said, opening up a file folder. No hand was offered, and I wasn't offended. I had an idea of where this was going.

"Mr. Cole, I'm looking for your cooperation."

"All right."

"You can imagine what we're up to, trying to determine who shot at Senator Hale yesterday, and why."

"Yeah."

"So I'm going to ask you a series of questions. All right?"

I looked behind him, at the mirrored glass. I wondered how many people were back there watching us, and how many recording devices were listening to us.

"Sure. That'd be fine."

He grinned. "Nice to have a cooperative witness, for once in my life. All right. Mr. Cole, were you at the campaign rally yesterday for Senator Hale?"

"I was."

"And why were you there?"

"As a favor."

"For whom?"

I gave him points for grammatical precision and said, "A lady friend. Who works for the senator's campaign."

That brought a knowing nod from him. "Right. One Annie Wynn of Boston, Massachusetts. So. You have no particular political interest in the senator or his political positions."

"Not particularly."

That brought a smile. "If you're a New Hampshire resident who doesn't have much interest in politics, then you're one of the few I've met in my time here."

"I'm sure."

"So you don't have any grudge against the senator, or the United States government, am I right?"

A brief snippet of memory of when I was with the Department of Defense, younger and less cynical, until a moment in the high Nevada desert, a training accident that took everyone's life save mine.

"Fifty percent right," I said. "No grudge against the senator. Perhaps a grudge against the government."

A knowing nod. "Your time in the Department of Defense. I understand."

"I'm sorry, I'm not allowed to say anything about my time of service in the Department of Defense."

He smiled again. "Really, I'm not interested in that particular part of your past. I'm interested in other things."

"Such as?"

"Such as your enrollment in Indiana University in Bloomington. When you were romantically involved with one Barbara Scott, a classmate of yours. Who later became the senator's wife."

"And what's your interest?"

He shrugged. "Just wondering...if you're jealous of the senator. For being with the woman you were once intimate with."

"No. I'm not jealous."

"Really?"

"Yes, really. Agent Reynolds, may I ask you a question?"

"Sure," he said, grinning. "I've been monopolizing the conversation since you've gotten here. Go ahead. Ask away."

"Why am I here? I thought I had been cleared by the Secret Service agent who saw me two days ago. Agent Harris."

"Agent Harris?"

"Yes. Agent Spenser Harris. From your Boston office. He came to see me two days ago, since I'm on one of your lists...persons of interest, he said. He talked with me for a while and left. Said that everything was just fine."

"Mr. Cole, like I said, I'm not much interested in your past. It's your present time that interests me. Especially what you were doing at the rally yesterday."

"Again, why me? You're interested in me as a witness? Because to tell you the truth, I didn't see much when I was at the rally yesterday. I was there for most of the speeches and then I got sick to my stomach and went outside. Where I then promptly threw up."

"Point noted," he said.

"So why am I here?" I asked.

"You're here because your presence at the campaign rally was reconfirmed, leading us to a few questions."

"Reconfirmed? By whom?"

Agent Reynolds's voice seemed to sharpen. "By our very dear and closest friend in the agency. Mr. Forensics."

"Sorry, I don't understand. What do you mean, Mr. Forensics?"

He went back to his folder. "Mr. Cole, do you own a stainless-steel Ruger .357 revolver, serial number 468723698?"

Something cold started touching the back of my neck and the back of my hands. "I do own a Ruger .357 revolver. I don't have the serial number memorized."

"They never do. Well, let's get right to it, shall we?"

"Let's," I said, now deeply regretting I hadn't called anybody before coming here.

"Mr. Cole, have you lent or given away this revolver recently?"

"No."

"Have you sold it?"

"No."

"Then can you tell us why your revolver, with your fingerprints and your fingerprints only, was found on the floor of the Tyler Conference Center yesterday? With three unfired and two fired cartridges?"

I said not a word.

"Two rounds were removed from the stage wall at the conference center. Ballistics conclusively show that they were fired from your revolver. And you were there."

"But I wasn't in the room when the shots were fired. I was out in the parking lot, puking up my guts."

"You see anybody in the parking lot? Anybody at all while you were out there conveniently being sick?"

"No."

Agent Reynolds carefully closed the folder. "Are you sure you don't want to change any of your previous answers?"

"Positive."

"Because there's an opportunity you have, right now, to make everything right."

"How?"

"By telling me why you brought your revolver to the campaign rally yesterday, and why you tried to shoot Senator Hale."

My hands were underneath the table, clasped tightly together. "I was at the rally, but I wasn't armed. And I didn't try to kill the senator."

"And that is going to be your story?"

"No."

"Good," he said. "Now we're getting somewhere."

"No, we're not, because you're not understanding what I'm trying to say. That's not my story. Those are the facts."

He stared at me and then made a crisp nod. "Mr. Cole, in a few minutes we're going to place you under arrest for the attempted murder of Senator Hale. You're going to be transported from this police station to the county jail nearby, and from there, I imagine the nearest federal facility, which will be in Boston. It's your choice as to whether you will then wish to have representation. I imagine you will."

"You imagine right," I said. "And you'll find out in a very short while that I had nothing to do with that shooting."

"Why? Because you're telling the truth?"

"Of course I am," I said.

"Interesting thought," he said, standing up. "Especially since I'm stationed in the Boston office, and I've never heard of a Spenser Harris." Some hours later, I was in a cell at the Wentworth County jail, staring at the stainless-steel toilet in the corner of my new little universe. While the processing in was efficient and proper, the ride over was anything but. After formally being placed under arrest and being handcuffed, I was quickly led out of the Tyler police station—not seeing Diane Woods in the process—and was taken to a dark blue van, pulled up to the entrance where I had earlier walked in as a free man. I was placed inside the van by two other agents, who carefully seat belted me in. We then left in a little convoy; the van was led and followed by dark blue Ford LTDs, similar to the one Diane drove.

When we turned the corner of the police station parking lot, we drove through a phalanx of television cameras, reporters, and news photographers, all flashing their cameras, all taking notes, all sucking in bits of information. One of the Secret Service agents said, "Hey, you're famous."

"Lucky me," I said.

"Too bad the windows are tinted. Your face would be seen by half the planet in an hour or so."

I didn't say anything more, and the agents also kept quiet on the drive west. We got out to Route 101, and along the way, I could see that the media interest was chasing us all the way along the state road. Other camera crews were stationed along the side of the road, and there was a moment, hearing the steady thrumming of an overhead helicopter, that I knew that live camera shots of this little procession were being beamed out to the insatiable cable news networks. Some people dream all their lives to achieve such fame.

I've never been one of those people.

At the county jail—an old brick edifice, stuck out in the middle of a field in the small town of Brennan—another group of journalists were waiting as we pulled in. Getting in was a challenge, as Wentworth County deputy sheriffs did their best to push aside the reporters in a manner that allowed an opening but didn't allow the trusty guardians of press freedom to charge police brutality. Still, some got close enough that I could see their cold faces, almost pressed up to the tinted glass, as they tried for more photos and shouted more questions in my general direction.

I said, "What are they thinking? That you're going to open up the door and hold a press conference?"

An agent sitting next to the van driver laughed. "The nature of the beast. It demands to be fed. Doesn't mean it's logical. It just means it's a beast."

And from there we went into a garage, and then through the booking area, and it was pleasurable to be standing up, handcuffs off, right up to the point where I was in my cell, alone, staring at the stainless steel toilet, just after making that always promised one phone call to someone far away.

I got up from the bunk, walked around, and then sat down again. My belt was off, and my footwear had been confiscated, leaving me with prison-issued paper slippers. My feet were cold. I stretched out on the plastic-covered mattress and waited, feeling okay, except that damn cold or whatever seemed to be coming back. Stress and lack of food, no doubt, but all in all, I had this serene sense of confidence while being held there. I guess I didn't expect to be in jail for long, for even if Agent Reynolds didn't believe me, I had been telling the truth. I hadn't tried to kill the senator. End of story.

I put my hands behind my head. All right. End of one story.

There was another story, about Spenser Harris, or the man who claimed to be Spenser Harris. Who in hell was he, and what had been his purpose in questioning me?

So I stared up at the cement ceiling—almost as attractive a view as the stainless-steel toilet—when a uniformed corrections officer came by.

"Cole?" he asked.

"That's right," I said, sitting up and swinging my legs over to the side.

"Your lawyer's here," he said. "Want to go see him?"

"Since I called him, yes, I would."

I knew that the tide had turned when I was let out of the cell, for handcuffs weren't placed on me, and the walk was a short one. I was led into an office area and then a meeting room—much better than the one at the Tyler police station—and I was pleased to see Attorney Raymond Drake was there, from Boston, a friend of Felix's and a mentor to Annie Wynn, and I was less pleased to see someone else in the room: Agent Reynolds.

But Agent Reynolds didn't look so happy, so that improved my mood.

I shook hands with Raymond and sat down. Raymond was smiling widely, I guess, at the thought and challenge of actually having an innocent client to represent, and a gold bracelet on his tanned wrist jangled a bit as he leaned forward. He was in his mid-fifties and owed a lot to Felix, back when he had ticked off one of Felix's relatives and was going on the usual and customary one-way trip out of Boston Harbor, before Felix had interceded. The conference room was warm, had no windows, but the chairs and table were almost brand-new, and there was a television with a VCR unit on a stand in the corner.

Raymond said, "Just to bring everyone up to speed, I'd like to show this news footage again."

Reynolds said, "There's no need for that. We can already stipulate that—"

It was like being in a courtroom, for Raymond had that demeanor, a man in his role and enjoying it fully. From the tabletop he picked up a remote for the television and switched it on, and once the blue screen came into being, he pressed another switch and up on the screen was the parking lot of the Tyler Conference Center.

I'll be damned, I thought, and leaned forward to get a better view.

The tape had a running digital readout on the bottom of the screen, denoting date and time. Besides the vehicles in the parking lot, it showed the side entrance to the conference center. I had no doubt what I was going to see next.

There. A figure, stumbling out of the doorway. Looked familiar, though pathetic, and I watched the digital avatar of Lewis Cole come out a few steps, lean over and—

Well. Perhaps it's embarrassing to see oneself on a secretly recorded sex tape, but I would guess seeing oneself become violently ill for eternity ranks right up there in the embarrassment department. Still, I was happy to see it.

Raymond held up the remote again, froze the image. "I know I've said it before, Agent Reynolds, but I still love saying it. Check the time stamp of the recording from this Boston television station. A full two minutes before the shots were fired inside the conference center. My client did not attempt to shoot the senator."

Reynolds said, "Fairly obvious, but it doesn't explain how his revolver was used in the shooting."

My lawyer turned to me. "Lewis, do you have any idea who shot at the senator?"

"Nope."

"Do you know how your Ruger .357 ended up at the conference center?"

"Obviously, it was stolen."

"Any idea when?"

"No," I said.

"Any idea by whom?" he asked.

"No," I said, lying for the first time that day, which I was sure would disappoint the good agent, but I didn't care right then.

Raymond turned back to Agent Reynolds. "There you have it, Agent Reynolds."

He said, "We still plan to ask him more questions. Especially about that so-called Secret Service agent he claims visited him."

"I'm sure," Raymond said, reaching into his coat pocket and removing a business card, which he slid across the polished conference room table. "And if you desire to do so, please contact me directly. You're not to contact my client without my say-so."

Agent Reynolds picked up the card delicately, as if it had contagious defense attorney germs on it, and said, "I guess we're through here."

Raymond shook his head. "No, we're not."

"Excuse me?"

"Agent Reynolds, I expect that within the next several minutes, you're going to hold a press conference out there at the main entrance of the county jail. You're going to announce to the world that the arrest of my client was made in haste, that he is not a suspect in the attempted assassination of Senator Hale, that all charges have been dropped, and that the United States government and the Treasury Department offer their deep apologies to Mr. Cole for putting him through this terrible ordeal."

The Secret Service agent's face reddened. "That's not my call."

"It better be, or we'll take action."

Reynolds said, "What? A lawsuit? Go ahead and try. You won't succeed. Nobody ever succeeds in suing the federal government."

My attorney said, "Who mentioned anything about a lawsuit? Here's a hint, Agent Reynolds. Look at my business card. Look at my firm's name. Consider I'm based in Boston, consider the contacts we have in the United States Senate and the House of Representatives. Wouldn't it be a marvelous coincidence if during the next budget cycle, your offices are slated for renovation, and that you have to spend the next two or three years in temporary offices...say, modular trailers at the old Charleston Navy Yard? Wouldn't that be an amazing coincidence."

There was a pause and Reynolds said, "You got your press conference. But your guy stays in the area, and you're cooperative if we want to talk to him again."

Raymond looked at me, I looked at him, and Raymond said, "Sir, you've got a deal."

Processing out was a heck of a lot more fun than processing in, and the staff and deputy sheriffs were cheerful and polite in getting my possessions back, after word had filtered through that the arrest had been a mistake.

Raymond led me out to his silver BMW and we soon left the grounds of the county jail, and I was surprised that the journalist scrum was gone from the gate.

But after we started driving out, it just took a moment to see Agent Reynolds, standing on a set of steps by the main building, talking to said scrum, and I said to Raymond, "Looks like he kept his word."

"For now, and that's a good thing."

"Ask you something?"

"Of course."

"The television tape," I said. "Where did you get it?"

"Friends and favors owed, Lewis. I know how well covered these events tend to be. Just our luck one television station from Boston had a camera trained on the exit door that afternoon."

"Let's hear it for luck."

"Sure," he said. "How does heading home sound?"

"Home would be wonderful."

As we got back onto Route 101, this time heading blessedly east, Raymond said, "Offer you a suggestion?"

"Absolutely."

"I don't have to remind you of the number of journalists scrambling around your fair state, trying to get a different angle, a different story on the primary. It's always a combination circus and revival meeting, and this assassination attempt has just spun out the reporters even more. Not to mention that little bit about you having a relationship with the senator's wife back in college."

"That was a long time ago."

"Still, it's newsworthy, if it gets out. And knowing how dedicated these journalists are, I'm sure it will come out one of these days, sooner rather than later."

"I know."

"Good. And you're going to see something else, Lewis. Despite that little show back there at the county jail, where you've just been set free on the side of goodness, you are now a story. Probably one of the biggest stories in the nation, right up to the time next week when the ballots get cast."

I said, "If you're advising me to keep a low profile and keep my mouth shut, consider it done."

Raymond said, "Good. I had a feeling you knew where I was going. Glad to see my high opinion of you is based on something."

"Not disappointing my attorney, that's always been a goal in my life."

He laughed at that and said, "Right now we've embarrassed the Secret Service. They thought they had a shooter, and we've just blown that right out of the water. So don't be surprised if they come back at you with lots more questions, lots more attention, usually at a time and place inconvenient for you. Don't worry; we'll ride it out."

"Thanks."

Off in the distance I could make out the thin line of the Atlantic Ocean, and Raymond said, "Now, this was a change. Usually I come see you because of some...adventure involving Felix. But you've managed to get into trouble all by yourself this time. Not sure that's an improvement."

"I just went to a rally and got sick. That's all."

"More than that, my friend. You've got yourself caught up in an attempt to kill a leading presidential candidate. When you die, that will probably be the first line in your obituary."

The approaching ocean looked good. I said, "I don't plan that anytime soon. Besides, something else might be the first line in my obituary. First man on Mars, for example."

He laughed. "I won't hold my breath, but if you do that, bring me back a rock or something."

"Or something."

Now we were crossing a long stretch of marshland, heading east to the ocean, and off to our right, squatting at the edge of the marsh, were the cement and steel structures of the Falconer nuclear power plant.

Raymond said, "Besides this campaign almost putting you in jail, it's lost me one of my best paralegals. How is Annie Wynn doing?"

"Doing well," I said. "Though yesterday was a pretty rough time. She's been taken in by the senator and his campaign. Question I have is, where is she going after the New Hampshire primary? She's made noises about going south if the primary goes well and if the polls improve for the senator."

"And how are the two of you doing?"

I eyed him. "Just fine, Counselor. Just fine."

That managed to keep him quiet. The road ended at Atlantic Avenue, which ran right along the edge of the coast, and he turned left, heading north. Empty parking spots flanked us all the way up to my home. I rubbed my hands across the tops of my legs. I knew I had just a few minutes left before we got to the Lafayette House parking lot.

"Raymond," I said.

"Yeah."

"I need to tell you a couple of things."

"Sure."

"I was set up."

He tapped a finger on the steering wheel. "That you were, son. That you were. Have you pissed anyone off lately?"

"Not that I'm aware of."

"Who do you think stole your handgun?"

"The fake Secret Service agent, that's who. He made sure I was going to be at the rally. And he knew me, knew about Annie...knew a lot of stuff. Which tells me he or his friends did their homework, did their research. They needed a patsy, and I was it. Lucky for me I got sick at the right time."

"Sounds good."

"Then how come that real Secret Service agent didn't press me?"

"Good question. I have a feeling Agent Reynolds knows a lot more than he was letting on. But I can tell you this, he does have his hands full. Trying to find out who shot at the senator, trying to find out who was impersonating a Secret Service agent. Just be glad you're not him."

"All right, I will."

He spared me a glance. "What's next, then?"

"What do you mean?"

"Not to worry, you're still under lawyer-client privilege, my friend."

I looked over at the wide cold ocean. "I'm going to find out who set me up. And why."

"Hell of a task."

"Don't think I've got much of a choice."

Raymond said, "You could let it drop. Let the professionals handle it."

"Not my style, Counselor."

He sighed. "All right. Just make sure you have my business card with you."

"Always."

The road rose up and went to the right and before us was the white Victorian structure of the Lafayette House, and across the street was the parking lot, the entrance to my house, and a mob scene.

The parking lot was a milling mass of reporters, photographers, news cameras, satellite trucks and vans, and assorted bystanders and passersby.

"Well," Raymond said.

"Understatement of the year, Raymond."

"Yeah."

He slowed down and I said, "You can let me out and—"

"Lewis," he said, his voice changing, sounding more like that of the guy who had gotten me out of prison a half hour ago. "I said I was going to take you home, and by God, I'm going to take you home. Just sit there, look straight ahead, and keep your face blank. Like you're holding a full house in a poker game with a motorcycle gang. All right?"

"Sure."

He made a sharp turn to the right, into the parking lot, and we moved forward slowly, like an icebreaker going through a mass of jumbled ice. I followed my lawyer's advice and stared straight ahead, as the enthusiastic members of the fourth estate pressed against the windows and sides of the BMW. We had a bumpy ride down to my house, and I felt a flash of anger as I saw another, smaller collection of reporters around the front door. Raymond said, "You let me handle this crowd, all right?"

"Sure," I said, thinking of the nice collection of firearms I have in my house, save for the one stolen two days earlier.

He pulled up and opened the door, letting in a burst of cold air and shouted questions, and he stood there for a minute or two, as the reporters gathered around him. He held his cell phone in his hand, smiled and said something, and after another minute or two, the reporters started going up the driveway. I turned and watched them trudge up the slight hill, and when they reached the parking lot, I got out.

"What magic words did you use to get rid of them?" I asked.

"Standard words. That they were all trespassing, and I was going to call the Tyler police to arrest their merry behinds. That's all."

I went up to the door. Raymond followed and I turned and shook his hand.

"Thanks," I said.

"Not a problem. Just remember my advice. All right? And if you don't remember my advice..."

"I remember. And yes, I've got your business card."

"All right." He slapped his hands together against the cold and said, "I'm off. Give my best to Annie."

"Consider it done. And Raymond?"

He was back at his BMW. "Yes?"

"Why don't you send me a bill this time?"

That made him laugh. "You're under the agreement I have with Felix, and with Felix, it's a lifetime of free legal services. It's taken care of, it will always be taken care of, and that's it. Now. Get your butt inside before you freeze it off."

"Sure. And get your butt back to Boston before some campaign up here hires you out."

"No chance, no chance, no chance," and with a smile and a slammed door, he was back in his BMW and heading up to the Lafayette House parking lot.

I went up to the front door, kicked the snow off my footwear, unlocked the door, and went inside.

Where I quickly determined I was not alone.

5

The house was too warm, there was a fire burning in the fireplace, and there was the low sound of music. The phone started ringing and I ignored it, knowing it was probably from one of the reporters up in the parking lot, checking in on me.

"Annie?" I called out.

"Yes, dear, I'll be right there."

But the voice sure as hell didn't match the sentiment. I went into the small living room, and in the kitchen, sitting at the counter like he owned the damn place, was Felix Tinios, a cup of coffee in front of him, his coat draped over a nearby chair. I suppose I should have been angry or upset that he had gotten in without telling me, but I knew how his mind worked. A friend of his was coming home from a stint in jail, so how could he not be here to greet me? The phone finally stopped ringing as I got to the kitchen.

He wore a thick green and black sweater and, I was a bit surprised to see, his shoulder holster and automatic pistol. "Carrying?" I asked. "That's a hell of an oppo research effort you're making."

He smiled, shook his head. "Not part of my oppo research job. Just part of getting into your house without having to answer lots of questions from those bottom-feeders out there in your yard."

"How's that?"

Felix toyed with the handle of the coffee mug. "Going to get all clichéd here and all, but most members of the press, they think the Constitution begins and ends with the First Amendment. They're not familiar with the particulars of the Second Amendment, and I've found that a flash of a shoulder holster and its equipment tends to shut them up. Oh, they bitch and moan about being threatened, but it's never come to anything. Funny how somebody who's brave enough to ask a mom how it feels to see her son drown gets all cowardly when he sees something made by Smith and Wesson."

"I see what you mean."

I sat at the counter, across from him, and he reached back and poured me a cup of coffee. I dumped in two spoonfuls of sugar and said, "I won't insult you by asking how you got in. Your usual skills, am I right?"

"Of course."

"I might have need of your other skills, if you can pull yourself away from finding out if Senator Pomeroy likes to surf the Net for big-breasted porn."

He said, "Somebody screwed you over."

"Correct. If it wasn't for the fact that I got sick at a certain time, I'd still be in prison, and I'd probably be going to trial in a few months."

"What happened, then? Just heard a radio report that a magazine columnist—you—had been arrested for trying to kill Senator Hale. Knew that you didn't have it in you. So what's the deal?"

"Deal was, two days ago, a guy came by to see me. Said he was from the Secret Service, was sent to my house to do an interview. Said I was on a list of 'persons of interest' and once he was satisfied that I was your run-of-the-mill nut, and not the kind of nut who blows up buildings, that was that. Wanted to know if I was going to the Hale rally the next day. Which I did. That's when somebody in the crowd took two shots at the senator, using my .357 Ruger. Revolver was left behind, with my prints and nobody else's. So I got arrested this morning and was released after your Raymond Drake came by and proved I wasn't in the building at the time of the shooting."

"How did he do that?"

"Got some television footage showing me throwing up in the parking lot of the Tyler Conference Center, about two minutes before the shooting started. Since I couldn't have been in two places at once, I was let go."

"You feeling better?"

"Better after having thrown up, or better after being released?"

"Both."

"Affirmative on both counts," I said.

Felix smiled. "Good old Raymond."

"That's not all. Right after I was arrested, I found out that the guy who was here talking to me the day before the rally wasn't really from the Secret Service."

Felix said, "This faux Secret Service agent. His name?"

"Spenser Harris."

"Show you ID?"

"Yes, he did."

He took a swallow from the coffee mug. "That's some serious scamming that was going on."

"I know. If I had been a bit more on the ball or suspicious, he would have been facing some hard charges of impersonating a federal law enforcement officer."

"Right. What else can you tell me about him?"

"Early thirties. Short black hair. About my height, though thinner and more muscled. Well dressed. Well-spoken. And...well. Yes."

"Yes what?"

"Yes, I'm sure that he's the one that stole my Ruger."

"Did he have a mysterious bulge in his pocket?" Felix asked.

"I wasn't looking for bulges, mysterious or otherwise," I said.

"But I saw something I should have noticed. It was snowing when I came home, and he was waiting for me. But his coat was clean. There was no snow on his shoulders. He had been in my house before I got here, long enough to steal my Ruger."

"Some setup," Felix said. The phone started ringing again, sounding sharp against my ears. I ignored it again.

I looked around at my small and snug and safe house, and while I was somewhat put out that Felix had let himself in, I really didn't like the thought of a stranger in here, a stranger who had gone through my belongings, looked at my belongings, stole one particular belonging as part of—

Part of what? The phone stopped ringing.

I said, "Setup. That's right. And look at what was involved. This guy knew me, knew my background, knew my relationship with Annie. He knew enough about my job with the Department of Defense to ask the right questions, look for the right answers. And he was confident enough to pull it all off, like he had help, somebody backing him up."

"More than one then."

"Yes."

"So. Who'd you piss off lately?"

"Excuse me?"

Felix said, "Look at the facts, my friend. Somebody tried to kill the senator. And not just any old run-of-the-mill senator. A guy who's trying to become president of the United States. And someone tried to pin that on you. More than one person. And if it's more than one person, ipso facto, it's a conspiracy. Organized. Smart. With resources. Not some nut lone gunman with a crush on a movie star or something equally stupid. So. Like I said, who's out there to get you?"

"Not a clue."

"Well, better get a clue soon, or next time you get set up, they'll do a better job."

"Felix, you're beginning to sound like bad late-night AM radio."

His eyes flashed at me. "Maybe so, but you should know better. You should look at things more closely, like you used to do, back when you were at the Pentagon."

"Really?" I asked.

"Yeah, really," he said. "Not that you've ever said word one about what you did back there, but I'm no idiot. I know what kind of things are looked at, what kind of things are researched. So research this. All these guys running for president—Senator Hale, Senator Pomeroy, the congressman, and the general—they're not out there on their own, with a stump speech and a smile. They've got people, lobbying groups, and corporations backing them, backing them with volunteers, phone banks, and lots of dollars. These people like power, they like to have power, they like to keep power.

And when things get tight, like this primary season, things happen. Dirty tricks. Whisper campaigns. And maybe an assassination. So watch your back."

"I will."

"Good."

He finished his coffee, put the mug down, and said, "I need to be going. If you'd like, I'll see what—if anything—I can find out about your fake Secret Service agent. Usually I can sniff around and find out about strange men bearing firearms and identification that show up in my neighborhood."

"I don't think you'll find squat."

"Probably not, but it'll make me feel good, and hopefully, you, too." He stood up, retrieved his long coat, and put it on.

I said, "A couple of days ago, you came to me seeking advice. Today, you're talking about feelings. You still surprise me, Mr. Tinios."

"Good." He started to the door and said, "Meanwhile, I'd stay away from campaign rallies."

"All right, but I can't stay away from campaign volunteers. Well, one particular volunteer."

"I can see why," Felix said. "You be safe now."

"I will. You watch out for the media up in the parking lot, all right?"

"Sure. Not a problem."

"And...thanks. Thanks for coming by."

He grinned as he opened the door, and I stepped outside with him. "It's wintertime, there's not much to do, and days like this, Lewis, you make a fine, distracting hobby."

And when my friendly hobbiest left, I went back inside.

At my phone, the answering machine announced in little red numerals that there were thirty-six messages waiting for me.

How nice to be so bloody popular.

I grabbed a pen and a slip of paper, sat down, and started going through the messages. It didn't take as long as I expected. Four of the messages were from pollsters or campaigns, thirty-one were from various media outlets— only one of whom I intended to contact—and in the middle of the mess, one from Annie.

"Lewis, call me on my cell, all right? I've heard about...your troubles. Call me when you can."

I called her back. No answer. I left a message, and then looked again at the phone. I made the call, and there was the cheerful voice of Paula Quinn, my reporter friend from the *Chronicle*.

"Lewis," she said. "How sweet you'd call me back. I'd think you'd be angling to go on one of those cable round-table shows. Or a major network. Or an exclusive with *The New York Times*."

"I'm not friends with any of them," I said. "Just with you."

She laughed. "One of the few advantages of being a reporter in a small newspaper during the primary. Look. Are you up to talking to me?"

"Absolutely."

"All right, I'm leaving friend mode and now going into reporter's mode, all right?"

"Sure," I said. "And I'm going into source mode. Fair enough?"

I could make out the tapping of her computer keyboard.

"Considering this is the biggest story in the Western Hemisphere today, you can go into any mode you'd like."

"Thanks. Look, everything and anything I say from now on, I'm not to be quoted by name or inference. Just say 'a source close to the investigation.' Does that work?"

"Works fine, and you're being a dear, but deadline is fast approaching. Can we get going?"

"Absolutely."

So I talked to Paula for a bit, answering the best I could, and despite my short answers, I think she was pleased that she was scooping the entire journalistic world with exclusive details on the attempted assassination attempt against Senator Jackson Hale. And to show her pleasure, she squeezed a lunch date out of me for later in the week, with a promise to pick up the check. Later in the afternoon the illness that had saved me from a longer stay at the Wentworth County Jail rallied and assaulted me again. The nausea had returned, along with a set of chills that made me shiver every few minutes. I had called Annie twice more and had left her messages both times, the last one saying, "I'm feeling awful again, so I'm unplugging the phone and crawling into bed. Join me if you can."

Which is what I did, but before crawling into said bed, I went around and made sure the windows were locked, that the door was locked, and the sliding glass door leading out to my first-floor deck was locked. I also did a quick weapons inventory, and aside from the missing Ruger, my twenty-gauge shotgun, my eight-millimeter FN-FAL, and my nine-millimeter Beretta were all in place. I went upstairs and retrieved my Beretta from my bedroom, took a long shower to warm up my chilled bones, and then slid into bed. I read for a while and soon enough, the sounds of the ocean put me to sleep.

The creaking door from downstairs woke me up. I reached over to the nightstand, grasped my pistol. It was cold and awkward and yet comforting in my hand. I sat up, moist and cool, and knew my fever had broken. There were footsteps on the stairs coming up to my floor, and I aimed the pistol out toward the open door, waiting. Waiting.

The wind rattled the windows in my bedroom. I waited and—

Damn.

I lowered the pistol and pulled the sheet over it, just as a figure appeared in the doorway. I called out, "Hello, Annie."

"Lewis," came the familiar and lovely voice. "Didn't mean to wake you up."

"You didn't, not to worry," I said.

She came in, and as she undressed, I tried my best to quietly put the Beretta back on the nightstand, and she said, "That's a new one, Lewis. Usually you can get me into bed with a soft word, not a weapon."

"The day I've had...sorry, I heard someone come in."

Annie came over, slid under the sheets. "But you invited me, didn't you?"

"That I did."

She cuddled up next to me and said, "You've been all over the news, but you knew that."

"Yes."

"Do you know why you are involved? Who did this to you?"

"Not a clue."

"Mmm...you intend to find out."

"That I do."

She said, "I...I cherish you, Lewis, but please. Please don't do anything to cause any more bad publicity for the senator. All right? I believe in him. I really do. And...I just want him to win next week, Okay?"

I stroked her hair. "Is this my Annie talking, or campaign Annie?"

"It's me talking, that's who."

"I understand, dear one, I do. Whatever I do, it'll have nothing to do with the senator. I just want to know how and why I was set up."

She touched my forehead. "How are you feeling?"

"Tired. Drained. Whatever I had before the rally seems to be going away."

"Good."

She kissed me chastely on the cheek and said, "You've had a long day. I've had a long day. Let's...let's just sleep, all right?"

"Fine. That'll be just fine."

She moved some more and in an instant was asleep. I held her for a bit, and then gently disentangled myself and rolled over. I lay there, listening to her breathing slow and deepen, until it almost matched the rhythm of the ocean's waves. I awoke with wet hair in my face. Annie was there, fresh out of the shower, it seemed, and she raised herself up. "You okay?" she asked. She was already dressed, and knowing Annie, breakfast was either ready or already consumed.

"Feeling better. I think."

Another kiss. "I've got to run. Campaign staff meeting in forty-five minutes, and I'm only going to be on time if I speed my pert little ass over to Manchester. I'll call you later, all right?"

"Sure. Thanks for coming by. It...it meant a lot."

"Meant a lot to me, too. Especially when you didn't shoot me."

I raised myself up and kissed her, and she smiled, and then she was gone.

I lowered myself back to bed, yawned, and thought about what I should do next, and when I looked at my bedside clock—keeping company with my nine-millimeter Beretta—I saw that another hour had passed.

Time to get up and get going.

Getting dressed after my shower, I felt like I hadn't eaten well in days, so I treated myself to a coronary-encouraging breakfast of scrambled eggs, bacon, toast, and some shaved potato bits that passed as home fries. I left the television off and switched on the radio to a classical station out of Boston that never broadcast news or political commentary, and with that comfort, I ate well.

After a quick wash of the dishes, I felt better than I had in days. I went out to the entranceway to get my coat, and then to walk across the way up to the Lafayette House, to get the morning papers, and then—

Something was on the floor, by the door. An envelope.

I picked it up. An interview request, no doubt, from some enterprising news media type who had snuck down my snowy driveway. It made me think about Felix and his direct way of dealing with the news media. I thought about wandering up to the driveway with my eight-millimeter rifle strapped to my back, and decided that was going against my lawyer's advice to keep what snipers call a low profile.

I opened up the envelope, and a heavy piece of stationery was inside, folded over in threes. I undid it and there were handwritten words penned there.

A clean, well-lit place with books and companions and soft chairs. What more can anyone want?

At eleven?

The sentiment and the handwriting were familiar. I could not believe it. I could not. But there it was.

I carefully put the paper back in the envelope, went upstairs, and placed the missive in a desk drawer. Saw the time. Just past 10:00 a.m.

I sat down in my chair, looked about at my collection of books, until I saw the ones I was looking for, old and unopened for so many years. There were four of them, large and flat and on the bottom of the farthest bookshelf.

I suppose I should have gone over there and pulled them free, to reminisce about what was and what might have been, but instead, I waited.

As the time passed, as the time always did.

Just before eleven—and after successfully driving past the lonely remnants of the media mob that had greeted me yesterday—I was in downtown Tyler, the small collection of office buildings and stores about a five-minute drive west of Tyler Beach. The beach is just a village precinct within the town of Tyler, and the two have always had a rocky relationship, like that of two brothers, one a barhopping ne'er-do-well, the other a sober, churchgoing type. But while the beach has much more to offer than the town proper, the town has one advantage the beach doesn't: a bookstore.

It's off Lafayette Road, on a small side street called Water Street, and, oddly enough, is called Water Street Books. It's in a two-story brick building, with small green canvas awnings. I walked in. There was a large area in the center, lined with bookshelves after bookshelves, and before me was a display with a current *New York Times* bestseller. I walked past that collection of books, with the eyes of Mona Lisa following me, and to the rear of the store, which had padded chairs and coffee tables.

There was a small table with fresh-brewed coffee and tea and some snacks that operated on the honor system, and I poured myself a cup of coffee, dropped a dollar bill in an overflowing straw basket, started browsing. It was, as described, a clean, well-lit place with books and companions and soft chairs.

I found her at the farthest end of the bookstore, curled up with a coffee table book about Shaker furniture. She was sitting in a large easy chair, windows behind her overlooking a small park, and she had on designer jeans and a dull red turtleneck sweater. A matching red knit cap was pulled over her head, her blond hair tucked up underneath, and as I approached, she looked up and smiled right through me.

"Lewis," she said.

"Barbara."

She stood up and I automatically came forward, and we exchanged hugs, the touch and scent bringing back old college-aged memories, memories I didn't even know I had anymore. She kissed me on the cheek, and I returned the favor, and then we sat down, holding hands, just for the briefest and most delicate of moments.

"You look great," I said.

"Right."

"No, I mean it. You look like you just left the Student Union, heading out to McGrath's Pub."

She smiled at the name of the old pub back at Indiana University, where we had spent long hours drinking cheap beer and solving the problems of the world, and she said, "You look good, too."

"Now you're the one who's lying," I said. "Face not as smooth, hair not as thick."

The smile was still there. "I like your face. It's got character. It's got life to it. Are you all right...with everything else?"

I nodded. "I am. I had nothing to do with the shooting."

"Of course. My staff tried to brief me last night and I told them not to bother. I knew you could have never done anything like that."

"Thanks. And was it your staff who delivered your note this morning?"

She nodded, the smile...oh, that smile. "Yes, an eager intern who knows how to keep her mouth shut, and who loved pretending to be a reporter begging you for an interview by sliding that envelope under your door."

I looked around the nearly empty bookstore. "Speaking of staff...how in hell did you get here without a media mob following you?"

The smile took on an icy edge I had never seen before. "One of the advantages of being the wife of the senator, and a possible first lady. The staff have their demands, but they also know I have a long memory, a memory of who's been helpful and who's been a pain in the ass, a memory I'll bring with me to the East Wing. And if I need a chunk of time here and there for personal time, without handlers, without staff, even without Secret Service protection, then that's the way it's going to be."

"I see."

Then the ice disappeared from the smile, and the old Barbara was sitting there before me. "Listen to me, a cranky and confident bitch on wheels. When I get to the East Wing. If I get to the East Wing, my old friend. There's a lot ahead, and New Hampshire's just the second step."

"How's the senator doing?"

"With the shooting? Jack's shrugging it off. That's one of his many admirable qualities. When he is focused on a goal, on something he desires so much, he won't let anything get in his way. His opponents in Georgia. Members of his own party who thought he should sit this one out. Or one deranged shooter."

"I saw you at the rally. You must have been scared."

The barest of shrugs. "It happened so fast...I don't think I had time to think about anything. The first shot sounded like a firecracker going off, but the Secret Service...they move very, very fast. I have bruises on my arms where they grabbed me. They don't fool around."

"I'm glad."

She shifted her legs in the chair. "What I found amazing was that I saw you in the audience. That was a surprise and a half. How did you end up in New Hampshire?"

"Long story," I said. "Quick version is that I ended up here after working for a while at the Department of Defense. I had some old memories about being a kid here on the coast, before my mom and dad moved us out to Indiana. And now I'm a columnist for a magazine."

"*Shoreline.*"

"That's right."

Barbara reached out, touched the back of my wrist. "Congratulations to you, at least. You and I, back at school, we were going to be great writers. Journalists who make a difference. To report from D.C., from conflicts in Asia and Africa. Struggle and fight to bring out the truth, to change the world."

"Not much change comes from a monthly column."

"Maybe, but at least you're still writing. Me...I'm lucky if I get to edit some of Jack's speeches. When he's in a good mood, that is."

I put my coffee cup down on the table between us. "Last I knew, back at school, you went out to D.C. on an internship."

Her voice was flat. "And never came back to Indiana. And never wrote or called you. I know. It's been a long time. I hope you've forgiven me since then."

I looked at her. "I have."

"Thanks. I mean that, Lewis. Thanks." She sighed. "Such a story. Went out there, just for a semester. Interning at Congressman Reisinger's office. Not supposed to do much of anything but answer phones and sort mail...but there was a vicious flu season that semester. Bunch of staffers got sick. So I got pushed into service, got myself noticed, and as time went on...I didn't want to go back to Indiana. And I didn't want to report the news. I wanted to be on the inside, making the news. So I transferred out to George Washington University, stayed and worked on Capitol Hill, and eventually, I got noticed by another congressman."

"The Right Honorable Representative Jackson Hale."

That made her giggle. "Such a mouthful, right? And if you had told me that I was going to marry a Southern congressman, a guy from Georgia, I would have told you, you were crazy. But I did...and you know why? Because I could sense he was going places. That he was going to make lots of news, and besides the fact that I was attracted to him, I wanted to be a part of it. So I got used to breakfast meetings, fried catfish, grits in the morning, and learning who races what kind of vehicle in NASCAR. Along the way, a wonderful son and a wonderful daughter. And here we are. All because of a bad flu season, all those years ago."

I made a point of looking around the store. "Yes. Here we are. A clean, well-lit place with books and companions and soft chairs."

"What could be better?" And then she looked down, as if suddenly fascinated by the cover of the book in her lap.

There was just the quickest of moments there, I think, when we were both in our early twenties, full of energy and good intentions, and recalling our shared love of bookstores, and our solemn vow to each other that if our relationship continued, that if we made it that much more, that we would always have to live in a place that had a fine bookstore.

Old promises.

She looked up and said, "My story. And what's yours? How did you end up at the Pentagon?"

"Senior year," I said. "I had done my own internship the previous summer, at the *Indianapolis Star*. I was getting ready to apply there for a full-time gig after graduation, when I saw this little ad in the campus paper. Something about did you think you were smart enough to work in an intelligence agency for the United States government. I don't know why, I just thought it was a bit of a goof, a bit of a challenge. So I applied, got a response, took an intelligence test with a few score other college students, and after a bunch of interviews and more tests, there I was, working on the inside."

"Regret not staying in journalism?"

"Not at the time," I said. "Later...yeah, there were regrets. But at the time, I thought I had the best job in the world. I was on the inside. I knew things that would never appear in newspapers, would never appear in print. I could spend the day reading, spend the day talking to people, following leads and tips, and then write reports. That's it. One week, a report prepared for one person, another week, a report prepared for the Joint Chiefs. That was my job. And at the time, I loved it."

"Now?"

"It's...the past. Some good memories. One very bad memory. And here I am."

"Why did you leave?"

My throat felt just a bit thick I wanted so much to let it all go, but yet...

"I'm sorry Barbara. I can't say. When I left, I had to sign a nondisclosure agreement. It...it was tough. But here I am."

"Married?"

"Nope."

She smiled. "A woman friend?"

Somehow, a tinge of guilt. Why? "Yes. A dear one. In fact, she's working hard to see your husband get elected."

"Good for her."

Barbara looked at her wristwatch, a delicate gold item that must have cost the good senator a chunk of change, some time ago. "Lewis...I've been here as long as I can. It's...it's been good to see you."

"The same."

She stood up and so did I, and there was another embrace, quicker this time around, and she said, "I just wanted to see you. Funny, isn't it? I saw you at the rally and, well...you look good. I'm glad you came." The old smile. "If we're lucky, I'll make sure you get another invite. To the inauguration, next year."

"That'd be great."

Another touch of her hand to mine, and then she was out the door.

I stayed behind for a while, browsing through the books, enjoying this time in a clean, well-lit place with books, all by my lonesome.

6

Back home, I passed through the dwindling crowd of news media, out there freezing for the dubious possible privilege of talking to me, including one enterprising type who wouldn't move from in front of my Ford Explorer. Considering I had gotten enough law enforcement attention already—and not wanting to dent the fender or hood of my Explorer—I let the driver's side window down and waited. The man was thickset, balding, with steel-rimmed glasses, and he said, "First things first, Mr. Cole. I'm not a reporter."

"Bully for you," I said.

He passed over a business card. "My name is Chuck Bittner. I'm with Tucker Grayson's presidential campaign. I'd like to talk to you."

I tossed the business card on the passenger's seat of the Explorer. "Sorry, Mr. Bittner. The feeling's not mutual."

He tried to lean into the open window. "Mr. Cole, look, General Grayson is what this country needs, and I'm dedicated to seeing him elected. Just a few minutes of your time, and I'm sure you'll agree with me, and agree to help his campaign by—"

I raised the window and kept on driving, and when I got down to my house, there was yet another visitor, standing outside the front door. I had an urge to keep on driving, to see if I could make my visitor run into the snowbank, but I was a good boy and turned into the garage.

I parked my Explorer, got out, and said, "Last time somebody stood there, he claimed to be a Secret Service agent. Glad to know your credentials seem to be in order. Or at least I hope."

Secret Service Agent Glen Reynolds didn't smile at my little gibe and said, "Do you want to see them again?"

"Nope."

He said, "I'd like to talk to you for a few minutes."

I scratched at my face. "Thought my attorney was pretty clear, Agent Reynolds. You weren't to talk to me without his say-so."

"Maybe I tried to call him. Perhaps I didn't reach him."

"Perhaps," I said.

"Or maybe I just wanted to see if I could talk to you without your hiding behind your attorney."

"I'm not sure if 'hiding' is an appropriate term, Agent Reynolds."

A quick nod. "My apologies then."

"All right. I guess we can talk away."

I stood there, and he stood there, and he said, "Well?"

"Yes?"

"Can we go inside?"

"Oh. Can you say the magic word?"

A slight grimace. "Mr. Cole, can we please go inside to talk?"

"Sure," I said, smiling at him.

I unlocked the front door, went inside, and dumped my coat on a nearby chair, and Agent Reynolds followed me and sat down on my couch. From inside his coat he pulled out a section of newspaper, which he tossed on the coffee table. I saw the familiar layout and typeface of the *Tyler Chronicle.*

"This article is not helpful," he said.

"Really?"

"Really. Not helpful at all."

"Then I suggest you talk to the reporter. Who was it?"

His voice got sharp. "You know who wrote it."

"So talk to her. Why talk to me?"

"Because of what she said in the story. Lots of juicy information and quotes about the shooting at the conference center, all of the quotes anonymous. None of them from me, none of them from the state police or anybody else officially involved in the investigation. So it was you. Why?"

"Seemed to be the right thing at the time."

"To interfere with the investigation?"

"Some investigation," I said. "You thought you had it wrapped up in a nice little package with my arrest. A one-day investigation, with everything all confirmed and concluded, no more work to be done. Right?"

His face flushed. "We followed the leads that were there. Beginning with your weapon, your fingerprints, your presence at the campaign rally. To do anything else would have been foolish."

"Well, it seemed foolish to me."

"Then consider yourself lucky that you don't have to worry about such things."

"All right, I'll do just that."

Reynolds said, "The investigation is continuing, Mr. Cole. Both into the shooting at the campaign rally and this supposed Secret Service agent who saw you the other day." He gestured to the newspaper on my coffee table. "Question I have is this. Do you intend to keep on interfering with our investigation?"

"Guess it depends on your definition of interfering, Agent Reynolds."

"All right. Here's my definition. Talking to the press again about what happened at the campaign rally. How's that?"

"Fair enough," I said. "And just to let you know, my press appearances have officially ended. That sound good to the Treasury Department?"

"That sounds excellent, Mr. Cole."

"Glad to be of service."

"Now, about this Spenser Harris. Do you have any information as to who he is, or where he came from?"

"No," I said. "Do you?"

He paused for a second, like he was debating what to tell me, and he said, "No, not a whit. We've done a canvass of what passes for a neighborhood around here, talked to the people at the Lafayette House and other nearby hotels and motels to see if someone by that name was registered. Nothing."

"Sorry to hear that," I said.

Reynolds said, "I'm sure it won't come as any surprise to you that we now believe this fake agent was connected with the shooting at Senator Hale's campaign rally."

"No, it's not a surprise."

"And you'll let me know if you find out anything about who he really is?"

"Of course."

"Thank you," he said, picking up the offending piece of newsprint and putting it back into his coat. He got up from the couch and I walked with him to the door, and before he left, he said, "One more thing, Mr. Cole."

I had to grin. "You know, there's always one more thing, isn't there. You learn that at the training academy or something?"

His smile didn't look particularly inviting. "Here's the deal. I'm in no position to tell you what to do with your personal life, but I think it would be a very good thing if you stayed away from the senator's wife over the next several days. Some of the senator's staff and supporters...well, they may make your life difficult if such news were to be made widely known."

"Really?"

"Really. Even if you both do enjoy spending time at the local bookstore. Have I made myself clear?"

"Quite."

"Good."

And then he left, and I went back into my house.

I called Annie and got her voice mail and then I sat on the couch and just brooded for a bit. Somewhere out there was Spenser Harris and his friends, and I so wanted to talk to him again, to find out who they were and why they wanted me to be their patsy. But where to start? Felix was out there, sniffing around, and I knew he would do a better, quicker, and more thorough job than I could imagine. Plus, trying to poke around on my own to find out who Spenser Harris was, coupled with the publicity tagged on me with the assassination attempt, that would pretty much take care of my promise to Annie not to do anything to disturb the Hale campaign.

So instead of spending the rest of the day on the couch, thinking useless thoughts, I went upstairs and tried to decide what kind of column I was going to write for the June issue of *Shoreline*. It being January, it was hard to get in the mood to write for an issue of the magazine that would be published in the season of bright sunshine and warm nights. Part of the fun challenges of being a magazine columnist: your writing clock is always three or four months off.

The phone rang and I picked it up, waiting for my old and trusty Apple iMac to boot up. "Hello?"

"Mr. Cole?"

"Yes."

"I'm calling from CNN and was wondering—"

"Sorry, not interested."

I hung up the phone, opened up my word processing program. Looked at my blank computer screen. I suppose I could write about the annual migration of tourists to the beach communities of New England, and how their presence changed the atmosphere of these little towns, and how this caused tension between the tourists and the year-round residents. I started writing down a few thoughts but then stopped. Practically every other newspaper or newsmagazine that covered this region did the same outsiders impacting-the-locals story, and who was I to inflict another such story upon the long-suffering readers of *Shoreline*?

The phone rang. "Hello?"

"Mr. Cole?"

"Yep."

"Mr. Cole, I'm calling from *The New York Times*."

"Really?"

"Um, yes, I'm from *The New York Times* and I was wondering—"

"Well, thanks for calling, but I get the paper from across the way. At a local hotel. It seems I can't get a subscription to my residence. Why's that?"

"Ah, Mr. Cole, I'm not calling from the circulation department. My name is George Mulvey, I'm a reporter from the *Times*, and—"

"Oh, a reporter. I apologize. I thought you were trying to sell me a subscription. But I guess you want to talk to me about a news story."

"Yes, I do, and I'd like to know—"

"Sorry, not interested."

I hung up.

Before me was the screen, still very much blank.

Why not a story about the islands of the New England shoreline? Too often my columns had been about the actual coastline of New England, about the communities and fishing villages, and why not expand it a bit? Across the way was the Isles of Shoals—All right, maybe not those islands, they'd been written about more than enough times. But there was Block Island down in Long Island...nope, overwritten as well. Nantucket and Martha's Vineyard? Please. How many forests had to die to churn out copy about those two special places every year? Long Island sound again, but Plum Island had been claimed by a well-known and well-regarded novelist a few years back, and there were the islands off the coast of Maine, all one or two hundred of them, and how could I choose, and—

The phone rang. "Mr. Cole?"

"The same."

"Mr. Cole, it's Chuck Bittner again, from the Tucker Grayson campaign. Look, I really think it would be in your interest to talk to me, so that your story can get the proper attention it deserves, about your relationship with the—"

"Mr. Bittner."

"Yes?"

I turned in my office chair. "You're an oppo researcher for the general's campaign, am I right?"

That seemed to make him pause. "Suppose...suppose I say no?"

"Then I'm not going to talk to you for even a second."

There was a sigh. "All right...yes, yes, I do perform opposition research for the general. But each campaign has such researchers, and I really need to talk to you, about you and the senator's wife. It's a story that really needs to be fleshed out, and—"

"Nope."

"But you said you'd talk to me!"

"No, I said I wouldn't talk to you if you denied being an opposition researcher," I said. "But you know what? I'm still not going to talk to you, even if you did admit to being an oppo researcher."

Then I hung up the phone. I was getting pretty damn good at it.

All right, back to the patient and blank computer screen.

Maybe it was time to think outside the box. Maybe I could do a column about odd aspects of history that had happened along the New Hampshire coastline that not many people knew about. Like the evidence that Vikings had settled here more than a thousand years ago. Or the case of the German U-boats that had been interned at the end of World War II up at the Porter Naval Shipyard. Or—

Or give it a rest, I thought. Who'd want to read offbeat stories like those two?

Another ring of the phone. "Hello?"

"Lewis? It's Annie. How's that sickness treating you?"

"Sickness seems to be bored with me and is leaving. How are you doing?"

There was pause, and I wondered if she hadn't heard me, and there was the briefest of sighs. "Lewis...I was talking to some senior staff here this morning. About you. And the shooting. And one other thing that somebody slipped out, a big-ass secret that only a few in the campaign know about."

"Yes?"

"Lewis...I've come to know you're a man with secrets. You've not told me much about the scars you have. Or what you did at the Pentagon. Or how you ended up in a prime beachfront home on a magazine columnist's salary. You've joked and fooled around and have really never answered my questions directly, and I've put up with that. Your other...your other assets have outweighed whatever questions or concerns I've had."

My hand tightened on the telephone receiver. I knew where this was going.

"So, having said all of that," she went on, "Would you mind telling me why you've never told me about you and the senator's wife? Barbara? Why you decided to keep that little secret from me? Good God, I can't believe the news media have picked up on it already...her former boyfriend being initially charged in the shooting. So far, it's only the staff who knows this."

"'We knew each other in college," I said. "Just for a while. It was...I didn't think it was that important, Annie."

Another sigh. "I'm working on a campaign for a man who might be the next president of the United States, and you used to date the future first lady when you were in college. And you didn't think to tell me?"

"I was...it just didn't...well, to tell you the truth, I didn't think Senator Hale was going to make it this far. So I didn't think it was worth bringing up."

Annie said, "Nope. Not good enough. I think there's something else. And once you figure it out, do me the favor of telling me. All right?"

It was my turn to sigh. "Sure. Look, there was no secret agenda, it was just—"

"Lewis, you're a man with secrets. Most times it's charming. This isn't one of those times."

"I hear you."

"Thanks. Look, we'll be pretty busy over here tonight. I don't think I'm going to make it over to your place later."

"Oh. I see."

"No, really...we're busy. I'll see if I can't come over tomorrow. All right?"

"That would be great."

A few more words here and there, and then she hung up. Before me again was the blank screen.

The hell with it.

I was done for the day. The next morning I went for a quick walk across the street to the Lafayette House to get my morning newspapers. Being in such an isolated location, newspaper delivery was out of the question, and since I got my mail from a post office box—which meant the usual drive into town—I most always got my newspapers from the gift shop at the Lafayette House.

The air was sharp and crisp as I walked up my driveway.

Hands in my pockets, I carefully made my way up to the hotel's parking lot, trying to decide what to say to any die-hard members of the fourth estate who might still be on stakeout duty. But when I reached the parking lot, I hated to say it, but I was disappointed. No one was waiting for me. The reporting hand, having writ, had obviously moved on to another story.

I took in a deep breath of the fresh sea air. Some other story was no doubt out there, being chased by the dedicated men and women of the news media, and I was now content to be left alone.

I went across Atlantic Avenue, up to the white colossus that was the Lafayette House, and then strode into the marble and glass splendor of its lobby. To the left was the gift shop, and I left a few seconds later, with five newspapers under my arm, after exchanging the usual pleasantries with the gift shop manager, a retired air force chief warrant officer named Stephanie Sussex. She had short gray hair, old-fashioned, black-rimmed glasses that were bowed like cat whiskers, a black turtleneck adorned by a simple gold crucifix, and the same old joke.

"Still reading for five people?"

"Looks that way, doesn't it."

She rang up my purchases and said, "Least you could do is make 'em pay for it. Have a good one."

"Thanks," I said. "I'll try."

I liked the feeling of the newspapers under my arm. I know that we are in a new world of computerized information, with most of the world's newspapers now available with the click of a keyboard or a mouse, but I still like the feel of newspapers in my hands. It just feels more real. Besides, the computer geniuses who brought us to this brave new world still haven't come up with a way of devising a personal computer that you can easily carry into the bathroom when the need arises.

I went through the parking lot on my way back, seeing a panel truck at the north end of the lot. JIMMY'S ELECTRICAL SERVICE, FALCONER, it said on the side of the truck, and I felt bad for Jimmy, having to hump his equipment up to the hotel.

Down the driveway I went, and back home, there was someone waiting for me at the doorstep to my house, sitting there, legs stretched out, looking quite comfortable. It looked like the fourth estate hadn't given up quite yet in their quest to interview me. I came down the driveway, focusing on my footwork, making sure I didn't slip and knock my skull against a piece of rock outcropping. I looked up once, and my visitor was still there, sitting patiently. Well, he could be as patient as he wanted. I certainly wasn't going to say much when I got to the doorway. I was done with the news media. The primary election was just a few days away, and I was going to keep my head down, ignore the senator's wife, and make nice with Annie Wynn after our last discouraging phone call.

When I got to my house, I stopped, as if the snow about my feet had suddenly turned into ice, keeping me still.

For before me was Spenser Harris, fake Secret Service agent.

I stood, waiting to see if he would say anything, but that didn't seem possible.

For he was dead.

7

I gingerly walked around, checking to make sure he was as dead as he looked. He was on the snow-covered ground next to the doorsteps, leaning up against the stone foundation. His legs were out in front of him, his hands were folded primly in his lap. His eyes were closed. Thank God for small favors. I looked to the side of his head and saw a mass of blood and torn flesh and splintered bone just behind his right ear. He seemed to be wearing the same coat and necktie and slacks combination from his first visit to my home.

I stepped back, taking a breath. I didn't like him, and didn't like what he had done to me, but still...I didn't like seeing him dead on my doorstep.

Another breath.

There were things to do, procedures to be followed, phone calls to be made.

I unlocked the door and went inside.

I left the dead form of Spenser Harris behind me.

I dropped the newspapers and went upstairs, taking the steps two at a time. Into my office, up to a small closet. Opened the closet, went through some boxes of papers and files until I saw a small, multicolored box stuck in the rear. I ripped the box open, tearing a bit of finger skin in the process, and sat on the floor, going through about twenty pages of instructions in

English, Spanish, French, and German, and then tossed the paperwork aside.

Before me was a prepaid cell phone, about the size of two credit cards together. I had gotten it as a Christmas gift the previous year from Detective Sergeant Woods, when she had told me that in this new age of ours, it was customary to be accessible through instant communications. I replied that I rather liked being inaccessible. And she had smiled and said next time I was driving in East Overshoe, New Hampshire, tracking down a story, it would be nice to have a cell phone in case my car died or I ran into a moose.

I had agreed and had promptly put the phone in my closet. Until now.

It had no charge in its little battery, so I managed to plug it into a free receptacle in my office. I fumbled through a few more minutes of trying to figure out what in hell to do with this marvelous instrument, when I started punching in the numerals.

By now, I guess shock was coursing its way through my system, for my hands were shaking.

But I still managed to dial the number. I waited as it rang.

And waited. Conscious that a body was cooling itself outside my front door.

The phone was answered. "Yeah."

"Hi, it's me."

"Oh. What's up."

"Got a situation," I said.

"A situation?"

"Quite the situation."

"Go ahead."

I said, "Remember that joke you told me a couple of months ago, about the difference between a friend and a true friend?"

"Yeah."

"I need a true friend. Right now."

"Where are you?"

"Home."

"You injured?"

"Nope."

The voice was as brisk and as professional as it had been from the first greeting. "Be there in under a half hour. Don't touch a damn thing."

"I won't."

"Good."

I hung up the cell phone. The joys of being accessible.

And somewhat untraceable. I wasn't sure just how untraceable this phone call would be, but there was no doubt that using the old landline telephone in my home would have been as visible as elephant tracks in the snow. Maybe this call would be harder to trace.

Maybe. I sure hoped so.

Then again, maybe I was just fooling myself.

However, after seeing what had been out there in the snow, I was probably in the mood for being fooled.

I tossed the cell phone across the room and went back downstairs.

I stood out there in the cold, hands in my coat, trying to ignore the body nearby. Hell of a thing. But I couldn't do it. I looked over at Spenser Harris. Still dead. Lots of questions and no answers were rattling inside my head. I toed a piece of ice-encrusted snow.

Just stood there. My breath was visible in the cold air. The sound of the waves just a few feet away were always there, and always ignored, until one listened. I was listening. The waves were constant, were a part of the background.

Toed another piece of ice. Waited. Another noise.

I looked up. A dark green Honda Pilot was maneuvering its way down the driveway, its four-wheel drive making the sloppy trip look easy. Something tight in my chest started to ease. I took my hands out of my pockets.

The Pilot stopped. Felix Tinios got out, looked at me and my uninvited guest. From his dark wool coat, he pulled out two sets of rubber gloves, tossed one set to me, which I caught with one hand. Damn, wasn't I good?

Felix said, "All right. Time for talking is later. Time for action is now. Got it?"

"Gotten."

He put on his gloves, and I followed as well. Instantly my hands felt warm and clammy. Felix went to the rear of the Pilot, opened up the hatchback. With the middle row of seats folded down, there was plenty of room back there. Felix reached in and pulled out a black rubberized body bag, and my stomach did a slow flip-flop, realizing once again what kind of man Felix was: the kind of guy who had ready access to body bags.

But I sure as hell wasn't complaining.

Felix made his way to the body of Spenser Harris, flipped the bag out on the ground. There was a heavy-duty zipper that started at the top, went down the side and then to the bottom, like a garment bag designed for undertakers. Felix zipped the bag open, the noise sounding obscene in my tiny front yard, and opened up the flap. He looked up at me, his face serious.

"Can you give me a hand? You going to be all right with this?"

"Yeah,"

"All right, let's move him. You get the legs."

Felix went to the rear of the body, reached under his arms, lifted him off the steps, and I grabbed the legs. The phrase "dead weight" rang through my mind as we moved the body over to the open bag. I slipped some in the snow and dropped Spenser's legs, but Felix had it under control, and got most of the upper body over the bag. I maneuvered the legs in and then Felix flipped the cover back over, zipped the damn thing shut. Suddenly it just felt better. There was no longer a body in my front yard. There was just a lumpy thing inside a bag, something without a face.

"Okay. Handles on both sides. Let's get him in."

As he always is, Felix was correct. Heavy black web handles were on each side of the bag, and we both grabbed on and got him off the ground. A handful of steps later, we had him in the rear of the open Pilot. Felix went forward to the passenger's side door and dragged the body bag in. When he had moved the bag far enough, I slammed the hatchback door shut. By now Felix was in the driver's seat and the engine was running. I joined him and he said, "You don't need to be here. I can handle it."

"You may think I don't need to be here, but I do. Let's get going."

"Sure."

Felix maneuvered the Pilot about in my yard, and then we were heading back up the driveway, to the parking lot of the Lafayette House, and in a minute or so, we were heading south, away from my home, away from Tyler

Beach. We both pulled off our rubber gloves. My hands felt moist and soft. I was feeling just a little bit better. But only a bit.

We didn't go far, only to Salisbury, the first town over the Massachusetts border. We took Route 1-A, Atlantic Avenue, all the way south. I was conscious of how tight my chest was as I sat next to Felix.

He said, "All right. Good job back there."

"Thanks. Coming from you that's a hell of a compliment."

"Do you know who he is? Or was?"

"Yeah. The fake Secret Service agent who scammed me a few days back. Spenser Harris."

"No shit."

"True. No shit."

Felix made a show of looking back at the shape in the rear and turned back. "Strange world, isn't it. Last time we were together, I said I'd do a little digging, see what I could find out about this guy, and now he ends up dead on your doorstep. Sorry I wasn't quicker finding him."

"You're forgiven."

"Gee, thanks. Well, I'll keep on digging, but having your Spenser Harris show up dead puts a damper on things."

"I guess so. And when did he become my Spenser Harris?"

Felix shrugged. "He was in your front yard. Possession being nine-tenths of the law, it seemed to be a logical assumption."

I told him what he could do with his logic, and that made him smile.

Traffic was light as we went by the deserted buildings of Tyler Beach, approaching the drawbridge that led into Falconer, the southernmost town in New Hampshire. Stuck in almost every snowbank was a campaign sign. HALE FOR AMERICA'S TOMORROWS. WIN WITH WALLACE. POMEROY/PRESIDENT. GRAYSON FOR PRESIDENT. Lots of signs, all with the same color pattern. Red, white, and blue. True imagination at work. It was good to look at the signs. It didn't require me to think of the body riding back there in the rear.

"His body hadn't gone into rigor yet," Felix said. "Figure he's been dead only an hour or so. That sound right?"

"Yes, it does. I was out at the Lafayette House, getting my morning newspapers. I was out maybe fifteen, twenty minutes at the most."

"Any idea who did it?"

"Not a one."

We went over the drawbridge spanning the small harbor of Tyler Beach. Off to the right were the concrete buildings of the Falconer nuclear power plant, quietly producing power, with nary a protester in sight. We were in Falconer for about a minute or two, and then we were in the Commonwealth of Massachusetts, in its northernmost community of Salisbury. For some reason I turned again and looked back at the body bag.

Felix said, "Any idea why this guy was killed on your front lawn?"

I turned back. The body bag hadn't moved a bit.

I said, "Have an idea or two. Main idea is...well, I think whoever did it wanted me to take the fall for trying to kill Senator Hale. When that didn't stick, they wanted another try by dumping Spenser Harris's body in my front yard."

In Salisbury, Felix maneuvered the Pilot through its nearly empty streets. "For what reason? If they wanted you to get arrested for Harris's death, why not keep an eye on the place and make a phone call when you arrive?"

I folded my arms. "They were probably counting on my civic duty. A phone call to the cops, the arrival of the cops and the state police Major Crimes Unit, followed by another media circus, all just before the New Hampshire primary."

"Then why didn't you do your civic duty, Lewis?"

"What?"

Felix said, "You're one of the more civic guys I know. Any other guy found a body in his yard, the call would go to the cops. Especially since you have such a fine relationship with the local constabulary's lead detective. So why no call?"

I said, "You can probably figure it out."

Felix grinned. "Women. Aren't they something? If this dump was from opponents of Senator Hale, wanting to give him another bucketful of bad publicity just before the primary, then you didn't want to give them that publicity, did you? All for your girl Annie."

I sighed. "That's as good a guess as any."

"Works for me."

I turned to him. "I suppose if the Pomeroy campaign was up to something nefarious like this, you'd let me know."

Felix laughed. "From what I know of the Pomeroy campaign, Lewis, they couldn't spell 'nefarious,' never mind knowing what it means."

Now we were in an industrial part of Salisbury, near I-95, and the buildings were one-story concrete and brick structures—printing plants, small businesses—and, there, just ahead, a barbwire enclosure, a self-storage business called, aptly enough, the Space Station.

The gate was open, and Felix drove in and went down one of the open lanes to the right, flanked on both sides by one-story buildings with roll-up steel doors. At the end of the building on the right, the doors were big enough to let a vehicle pass through, Felix stopped the Pilot at the stall at the end of the lane. He got out, undid the combination lock at the side of the door, and rolled it up. He flicked on the interior lights for the now open storage unit and got back inside.

"Where did you get the Pilot?"

"A business associate. Let's leave it at that."

"Some business associate."

Felix slowly backed the Honda into the storage room. "Didn't think I could use my Mercedes. And I didn't want to use your Ford. And when we're done with the Pilot, it's going to get steam-cleaned and detailed. Just to be on the safe side, which is a side I love being on. Come on, we've still got work to do."

We both got out on the concrete floor of the storage room, and Felix went to the entrance and lowered the steel door. It was now quiet, and it felt good to be inside with the door closed, away from any curious neighbors. I followed Felix as he went forward. There were storage lockers on both sides and, at the end, a large top-opening refrigerator. He propped open the cover to the refrigerator and said, "He'll fit."

"How come I get the feeling you've done this before?"

While there was humor in his voice, there was no humor in his expression. "Don't make me answer dangerous questions, Lewis. Deniability is a wonderful gift."

Back to the Pilot we went, and up went the rear hatch. Felix reached in and said, "I want to open up the bag for a moment and examine our guest."

"I'm not going to stop you, so go right ahead."

The interior was roomy enough so that Felix knelt down and opened the bag up, the zipper sounding better here than at my house. He worked for a while, his hands busy inside the bag and the clothing of the dead man, and he looked at me, his face impassive. "Dead people are hard to work with. Frozen, not moving, resisting."

"Yeah, well, we've all got problems."

"At least we're doing better than your friend here."

"Not my friend."

"If you say so."

He worked for a couple of minutes more and said, "Lewis, he's been cleaned up. No driver's license, no money, not even a scrap of paper. Very professional."

I thought about a promise I had made the day before to the very real Secret Service agent Glen Reynolds. I had promised to let him know if I found out the man's true identity. So far, I hadn't, so at least that was a promise I could keep.

"Thanks for looking," I said. "Can we get this wrapped up?"

"Sure."

The zipper went shut and Felix came back out and started pulling at the body bag, and I followed suit. A few steps later, the body of Spenser Harris went into the refrigerator, and the lid shut down.

Felix looked at me. "You okay?"

"Sure am. Could use a drink, though."

He smiled. "Damn it, man, it's not even ten in the morning."

"What does that have to do with anything?"

He shrugged. "Not a damn thing. Let's go get those drinks."

We had a late breakfast at the Lafayette House, in the main dining room, with coffee and Belgian waffles and eggs Benedict and mimosas in tall, cold glasses and bacon and sausage. With each passing minute in the luxurious comfort of the hotel, I felt the tension slide away, like a solid block of ice exposed to the warm April sun. We were in a part of the dining room that had a fine view of Tyler Beach, the parking lot, and if you looked real hard, the top of the roof of my house. Another reason I felt good is that the parking lot had the standard collection of vehicles belonging to hotel guests and visitors. There were no police cruisers or television vans out there, looking to record Lewis Cole's next misadventure with the criminal justice system. Nothing at all. Quiet is a wonderful thing.

Felix said, "What now?"

"I find out who the hell's drawn a big bull's-eye on my back, that's what."

"Going to be hard to do, with your only link to them now resting comfortably in Salisbury."

"I'll think of something, I'm sure."

"And then what?" Felix asked. "Make them stop?"

"Sure. I'll appeal to their better nature. Or something."

"Or something."

I took a swallow of my mimosa, enjoying the mixed sensation of orange juice and champagne in my mouth. "Ask you a question?"

"Ask away."

"Why store him in the refrigerator? Why not the ocean? Or the proverbial shallow grave?"

Felix thought for a moment and said, "You dump a body, you can never get it back. Keep it in a safe place, you need it for something down the road, no matter how nutty or off the wall, you can get it."

"What in hell do you think we might need that body for?"

"You never know."

I took one last swallow of the mimosa. "So. If this goes south on us, what kind of trouble are we looking at?"

"The usual and customary. Concealing evidence. Obstruction of justice. Illegal transport of a dead body. Hell, maybe even suspicion of income tax evasion when it's all said and done."

I toasted him with an empty glass before putting it down on the tablecloth. "At least we have the best in legal representation."

Felix said, "You know, the night I saved Raymond Drake from a one-way trip out to Boston Harbor was the second-best investment I've ever made."

"And what was the first-best investment you've ever made?" Felix picked up the check, a nice surprise. "Some secrets should stay secrets, my friend. Let's go. I've got a Honda to clean up."

We walked outside to the main parking lot, and Felix said, "What's up for the rest of the day?"

I had to smile. "It's been a full day already. I think I'm going to take it a bit easy, but first I'm going back to the Lafayette House for a moment."

"What for?"

"Just to follow up on a hunch, that's all."

He held out his hand, and I gave it a firm shake. "Thanks. And thanks for the joke. It paid off."

"Sure," Felix said. "So. As a reminder: What's the difference between a friend and a true friend?"

And like clockwork, I answered, "A friend will help you move. A true friend will help you move bodies."

Felix laughed, slapped me on the shoulder. "Good job. Let's see if we can't keep this joke to ourselves for a while. You take care."

"You, too."

I stood in the parking lot and watched Felix drive out in his borrowed vehicle. No police vehicles followed him in pursuit. No helicopters descended with SWAT teams at the ready to intercept. Felix drove off, unimpeded.

I turned and went back into the Lafayette House.

8

Into the gift shop I went, and Stephanie was waiting on a couple that spoke English with a heavy German accent, and I wondered what would bring someone from Europe to my little corner of New Hampshire in the middle of winter. When they left, I went up to Stephanie and she raised an eyebrow at my approach.

"Drop your newspapers in the ocean already?"

"Nope. Not yet. German tourists?"

"I wish. Belong to some German television network. Here for our quadrennial circus. If you think local news media are goddamn divas, try those from Europe. Who the hell ever heard of copies of *Der Spiegel* ending up in a gift shop like this? Jesus. So. What's up?"

"Wondering if I could ask you a question."

"Sure."

"Who's the manager nowadays?"

"Paul Jeter."

"What's he like?"

"Truthfully?"

"Yeah. Truthfully."

She smiled. "Truthfully, he's a prick."

"Please, Stephanie, don't sugarcoat it."

"Well, that's how it is. Don't know any way around it. Used to be, under the old management, how this shop was run was mostly my business. If I made a nice little profit each month and there were no complaints from the customers, then I was doing all right and I could be left alone. Now...don't get me going. Some days, I think that man counts the number of toilet sheets in each stall just to keep track for tracking's sake and nothing else."

"Think I could talk to him?"

"Sure," she said. "For a prick he's open to seeing people. But Lewis...don't confuse being seen with being helped."

I thanked her and went to the main desk at the lobby, asked a perky female clerk if I could see Paul Jeter, and in a few minutes, I was ushered into his office on the same floor and with a stunning view of the side parking lot and assorted Dumpsters. I guess hotel management wasn't all it was cracked up to be. Jeter was about my age, heavyset, wearing a dark gray suit, white shirt, and dark gray tie. He had the look in his eyes of the kind of guy who couldn't walk past a mirror without checking his appearance. I passed over my business card, identifying me as a columnist for *Shoreline,* and he passed the card back.

"What can I do for you, Mr. Cole?"

"I was hoping for a favor from a neighbor."

"A neighbor?"

"Yes, I live across the street. At the old lifeboat station."

His eyebrow lifted just a bit. "Ah, yes, the writer. The one we allow to use our parking lot as an entry to his house."

"That's right."

"And what kind of favor would you like? Free towels? Free hotel room? Gift certificate to the restaurant?"

So far, Stephanie had been dead on in her description. Not that I had doubted her. I was just being hopeful.

"Nothing like that. I've heard that the past month or so, there's been a series of break-ins among guest cars across the way."

He seemed to take that in for a moment, and said, "If one has a large number of cars, there will always be some incidents of vandalism or theft. That's just normal. Why do you ask? Do you know anything about who might be breaking in?"

"No, I don't."

'Well...no offense, what do you know then, Mr. Cole?"

"I've heard that the hotel might have set up a camera surveillance system in the parking lot. To see who might be doing the break-ins."

Jeter shifted just a bit in his seat, enough to make the leather creak. His already chilly mood cooled even more. "Perhaps. Perhaps not. And what's the favor?"

It was my turn to be a bit cool. "The favor is...somebody came to my house this morning. I'd like to know who it was."

"Did the person break in? Commit some other offense?"

"He didn't break in. But in a manner of speaking, yes, he did commit an offense." Well, that was certainly one way of putting it.

He folded his hands across his chest. "Then I suggest you contact the police. If they are interested in what kind of surveillance system the Lafayette House may or may not have, then I'll have my lawyer talk to them."

I leaned forward a bit. "You see, that's where the thought of doing a favor comes in. I don't want to involve the police."

"No police. I see. But you'd rather involve the hotel in whatever you're trying to prove involving your visitor this morning. Thereby opening up the Lafayette House to certain legal liabilities. And I don't see why we should do that."

"All I want to do is look at the surveillance tape from this morning. That's all."

There was the shortest shake of the head. "I'm sorry, Mr. Cole, I'm forced to decline. While, of course, neither confirming nor denying that such a surveillance system exists."

"I see. So much for being neighborly."

The cool factor seemed to be enhanced by another ten degree drop in temperature.

"Neighborly is allowing you to continue using the Lafayette House ·parking lot as a gateway to your driveway. Not being neighborly would be putting up a concrete berm at that end of our lot. Catch the difference?"

It was time to leave, so I stood up and said, "Difference caught."

In the lobby of the Lafayette House, I was ambushed by a guy with a familiar face. Chuck Bittner of the Tucker Grayson for President campaign stood in front of me and said, "Mr. Cole. Please. Just five minutes. That's all I ask."

I wasn't in the mood, but I was also tired of being stalked by him, and with the primary just a few days out, defusing him now might save me some aggravation later on.

If I was lucky, but Lady Luck seemed to have been taking a vacation lately.

"Five minutes," I said. "Three hundred seconds. Make them count."

We sat in a secluded corner of the lobby, in nice, comfortable chairs, and he leaned across a glass-topped coffee table and said, "You're a New Hampshire resident, so I won't insult you by asking if you know anything about General Grayson and his career. We've been publicizing his career very heavily these past few months."

"Career United States Army, former head of NATO, roving ambassador to the Mideast and Southeast Asia, or wherever else the current administration believes a firestorm can be snuffed out by his charming presence."

"Very good." He suddenly smiled, which I found disquieting for some reason. "There are those who hate your little state, hate the fact that it has such impact every four years. Every four years, the same arguments. Your state is too rural. Your state is too white. Your state is too rich. So forth and so on. But you know what? Your state takes its presidential primary role seriously. That's what I love. Retail politics, right on the ground. Candidates forced to think on their feet in living rooms and town halls, to answer questions from real voters. Quite refreshing. Suppose we gave the first-in-the-nation primary to Michigan or Ohio or California. What then?"

I said, "Might give us a break from all the attention and accompanying nonsense. Like dozens of phone calls every day, mailboxes filled with flyers. That sort of thing. Though I'd imagine the restaurant and hotel owners might complain."

"Maybe so," he said. "But a campaign that would start anywhere else but New Hampshire wouldn't be a true campaign, a true way of sorting out the best candidate possible by going to the people. It would be an airport tarmac and television studio campaign, that's what. And the only way the average voter would meet a candidate, or vice versa, would be through a television screen."

I said, "You're using up your precious three hundred seconds, Mr. Bittner."

He nodded. "I'm former U.S. Navy. Tend to get into briefing mode, and it takes me away from the point sometimes. So let me tell you this. You're an educated voter. You're a resident of this state. You have an important background."

"What kind of background?"

He looked about the lobby and lowered his voice. "Your time in the Pentagon. In the Department of Defense. In a little research group that you and your fellow people called the Marginal Issues Section. Researching and analyzing issues that fell through the cracks from the bigger boys in national intelligence."

I said not a word. The bastard had gotten places so very few had ever done. He seemed to note the look on my face and said, "You, more than many others, know what kind of president we need for this country, Mr. Cole. Someone who won't rely on paper treaties, won't rely on world organizations, won't rely on the supposed good nature of our adversaries. We need somebody with sharp elbows, who doesn't mind trusting as long as it's matched with verifying, and who's had experience making life-and-death decisions. In short, this country needs General Grayson."

I cleared my throat. "So far, it seems the majority of voters in Iowa and probably New Hampshire would disagree with that assessment."

"Perhaps, but that assessment can change. The right words from you, a former research analyst with the Department of Defense, who has, shall we say, an intimate familiarity with the senator and his campaign, could go a long way to taking the steam out of the Senator Hale campaign. And boost General Grayson's chances of making a respectable showing."

Out in the lobby there was a flare of light, and I looked over, saw a well-known television correspondent from one of the major networks doing a stand-up. He was wearing a suit coat, tie, and dirty blue jeans and wet boots. But who cared? The camera would only capture his serious tone and nature from the waist up.

I turned back to my inquisitor. "You seem to forget that a few days ago, I was the leading suspect in the attempted assassination of Senator Hale. Anything else I might say would probably be seen as the ravings of someone with a grudge against the senator."

A chilly smile. "So what? It means publicity, bad publicity for the senator, and a chance for you to contribute something to this country again."

Suddenly I stood up, my legs trembling, and I pulled up my coat and shirt to reveal a scar on the side of my abdomen. "I have five others like this on my body, and the chances of more appearing in the future, thanks to something that happened to me while in service of my country. I've already done my part. Don't ask me again. You and your general will have to do it on your own."

I stalked out, with Bittner calling after me, "We can still make a fuss, Cole, with or without you! It's your choice!"

I went out of the Lafayette House, fists clenched, trying to forget Bittner and trying to focus on my original intent in revisiting the damn place.

I stopped for a moment, looked up at the elaborate design of the building, a Victorian appearance from the times of the grand hotels at the turn of the twentieth century. I examined the windows, turrets, and moldings, looking for some telltale sign of some sort of recording device, and then I gave up. Surveillance cameras were no longer the big, bulky units that looked like they came from a 1960s science fiction movie. They could now be the size of one's thumb—or even smaller—and there were so many different places to hide them, up there in that elaborate building design.

Of course, allowing for the fact that they even existed, a particular fact that the hotel's manager was in no rush to confirm.

My hands went back into my coat pockets. The wind was coming up from the ocean at a stiff clip, and I walked away from the lobby entrance, across the bare pavement of Atlantic Avenue, and made my way through the parking lot again. As a joke, I counted the number of bumper stickers on the cars at rest in the lot. There were two for Senator Jackson Hale, five for Senator Nash Pomeroy, and one for General Tucker Grayson.

There was none for Congressman Clive Wallace. Most of the good congressman's voters and supporters didn't have the financial means to spend a night at the Lafayette House, which didn't mean much, since neither did I.

At home I hesitated outside my front door. There was a disturbance in the snow where Spenser Harris had rested, and where Felix and I had worked to get him bundled up and out of here. I went up to the stone foundation and the dark gray clapboards of my house. They were clean of any blood spatter, brain tissue, bone fragments, and clumps of hair. The mess had all been in the snow where he had lain, and Felix had taken care of that. A nice small gift. I stood up, breathed in hard. I guess I should have been thankful for small favors, but my thankfulness quotient was pretty damn low.

I went inside, glad to be inside and away from my front lawn. The day dragged by and as it got dark, I was thinking of dinner—which usually meant rummaging through the pantry and the freezer to see what was available—when the phone rang. I almost ignored the damn ringing, for it would probably mean a poll, yet another inquiring reporter, or the charming Chuck Bittner from the Tucker Grayson campaign.

I went to the phone and picked it up. Damn, it wasn't time yet to cower here.

"Hello."

"Good evening, sir," came a familiar female voice. "Was wondering if you had time for a brief survey."

"Sure," I said, sitting down on the couch. "Yes, yes, no, yes, and briefs."

Annie laughed. "Just what I was looking for. How are you doing?"

Hell of a question, considering what had gone on that morning, and I told her the truth. Or at least part of it.

"I'm doing fine. And you?"

"Great. Look, I was hoping I could combine my two passions tonight. Interested?"

I looked out the window, into the darkness. "Go on. You've definitely got my interest."

She took a breath. "Before I get into that I just want to say I...I felt bad, the way our last talk went. I...I just want to go on with you, my dear one, all right? Just go on, don't bitch and moan about the past or whatever you did or didn't do with the senator's wife back in college. So I want to focus my attention on two passions, you and this damn campaign, and I've come up with a way to balance both."

"Quite a job. Maybe I should call the campaign manager, give him a glowing review. If that'd help."

"Hah. Who knows? All right, here's the deal. Senator Hale is holding a private reception, up in Wallis, with some of his money people tonight. Free food, free booze. You and I get a chance to eat something nice, maybe chat and grope each other in a deserted corner...and you get to see the senator up close. Lewis, I'm working so hard to help him become the next president. It's important to me...and I want you to see why."

I cleared my throat. "The news media will make this a horrible circus, you know. The senator's alleged assassin, perhaps coming back for another round. Have you thought about that?"

She laughed. "Of course, silly. Which is why this reception is going to work. It's media free, and I've already cleared it with the higher-ups. Your name will be on the list. What do you say? Dinner, drinks, a talk with the next president of the United States, and if you're really, really lucky, I'll come back to your place for some constituent outreach. Just show me you care by staying away from his damn wife."

I looked out the window again, at the rise of land that went up to Atlantic Avenue and blocked the view of the Lafayette House. I couldn't see the hotel, but I could see the glow of light that represented its presence, in all its high-priced glory. I wanted to be up there tonight, doing illegal things, but important things, to see if the damn place had what I needed to find out why and how Harris had ended up dead in my front yard.

I needed to be up there tonight. Had to. The phone receiver was still in my hand. But there were other needs as well.

"Sure, I'll be there," I said. "I'd love to."

9

Which is how two hours later, freshly showered and dressed in clothing that included one of my three neckties, I found myself driving up to one of the mansions that are scattered along the shores of Wallis, two towns north of Tyler Beach. While Tyler Beach is all cottages and condos and hotels and restaurants and nightclubs and T-shirt and souvenir stores, its sister town to the north—called in a burst of imagination some decades ago North Tyler—is like a junior partner, with a couple of state parks, some cottages, no hotels, and few stores and restaurants.

And to the north yet again, in some sort of example of declining sprawl and increased property values, was the town of Wallis. Along this particular stretch that I drove, the home values started in the low millions and worked their way up with each passing mile, and the homes were set back a ways from the rocky shores, with long driveways flanked by stone and metal gates.

In other words, it's about a fifteen-minute drive from a booth that sells fried dough to Massachusetts tourists to a home whose owners had probably never touched a piece of fried dough in their lives. Sometimes quite a shock to the system to those who, for the first time, drive the coastal route along my fair state.

I turned into a driveway that was reached by going through an open gate supported by two stone columns, each with a brass numeral 7 set in the stone. On either side of the gates were Wallis police officers, providing crowd and traffic control, and a small knot of reporters and supporters from the Hale campaign and the other campaigns as well, waving signs and banners at one another. I was processed forward and about fifty feet up into the driveway, I ran into a more formal checkpoint. Smart work. That way, traffic wasn't backed up on Atlantic Avenue from the arriving guests, such as we were.

The checkpoint was manned by a uniformed Wallis cop—no doubt on paid detail—and a Hale campaign rep, a young man who checked my name on the clipboard. There were portable lights set up on a pole and a kerosene heater at their feet.

"Cole, Lewis Cole," he said, shivering a bit in the cold, holding a clipboard in one gloved hand, holding a small flashlight in the other. "Yep, you're on the list."

"Thanks."

"Hey—quick question, if you don't mind. You're not the Cole who was arrested a few days ago, are you?"

I decided the truth wasn't in my favor. "Nope. That was my evil twin."

"Oh." I guess the guy wanted to ask me more questions, but headlights were appearing behind me, so I kept on driving.

Up ahead, the driveway curved to the left and I parked among a host of other high-powered, high-priced SUVs to the side of an expansive two-story brick home with black shutters and a white-columned entrance. One vehicle was parked right near the door, a black Jaguar XJ8 with vanity plates: WHTKER. Based on the parking lot population, I guessed the topic tonight wouldn't be alternate energy sources or our never-ending reliance on Middle East oil. Outside it was bitterly cold. Inside, I was glad to be someplace where the cold didn't make my nostrils seize up, and I dumped my winter parka on a long counter in a foyer that was serving as a coat check.

Before me was a wooden table, manned by yet another collection of eager volunteers, and after making sure I was on the all-powerful list that either allowed me entrance with a smile or a curt dismissal with a sneer, they passed over a contribution folder with an attached envelope for the good senator. A nice picture of the senator and Barbara was on the outside of the folder. Inside were some stock paragraphs from his campaign speeches, and little boxes one checked off to make a donation. The smallest box was a hundred dollars, the largest—due to campaign financing restraints—was one thousand dollars. I shoved the envelope in my pocket and walked away.

I grabbed a Sam Adams beer from a young waitress with tanned skin and went into the main dining room. Unlike the last campaign rally, this one was smaller, more manageable, and I didn't feel sick to my stomach. A good combination. The hall was wood paneling and high ceilings and wooden chandeliers, and it looked like the place had been magically transferred from medieval England. Around me, talking and drinking and eating, were what passed for high political society in Wentworth County. Annie wasn't here yet. To say I felt out of place was like calling the sinking of the *Titanic* a minor setback for steamship travel.

I took a swallow of my beer and looked around the dining hall, went over to a bookshelf that had a collection of leatherbound volumes. Some history books, a few biographies, and a collection of seafaring tales from Edward Rowe Snow, a New England historian who had a flair for storytelling that made a lot of young men and women—including a writer from *Shoreline*—fall in love with this region.

"Admiring my first husband's collection?" came a voice.

I turned and there was a woman, dressed in a fine light blue wool dress with a string of pearls about her throat. Her dark brown hair was carefully coiffed, and her skin and face were those of a woman in her late fifties, perhaps mid-sixties, and even early seventies, depending on the light. But her eyes were that of a young woman who could not believe that her girlish spirit was still trapped in a body determined to grow old. I had the oddest feeling I had met her before.

"Yes, I was," I said. "A nice collection."

She held out her hand, which I briefly squeezed, and she said, "My name is Audrey. Welcome to my home."

"Thanks for having me," I said. "I'm Lewis."

"Are you part of the senator's campaign staff, or a local?"

"A local."

She cocked her head in a little display of amusement. "I'm afraid I haven't seen you at any party functions these past several years. Are you a newcomer to politics?"

"Hardly."

"And what, may I ask, is your political persuasion?"

I sipped from my Sam Adams. "I'm a drunkard."

She laughed and laughed at that one. "Oh, that's a good one. The great line from Rick Blaine, in Casablanca. Of course, he was asked about his nationality, not his politics. Still, such a wonderful, wonderful movie, filled with classic lines. That was George's favorite movie—George being my first husband. You know, he always thought he had the rakish charm of Bogart, when he wasn't too busy making money...such charm."

She seemed lost for a moment and smiled again. "Charm brought him a long way, especially in business. But charm is what killed him, because of his hobby."

"His hobby killed him?"

Audrey nodded. "Yes. George loved to fly. Owned a small plane that he kept at an airport up in Rochester. He charmed his way through flight school and pilot licensing and all that, but the night he was trying to get to Nantucket and his instrumentation failed...well, the sky and the ocean weren't impressed with his charm."

"I'm sorry," I said.

She shrugged. "It happened a long time ago...and now I'm married again. To Henry, over there in the corner."

I looked to where she was pointing, at a great stone fireplace that was roaring right along. A man about ten years Audrey's junior with a red face and too fine blond hair and wearing one of those funky navy-blue jackets with a crest over the breast pocket was holding court with a couple of young, attractive women dressed in cocktail dresses that looked more suitable for June than January. Even with the low roar of conversation in the room, I made out the sigh of disappointment from my newfound conversationalist.

"Henry doesn't have as much charm, but he is a fair companion...though you can probably guess about his particular hobby. But I'm of an age and condition that I don't particularly care. But what I do care about is giving back."

I nodded and she said, "And I've been entirely too rude, prattling on and on about my personal life. And you, Mr. Lewis. Where are you from?"

"Tyler Beach."

"And what do you do?"

"I'm a columnist for a magazine. *Shoreline*."

The smile on her face froze just a tad. "The understanding, of course, is that tonight's event is entirely off the record, and not open to members of the press. I'm not sure how you gained entrance."

"I'm sure it is off the record, and I guarantee you, I don't consider myself a member of the press. I write about the seacoast of New England and its history. I don't write about contemporary politics. And I gained entrance through the good graces of a woman friend who works on Senator Hale's campaign."

The frozen smile defrosted back to its original state. "That's fine. I once considered becoming a reporter, back when I was in college, in the Stone Age, when writers worked on manual typewriters and television crews used real film in their cameras...but I decided life was too short and too grand to be just an observer. I wanted to participate, to be in the arena, not in the audience."

"I see."

"Mmm...perhaps not. I believe I think you see an old, rich, idle woman, throwing a party for her equally rich friends, all for the privilege of seeing another lying politician up close." She leaned into me, her voice crisp. "But that's not the case. I can't sing, dance, or run for office. But what I can do is write checks, and convince my friends to write checks, to men and women and causes that I believe in. And tonight, I believe in Senator Hale. And I hope you do as well."

"We'll see," I said, feeling light now as Annie approached me through the crowd, smiling, wearing a tan turtleneck sweater and a long black skirt.

Audrey saw where I was looking, and she touched my wrist.

"So glad to meet you, Lewis. Enjoy yourself...and someday, why don't you come play with us? It can be so much more fun than kibitzing from the sideline."

She moved into the crowd and Annie came up to me, we kissed, and she squeezed my hand and said, "I get here a few minutes late, and already I see you're trying to bed one of the wealthiest women in your state."

"I was?"

"Certainly. The former Mrs. George Whittaker, whose late husband was a developer who cheerfully raped the southern portion of the state and built lots and lots of malls and strip housing developments, and who ended up in the bottom of the Gulf of Maine some years ago. His wife has his fortune and not his politics, and she's been a heavy hitter and kingmaker—or queen-maker—during the last three New Hampshire primaries. Having her in Senator Hale's corner has been a real break for him."

I now knew who owned the impressive Jaguar parked outside. I saw Audrey Whittaker pause and talk to some people, and then it clicked. I had seen her before, at the campaign rally where the shots had been fired. At the Tyler Conference Center, she had been holding court as well, but even though I now knew where I had noticed her before, something odd was niggling at me.

Annie squeezed my hand. "I'm starved. Let's get something to eat."

"And the senator?"

"Another thirty or so minutes out. We've got plenty of time." Still holding my hand, she led me through the crowded dining room and through a set of swinging doors that led into a kitchen, which looked like it belonged in a small restaurant. A catering crew was working there, and lots of pans and pots were being banged around, and steam was rising up from a couple of cooking stations. Annie let me be and came back a few minutes later, carrying two Sam Adams by their long necks, and two full plates, which she managed to balance on her wrists. I grabbed a plate and a beer and kissed her on her nose for her effort.

"Nice balancing act, Counselor," I said.

"Old waitressing trick. You never quite forget them, no matter how old you get. Let's find a quiet place."

Which we did. From another door we went into a small hallway leading to a breezeway that looked like it headed out to a garage or some other outbuilding. The breezeway had tall windows with recessed padded window seats, and we shared one while balancing the plates on our laps. Annie, knowing me so well, had filled my plate with scallops wrapped in bacon, slices of prime rib, rice pilaf, and a chunk of salad for roughage. I raised my bottle in salute.

"Thanks for dinner."

"Don't thank me, thank your new friend, Mrs. Whittaker."

"If I can, I will." I looked around the paneled walls and fine wooden floor and said, "How do you know your way in and around this place so well?"

Annie was being good in her food choices tonight, with lots of salad, lots of rice, and a couple of small pieces of haddock and a fine collection of steamed vegetables. Murmuring through her first bite, she said, "Been here a few other times for fund-raisers. Get to know the lay of the land after a while. Mrs. Whittaker is a real sweetheart in lending out her home to the campaign."

I ate some and said, "Ask you a campaign-related question?"

She delicately dabbed at her lips with a napkin. "As opposed to asking a bosom-related question?"

"That can come later. I was just wondering...how many fund-raisers can one person like her support? I mean, I thought the federal limit on making campaign contributions is one thousand dollars per person. There must be a limit on one's pool of friends."

Annie smiled at me and raised up her bottle in a mock salute.

"One of these days, you really need to show me that cabbage patch you were raised in, my dear."

"What do you mean?"

"Yes, campaigns are limited to what they can receive. But not, quote, independent political action groups, unquote, which can get as much money as they want to pump up any message they want. Especially if said message by some wonderful coincidence manages to complement a certain campaign's message. Tonight's soiree is being held by something called the American Fund for America's Future. Or some such nonsense. But what it does is raise oodles and oodles of cash to help Senator Hale, without being constricted by the Federal Election Commission. Because it's a so-called independent committee, it can attack the other candidates and make them look bad without being an official part of the Hale campaign. Is this a great country, or what?"

"I don't know if I ever had political virginity," I replied, "but if I ever did, I think you just took it."

She gave me a wicked smile. "Keep on hanging around with me, and we'll see whatever forms of virginity are up for the taking."

We finished our meals and dropped off our dishes with the busy catering staff in the kitchen, and went out to the main dining hall, which was now even more crowded. There was a hum in the atmosphere, something anticipatory and electric, and I looked at all the young and old eager faces, all sizes and shapes, male and female, all of them looking forward to that one moment in time, the one in which they shared a room with the next president of the United States.

At the far wall was a doorway and a crowd of campaign officials, and I recognized one of them: the red-bearded gatekeeper who had tried to keep me out of the last disastrous campaign rally. Not wanting to encounter him yet again, I moved to another side of the room, just as Annie got swept up by a couple of her friends from the local campaign office and managed to wave at me as she was dragged away. I found myself standing by the bookcase as the door at the far wall opened and the cheers and applause began.

Senator Hale came into the room, accompanied by his lovely bride, and I took a breath, for seeing Barbara again rekindled those old thoughts and memories, and though I did my best to ignore them, they were still there. I was angry at myself for thinking of the times we spent in her apartment or my dorm room, the young and eager lovemaking and long, wonderful conversations that never seemed to go anywhere but always seemed so important, and both the conversations and the lovemaking had an energy to them that I had forgotten even existed.

And even though I knew that the passage of time was a great editor, that my memories had been enhanced and cleaned up like some old photograph, the memories were still there, and I was surprised at how powerful they still were.

I looked for Annie again. I couldn't find her. That made me feel guilty for a moment, and then there was more movement and it was time for the politicking to begin.

I folded my arms and listened to Senator Hale go into his stump speech, as Barbara stood by his side. As he spoke, his face animated, his eyes lively, the gaze he gave out as if each and every single person in the room were his friend, I realized that he had it, the almighty "it" that separated mere mortals and mere politicians from those who would be president. There was energy and confidence and strength in his voice and his presence, and though the words on paper would most likely be the same clichés that other politicians, future and past, have used ("strength at home and abroad," "a compact with our old and young," "a nation with more than just friends, but true partners"), his gift brought them a certain power. The words seemed to roll over me with their strength, and I thought about the contribution envelope in my pocket and how now it seemed quite right to make a campaign donation.

I shook my head, no longer thinking about a possible contribution. I kept my focus on the senator from Georgia, seeing the light in his eyes. It must be a strange and horrible thing to have such a gift, for once your goal of being president is in sight and almost in hand, would anything else ever be as worthwhile, ever again?

The applause startled me. His speech was over, Barbara still at his side, and right then and there, in the close confines of this magnificent home in Wallis, I knew two things: I was looking at the next president of the United States, and I was being used by someone to prevent that event from happening.

10

The crowd jostled and people moved around, and in the movement of people about me, I started looking for Annie. Somebody bumped me hard, propelling me between two older women, and before I had a chance to apologize, Senator Jackson Hale was there, right before me. He smiled and I found myself smiling back, and I shook his hand as he said, "Thanks for coming tonight, appreciate it."

I said not a word as he moved past me, and then, I found myself facing his wife. She had a bemused smile on her face as she shook my hand as well.

"So nice to see you," Barbara said.

"Me, too," I said, as I felt a slip of paper pressed into my hand. She joined her husband and maybe the smart or rational thing would have been to drop the piece of paper on the floor.

Instead, I slipped it into a pocket, and went to find Annie.

I found her in a corner, talking to a couple of energetic young men, and they looked closely at me as I approached, as if I were her father, ready to collect her after the junior high school dance. It was good to see her work, good to see her fulfilling her passion, her dream, and that little surge of affection seemed to drive away the thought of Barbara and the mysterious slip of paper. As I got closer to her and her friends, she said, "and that's why importing a lot of out-of-state talent to knock on doors, day after day, doesn't work. Just pisses off the voters. The locals don't want to be told how to vote by a lot of eager out-of-staters who think they're smarter than everybody else."

As I came up to her, she squeezed my hand and turned and said, "Get me out of here, will you?"

"Sure," I said.

As we walked away, I said, "Must be nice to be so popular."

"Yeah, right," she said. "I've been with the Hale campaign for six months, and that makes me an old vet."

I thought of something and said, "Saw a familiar face tonight. Guy with a red beard. He was running media interference at the conference center rally. Who is he?"

"Hah," she said. "You've got a good eye for imported assholes. That's Harmon Jewett, campaign flak for the senator. From Georgia, a true believer but with a temper that can curl paint off the side of a house from fifty yards. He was with Hale when Hale was just a state senator and helped manage his congressional campaign. Said ten years ago, if you can believe it, that Jackson Hale would be the next president and he'd kill his own grandmother to make it so. And that little story has made more than one reporter look into the circumstances of that poor woman's death."

"So why is he up here in New Hampshire?"

Annie grimaced for a moment. "One of the senator's least best traits is loyalty, combined with forgiveness. He's never forgotten that Harmon got him started in politics and managed to usher him through some very tough campaigns. So the senator keeps him on, even in a job as simple as a media gatekeeper. But that temper...once it lets go it could really hurt the senator. Any other guy would have cut Harmon loose years ago. But not our Jackson."

We gathered our coats from the official coat drop-off place and stepped outside, Annie also carrying a bulky over-the-shoulder leather bag. I think we both shivered at about the same time as we went down the stone steps. It was damn cold, but the stars sure looked fine. I stopped to admire my favorite constellation, Orion, rising up in all his glory in the east, the mighty hunter, his club holding arm still there, at the ready, thousands and thousands of years later.

Annie nudged me in the side. "Come along, star boy. I want to get to your place before some of my favorite—and your favorite—extremities start freezing."

I looked around the rapidly emptying lot. "Where's your car?"

"In Manchester, silly. I got a ride from some of the staff. You don't mind bringing me back to Manchester tomorrow, do you? Please, pretty please? I'll be your best friend."

And then I knew that bag she was carrying contained a change of clothes and other essential items. Sometimes even when I was being observant, I could be as blind as a chaplain at a cathouse.

My Annie, always thinking.

I tried to keep thoughts of the Lafayette House and the mysterious piece of paper, weighing down my pocket like a chunk of lead, out of the way. I leaned over, kissed her. "I'd take you to Manchester, England, if that's what you'd like."

"What I'd like," she said, her voice just a touch curt, "is to go someplace warm."

And someplace warm is where we ended up.

At home I built a fire and went to my liquor cabinet—all right, the space next to the handful of spices and condiments that I have managed to collect over the years—and pulled down a bottle of Australian sherry. I poured some in tiny sherry glasses and set them on the counter. Annie was on her cell phone, talking campaign talk yet again, and when she moved to the sliding glass doors that led out to the deck, I went back to the fire and looked at what Barbara had handed me.

It was a slip of notebook paper, from the Center of New Hampshire Hotel and Conference Center in Manchester, with a short note: Room 410, between 8 a.m. and 9 a.m. B.

I reread it and tossed it into the flames, where it curled up and disappeared. Annie's voice rose a bit and then she said, "Fine!" and snapped her cell phone shut. "Asshole," she murmured, and she came into the living room and said, "You might not like this."

"All right, try me," I said.

"There's an all-hands meeting tomorrow at seven a.m. Which means—"

Ugh. "It means getting up early. That's all right."

She raised the glass of sherry. "Take our drinks and go to bed?"

"Absolutely."

We climbed into bed after tumbling out of our clothes, and as I held my sherry glass, Annie leaned against my shoulder. I said, "Your feet are cold."

"Tell me something new."

"I mean really, really cold. Were you eating ice cream with your toes before going to bed?"

In response, she moved her feet briskly up and down my shins, causing me to shiver. "There," she said, "take that, you insensitive man."

"My legs are now insensitive," I said. "Not sure about anything else. Hold on while I try to warm up."

I took a stiff swallow of the sweet sherry and Annie said, "I ever tell you the two types of campaign people?"

"No, but I think you're about to."

"Meanie," she said.

Annie knocked her sherry back with one swallow and said, "Two types. Type one is the true believer. He or she really believes in his or her candidate, will follow the candidate around the country, will work for free pizza and a place to crash on the floor at two a.m. These are the ones who man the phones, stuff envelopes, and go door-to-door handing out campaign brochures, and will stand outside in a polling place on primary day, holding a sign, in the pouring rain, sleet, or snow. They can be a bit nutty, but you can't run a campaign without them. They get teased, they get overlooked, but you can't kill them. They're like those blow-up clowns that you can punch in the head. They always bounce back."

"I think I know who the second group are."

She nuzzled my ear. "Then you've been paying attention these past months, Grasshopper. But let me remind you. The second type are the professionals. The poll takers, the money men and women, the consultants. They parachute in and try to stitch things together so that the true believers don't run things into the ground. Sometimes they believe in the candidate and sometimes they hate him or her. A lot of it depends on who's paying the most, and in a campaign, a lot of times, a lot of energy that should be

spent on the actual campaign is spent on gossip, revenge, and bitching over
who has the biggest office. You would not believe some of the war stories
I've heard since I've been with the campaign."

"And what does this have to do with the meeting at seven?"

"Oh, one of the pros wants to rein in us amateurs. Stop playing around
and focus on winning the damn primary, and don't be so pie-in-the-sky,
trying to be everything to all voters. We have a candidate who is hungry for
this win, despite his wife, so knock off the amateur hour. Blah, blah, blah."

I carefully put my now empty sherry glass on the nightstand.

"What do you mean, despite his wife? I thought she wanted to become
first lady in the worst way. And that she didn't make any secret of it."

Annie laughed and rolled over. "Lewis, I don't know what she was like
in college, but Mrs. Senator Hale is one prime bitch diva, and coming from
one who admires prime bitch divas, that says a lot. She hates campaigns,
hates campaigning, and most days, she's a goddamn drag on the campaign."

"I see."

She finished her own sherry and said, "So...do tell me. What was she
like in college?"

"Barbara?"

"No, silly, the mysterious woman who lives in your basement, that's
who."

"Oh," I said. "Very fair question. We worked on the student newspaper,
which is where we met. Typical student paper for the time. Lots of long
hours into the night, writing and composing and pasting up. Sometimes
you'd skip classes to be able to work on the newspaper. I'm sure I lost a
point or two on my grade point average due to all the time I spent there."

"What was the name of the newspaper?"

"The Indiana Daily Student."

She laughed. "Such an original name. What else can you tell me about
her?"

"Typical college student, I guess. Full of energy and the feeling that
once you get out, you can do anything. Long story short, we dated for a
while, and then summer came and we went off to our respective intern-
ships. I did one at *The Indianapolis Star*. She wanted to dabble some in poli-

tics, so she went to D.C. to work for a congressman. I came back to Bloomington and she stayed in D.C. End of story."

Well, sort of, I thought, thinking about the note I had received earlier.

"She break your heart?"

"At the time, yeah."

"Bitch," Annie said, and we both laughed and Annie then sighed and said, "Dear one, do cuddle me and keep me warm, will you? I'm about ready to fall asleep, and it'll be so much better if you're holding me at the time."

I turned the light off and rolled over, holding Annie in the dark. We nuzzled and kissed for a while, her warm body—now even including her feet—in my grasp, and I held her for a time in the darkness, hearing her breathing deepen and slow, as she fell asleep. It took me a long while to join her.

To get from Tyler Beach to Manchester is pretty much a straight shot, from Route 101 all the way west to the interior of our fair state. It's a trip of just under an hour, and we both skipped breakfast before we left, though Annie did find time for a quick shower. Her fine red hair was still wet as we joined the other travelers on the two-lane highway, the rising sun shadowing us as we raced west. I listened to a bit of the morning news as I drove, hearing about a snowstorm heading our way this evening, and then I got a look from my companion, and switched the radio off, as she dug her cell phone from her purse.

For most of the time we drove, Annie was on the cell phone, checking with her staff, coordinating the logistics of a luncheon meeting later that day, and basically juggling about a half dozen questions, concerns, and complaints. It sounds odd but while any other man may have felt ignored or slighted at the lack of attention, I felt a sense of pride. She was damn good at what she was doing. The highway raced through mostly open rural areas that were only developed with homes and service stations at the different exits, and though the speed limit was sixty-five and I kept my Ford Explorer at seventy, I was passed on several occasions.

It was something to see her work, but what pleased me most was that during one break in the call, she reached over and gave my thigh a quick squeeze. "Thanks for the drive in, and a promise for better things later," she said.

I returned the favor, squeezing something else, and she laughed and returned to her cell phone as the buildings of Manchester came into view. The state's largest city, it's a mix of poor neighborhoods and office buildings in the center of town. New immigrants from Latin America and Asia jostle for jobs in places where the accents were once Irish or French-Canadian. The headquarters for Senator Hale were on Elm Street, the main drag for Manchester, and I pulled in next to a fire hydrant. Highly illegal, but I planned to be there only for a few moments.

Annie dumped her cell phone in her purse and reached behind her for her overnight bag. I kissed her a few times and she said, "Thanks, dear one. I'll see you later."

"Bad weather coming tonight," I said. "Are you coming back to Tyler, or are you going to stay here?"

"Stay here, I'm afraid," she said. "But look at it this way. Less than a week to the primary, and then you get me all to yourself."

"Lucky me."

She made a wrinkling gesture with her nose. "I'd like to think I'm lucky as well. Take care."

"You, too."

She walked into the storefront, each and every window obscured by HALE FOR PRESIDENT signs, and already she must have been in campaign mode, for Annie didn't turn and wave at me as she went inside.

But that was okay. I drove away and in a matter of minutes, I was in a parking garage that was adjacent to and serviced the Center of New Hampshire.

I was early so I bought a *New York Times* and *The Wall Street Journal* and settled down in a lounge area next to the check-in counter, and I surprised myself by letting the papers go unread. There was a floor show going on near me, and despite myself, it was fun to watch. Guests and assorted hangers-on were moving about the lobby, talking and arguing and speaking into their cell phones. Camera crews were stationed by the doors, gear piled at their feet, like soldiers on a long campaign. The reporters from different organizations came to and fro, and I recognized a few network and cable television correspondents. They always had the best skin. The reporters made it seem a point of pride to wear their IDs and credentials around their necks, as if they were some well-bred species of animal that had been awarded a number of blue ribbons.

It was amusing to see the looks on the faces, to hear the snatched bits of conversation, and in some way, it was like a high school reunion, as old relationships were started up again. And more than a few times, I heard, "See you in South Carolina!" knowing that was the next big primary after New Hampshire's.

And before I knew it, it was time.

I gathered up my newspapers and walked to the bank of elevators.

At 8:01 a.m. I knocked on the door to room 410, and it opened quickly, as if she had been waiting for me. Before me was the wife of the senior senator from Georgia, barefoot, wearing blue jeans and an Indiana University sweatshirt.

I went in and she kissed me on the cheek and said, "Old reliable Lewis. I knew you'd be here if you could, right on the dot."

"Thanks, I think," I said, and followed her in, and I was surprised at how small the room was. It was a typical hotel room with two double beds and a television and bathroom and small table with a chair, but for someone like Barbara, the possible future first lady, it seemed all wrong. She sat on the bed and curled up in a familiar pose that made something inside me ache with memory, and I took the chair across from her.

I said, "Another way to keep your sanity, above and beyond sneaking out to bookstores when no one's looking?"

"You know it, Lewis." She rubbed her face and said, "When you are where I am, you're constantly on. You're surrounded by staff, by consultants, by campaign workers. They all demand and expect the perfect candidate's wife, the perfectly scripted fembot, the perfect arm candy for the next president. I have a room here paid for by the campaign that's the size of my first damn apartment. This one's been rented in the name of my mom. It's nice to slip away and wear old clothes and watch television programs that aren't news shows and know that the phone won't ring."

"Sure is." I looked at her and she looked at me, and I recalled what I had done less than an hour ago, dropping off Annie at her place of work, and I tried to keep my voice even and gentle. "Barbara, what's up?"

It was amazing, seeing the look on her face change from that of an old college friend to that of a candidate's wife, morph from relaxation to cool hostility. For a moment I felt a flash of sympathy for this woman who could never be quite comfortable with new acquaintances, could never know if someone wanted to be her friend because of who she was, or because of her position and power.

"I'm not sure what you mean," she said.

"Barbara...this has been wonderful, catching up with you and our times back in college, but in less than a week, the primary will be over and you and your husband and the campaign will be heading to South Carolina. I'll still be here, in Tyler Beach. In the meantime, you and I are playing 'remember when,' and the only thing I can do is damage the campaign. Some smart reporter, still wanting to know how and why I might have been involved in the shooting, might decide to tail me for a bit. And can you imagine the headlines if a story comes out that you and I have been seen together?"

"Sounds cool and logical."

"It sounds right, Barbara, and you know it. So. What can I do for you?"

"I need your help," she said.

"How?"

She folded her arms tight against her chest. "I...I need you. I need you...because I think someone's trying to kill me."

And then she started weeping.

I was on the bed with her, holding her, the scent and touch bringing back memories of college years so hard it made me feel lightheaded for a moment, and there was that sour tinge of regret, of what might have been, how our lives would have been different if she had come back from D.C., if I had been more aggressive in tracking her down, in finding out why she had gone east and had never come back.

Old regrets, still feeling fresh.

She turned to me and said, "All right, all right, maybe I'm being a bit hysterical...but, Lewis, I don't know who to talk to, who I can trust."

"What's going on?"

"There's been two attempts. The first was a month ago, outside Atlanta. I was driving our Lexus and I got in a car accident. Flipped right off the road and into a drainage ditch. Almost broke my damn nose when the airbag popped open. It was at night, a light rain...but no reason why it should have happened. The Georgia Bureau of Investigation kept Jackson and me informed through their investigation...managed to keep most of it out of the newspapers. Seems like my Lexus was sabotaged. Brake lines were cut, the tires were underinflated, making it easier to roll over."

"Who did it?"

She smiled, though her eyes were full of tears. "Who the hell knows? The Georgia Bureau of Investigation is still investigating and Jackson...he just nodded at the right places and told me that the professionals should handle it, and by then, the Secret Service was with us, and there was a campaign to run."

"The car accident was the first attempt. What was the second?"

"You should know," she said. "You were there."

"The campaign rally?"

Barbara nodded. "Nothing I can prove, Lewis. But I managed to see a preliminary report from the Secret Service on the shooting. From where the bullets impacted the wall behind the stage, it was apparent that I was the target. Not my husband. Me."

"Why?"

She rubbed her arms, as if the room had suddenly gotten cold. "Despite all the polls and predictions, the Hale for President campaign is a hollow shell. We're running on credit and optimism. We need to nail down the New Hampshire primary for another round of funds and campaign people to come streaming in. You see, there comes a point in any campaign when the well goes dry. And it remains dry unless the landscape changes. A scandal in another campaign. Some string of good news. Other things."

Now I felt cool as well. "Other things...like the shooting or killing of a candidate's wife just before the primary."

A sharp nod. "You have no idea how much politics is a dirty business. Not as dirty here as in other places but when certain people and certain groups have an idea and confidence that they are going to be part of the new crew come next inauguration, then they can get a bit crazed. They get so close to those centers of power and influence that they do things they wouldn't otherwise do."

"So if a candidate's wife is wounded or killed..."

"My God, an orgy of publicity...can you imagine it? The sympathy vote would roar right in, the funding would increase, they'd have to drive away the excess volunteers with a fire hose. And those people backing Jack would be very, very happy."

Having her in my arms now seemed to be quite wrong, but I couldn't move, couldn't disturb the moment. "All right, having said all of that, Barbara, what can I do to help?"

She sighed. "I'm not proud of what I did, Lewis, but after seeing you at the bookstore, I wanted to know more...wanted to know more about what you did after college. So I had you checked out."

"Lucky me."

"Your time at the Pentagon is still in deep black, but not what you've done with yourself afterward. You write a snappy column for *Shoreline* but you've been involved in some criminal matters over the years, poking around, asking questions, working as an investigator without a license. And that's what I need."

I squeezed her gently with my arms and got off the bed and back into the hotel room's chair. "What you need is beyond what I can offer, Barbara. You have the Secret Service, the Georgia Bureau of Investigation, the New Hampshire State Police, probably even the FBI at your fingertips. You don't need me."

"Right. And in any one of those agencies, there might be people supporting one of the other candidates, who'd take great pleasure in leaking a story about a crazed wife, who's gotten paranoid and thinks someone's trying to kill her."

"And what can I do?"

"What you've done in the past. Poke around. Ask questions. See what you can find out from the locals, from the cops to the party organizations. I know I'm grasping at straws, Lewis, but..."

I looked into those familiar blue eyes, listened to the soft cadence of her voice, and I knew I couldn't do a damn thing. The election was just a few days away and my contacts were limited, no matter what Barbara thought about my talents. There was no way I could find out who was trying to hurt her—if, in fact, somebody was trying to hurt her—before the primary election. Not a chance in hell.

So I should gracefully decline, and get out of this room, and let her go on with her life with her maybe soon-to-be-president husband, and in less than a week, she and her husband would be gone from my state and my life.

Just a few days.

I looked at her again. It looked like she hadn't gotten a good night's sleep in days. If I told her no, I knew what would happen. More stress, less sleep. And maybe this whole thing was why Annie and the others thought she was a diva. No wonder they had the impression that Barbara hated the campaign, if someone was actually trying to hurt or kill her.

And if I said yes...perhaps a chance at some peace and relaxation over the next few days. Then she would leave, go to South Carolina and beyond, and in the crush of campaigning that would follow, other issues would rise up, other demands on her time, and I think she would eventually move on. And maybe I would get an inaugural invite sometime next year.

Maybe.

"Okay," I said. "I'll do it."

She held her hands up to her face and then lowered them.

She swung over a bit to the nearest nightstand, scribbled something on a piece of paper. "My private cell phone number. Call me if you have anything, all right?"

"Sure."

She came over to me and I took the number from her hand, and I looked at her and she looked at me, and it was like the flow of water, reaching its natural state. She just sat in my lap. The smell and the sense of her being there...I put my arm around her still slim waist and pulled her close. A bit of her hair tickled me. I kissed her and she kissed me back, and before it got any farther, I said I had to leave.

Which wasn't much of a lie, but it worked.

I got out of the hotel room and a few minutes later, left to go home. By the time I got back to Tyler Beach, an hour later, clouds had rolled in, thick and gray and threatening. I listened a bit to the radio as I drove back east;

we were going to have a nice dump of six to eight inches of snow overnight. Of course, given the time of year, most of the weather report was centered around campaign speculation, over who it might help and who it might hurt. As I went up Atlantic Avenue, heading to my home, I had a thought of what the snow might achieve, in terms of cover, and I was thinking so hard that I missed the turnoff to the Lafayette House parking lot.

And as I made an illegal U-turn to come back, I had another thought. I went into the short-term parking area and after parking my Explorer went inside to the gift shop, where Stephanie Sussex was at work, handling a small crowd of people. Before me was a group of Japanese visitors, talking slowly and with great precision to Stephanie, and I waited in an area of the small store that had Tyler Beach T-shirts and sweatshirts for sale, as Stephanie carefully packed up the group's purchases.

When they left, I walked over and Stephanie placed my morning ration of newspapers on the glass-topped counter. "You're late," she said.

"Yes," I said. "And good morning to you, too."

That brought a laugh and as she rang up my purchases, she said, "There's a lesson there in the passage of time, if you saw it, Lewis."

"What's that?"

"That little overseas group. From a Japanese television network. NTK or something like that. The woman reporter, the one who does the on-air work, she was talking about a visit she had up to Porter. We tend to forget that's a very important place for the Japanese."

"Some forget, others don't. The Russian-Japanese peace treaty. Where Teddy Roosevelt got the Nobel Peace Prize for manhandling Japan and Russia into a peace agreement, about a hundred or so years ago."

I paid her and she passed over the change. "Good for you, Lewis."

That bit of history got the two of us talking, and she mentioned that her father was a naval aviator in World War II. Barely made it through the war alive. And I told her that my dad flew Wildcats off the Enterprise at about the same time. That's when we both realized our dads may have shot at each other once or twice. We both laughed, but you know what? A funny world, isn't it, how sworn mortal enemies, more than a half century later, can have their children share a moment without trying to slit each other's throats.

The newspapers were now under my arm, and I said, "History sure is a funny thing. Ask you a question?"

"Sure, go ahead."

I made a quick scan of the store, noted that we were alone, and said, "The parking lot break-ins, last month and before."

She looked cautious. "Yes?"

"They've mostly stopped now, haven't they."

"So I've heard."

"Is it because of the surveillance system, keeping an eye on the outer parking lot?"

Stephanie took a bottle of glass cleaner and sprayed some of the blue stuff on the counter. "Well, I've got to give you that. That was a question. I guess your visit with our local insufferable prick didn't pan out. So is it now dumped in my lap?"

"What's the problem?"

She tore off a sheet of paper towel, started wiping down the glass. "The problem is, it's how the Lafayette House has changed the past year. We used to be an overpriced white elephant, charming and fun with water pipes that banged in the middle of the night. Sort of a genteel snobby place, pretending to be one of those old New England upper-class resorts. Hung on by our teeth, year after year, until a sharp little hotel investment group from Switzerland took over and brought in Paul Jeter to run things. Which meant a new regime. A new approach. And new rules."

"What kind of new rules?"

The paper towel was now wadded up in her fist. "Rules that change the nature of this place. No longer are we the shabby, overpriced place where your parents and grandparents once stayed. Now we are trying to appeal to the very upper reaches of wealth, to offer them an experience that they can't get anywhere else. And part of that experience is anonymity and privacy. So if a guard for the Boston Celtics allegedly has a permanently rented room here, where he keeps his two mistresses—"

"Two?"

"Allegedly, he has big appetites...and as I was saying, if this supposed basketball player knows he can stash his two mistresses here, away from the eyes of the Boston news media, he'll pay dearly for that privilege. And the word will get out to other folks in similar circumstances, who wish to keep their hobbies and tastes secret. So the Lafayette House develops a nice little reputation for quiet and discreet service. Publicizing the supposed fact that the parking lot is under surveillance doesn't help that reputation, now does it?"

"No, it doesn't. Where...where might this alleged surveillance system be set up?"

Stephanie threw the wadded paper towel away. "That's why you wanted to see Paul Jeter yesterday, right?"

"Right."

"Something happen over your place that morning, you looking to find out what's what?"

"You could say."

Her face was firm. "Lewis...I'm sorry." There was noise at the entrance of the gift shop and a couple of kids tumbled in, wearing swimsuits, carrying towels, and expressing joy at the pleasure of being able to swim in a heated pool in January.

"I see,"

Stephanie shook her head. "No, you don't. I need this job. It's relatively easy, pays reasonably well, and I get nice benefits. Nice benefits to help support a sick husband and help me do things for my church. That means a lot to me and...I'm sorry, I can't help you."

I managed a smile. "No problem, Stephanie. No problem at all."

And so I left, newspapers under my arm, leaving her behind with her job and her history.

11

At home I was in my upstairs office, looking out the window, watching the snow start to tumble its way down. Up above the rise of land stood the Lafayette House, and somewhere in there was the surveillance tape of the nearby parking lot. I had an idea of where it might be, and I also had a couple of ideas of how I was going to get it.

But there were other things to do, as well.

From the Internet, I was able to call up a story from *The Atlanta Journal-Constitution* and found out that yes, the good senator's wife had been in a car accident the previous month, while driving to a political function outside Atlanta. The story rated about four paragraphs and mentioned minor injuries on the behalf of Barbara Hale, and the usual and customary, "the accident remains under investigation."

All right, I thought. Step one complete. Time for step two. In the bad old days, before information got digitized, to find out about the Georgia Bureau of Investigation would have meant a call to directory assistance, a phone call to a central number, and maybe a half dozen more follow-up phone calls, as you navigated the bureaucracy and killed most of an afternoon. Yet now, it was all there, at your fingertips; it took only a few minutes before I got a public information officer's name and phone number from a quick Internet search.

Of course, this bit of information revolution didn't necessarily mean you got your information faster. Sometimes it just meant you hit the road-blocks that much sooner.

The public information officer's name was Samantha Tuckwell, she sounded like a charming lady from the Deep South, and while she would give me the time of day in Atlanta, Greenwich, and no doubt Murmansk, that's about as far as it went.

"So, tell me again what you're lookin' for, Mr. Cole?" came the sweet voice from some office park in Atlanta.

"As I said, I'm a writer for a magazine based in Boston. Called *Shoreline*. I'm looking for some additional information about a traffic accident involving Senator Hale's wife, Barbara. It happened about a month ago."

"And this story...all about a traffic accident?" Although there was a fair sprinkling of Southern charm and hospitality in that silky voice from hundreds of miles away, there was also about a ton of skepticism.

"Not just the accident. A profile piece about the senator and his wife, and the accident's just part of the piece. A bit of human interest, that's all."

"Well, hold on, will you?"

"Certainly."

I held on as instructed and looked out at the heavy snow and the increasingly dark sky. I wondered what the weather was like in Atlanta. My Apple computer was humming along contentedly in front of me, and it would just take a few keystrokes to find the exact temperature and nature of Atlanta's weather, but I decided not to. Sometimes, mysteries are best left mysteries.

"Mr. Cole?"

"Right here."

"Mr. Cole, that accident took place on Tuesday, December twelfth, at six ten p.m., on Interstate Twenty. Mrs. Hale was the sole occupant of her auto-mobile, a Lexus. She received minor injuries and was treated at the scene. The vehicle had to be towed away. The accident remains under inves-tigation."

"I'm sure it does," I said. "But it's been over a month since it happened. What was the cause of the accident?"

"I can't rightly say, Mr. Cole. It remains under investigation." I switched the phone from one ear to the other. "Yes, I know. But could you get an update for me, please."

"Why?"

I pondered what to say, decided to go for broke. "Well, Miss Tuckwell—"

"Mrs. Tuckwell."

"Sorry, Mrs. Tuckwell, I would think that it would be your job. To answer questions from legitimate news organizations and writers."

"And your question is?"

Could someone be so dense, or so crafty? I said, "I'm looking for an update on Barbara Hale's traffic accident. To see if a cause of the accident was determined."

"Oh," she said, her voice cheerful again. "I certainly can find that out for you."

"Wonderful. When do you think you can get back to me? Later today? Tomorrow?"

"How does next Wednesday sound?"

"Wednesday? Next Wednesday sounds awful. Why so long?"

A soft chuckle, and I felt a bit of admiration that I was being played so well by this fine example of Southern womanhood. "Mr. Cole...you seem to be a bright fella, and I've really enjoyed talking to you, but I'm sure you can figure out all on your own why I'm gonna give you a call next Wednesday."

"Because it's the day after the New Hampshire primary."

"Right," she said, almost purring. "That is entirely one hundred percent correct."

"But I'm not going to do anything—"

"Mr. Cole, I've been on my job for a while and know all the ins and outs of dealin' with the news media. That means the rest of this conversation is off the record, and I'll ever deny saying it, but here it goes: we're awfully proud of our senator, we would love to see him in the White House, and we don't like the fact that your pissant little frozen state is gonna have a key part in whether or not our man gets there. Understand? And you may be doing an innocent story and all that, but it sounds like bad publicity to me, professionally speakin'. And even if it is bad publicity, I'll still be doin' my job by callin' you back. But I'm just gonna be doin' it next Wednesday. All right?"

"All right. I understand completely. And Mrs. Tuckwell?"

"Yes?"

"You're very good at what you do."

A throaty laugh. "Why, thank you, Mr. Cole. And you have yourself a real good day, okay?"

"Sure."

After I disconnected from this underpaid public servant, I stared for a while at the computer screen. In doing a search for Barbara Hale and her car accident, other links had come up as well. Including one involving the actual shooting at the Tyler Conference Center. I had been inside the conference center, I had seen the shooting's aftermath from the parking lot, and I had missed some of the news coverage.

So I had never seen the actual shooting footage.

I moved the mouse and double-clicked a few times. That was going to change.

The first link didn't work, because my Apple software—being old and being Apple—couldn't read the movie file. But the second link worked, and I felt the back of my neck tense up. I was back there in the conference room, feeling sickly and warm and—

The footage went on, and there she was, up onstage with her husband. She was standing next to him at the lectern, just as I recalled. The speech went on and even though I knew what was going to occur in the next few moments, I had a dark sense of something bad about to happen. It was like the very first time, so many years ago, when I had viewed the Zapruder film of JFK's assassination. You wanted to stop the film. You wanted to shout out a warning. You wanted someone in the crowd, somewhere, to look up at the right time at the Texas School Book Depository.

And you felt so powerless.

A round of applause, the sound coming out quite nicely from my computer's dual speakers. Senator Hale was smiling. Barbara was right next to him, applauding along, and then she moved to the right a few feet, still applauding, and the applause died down and Senator Hale said, "Who among us—"

The gunshots were loud and rapid, and the crowd screamed and shouted, and Senator Hale flinched, and in a matter of seconds, a crowd of

Secret Service agents were upon Senator Hale and Barbara, and they were gone, just like that, as the camerawork got jerky, out of focus, and—

My breathing was rapid. I swallowed. Barbara.

I shut down my computer and went downstairs.

Dinner was a ham and cheddar cheese omelet, and I sat on the couch and balanced the plate on my lap as I ate. I ate with Annie in mind and watched some of the cable television shows, all of them with breathless reports of who was up in the polls, down in the polls, when the next poll was going to come out, and what was going to happen then. There was shouting, there was yelling, there were accusations, and there were talking heads from the Hale, Pomeroy, Grayson, and Wallace campaigns.

I watched for about an hour, and in those entire sixty minutes, if anyone had talked about what was going on in our corner of the world, what was wrong, and how we could work together to improve it, I must have missed it.

After washing the dishes and putting them away, I was planning to take a walk across the way, when there was pounding at my door.

I was in the living room and the sudden sound made me jump. Usually my visitors announce themselves through a phone call or such, and I don't like surprises. I thought quickly of securing my .357 Ruger—usually kept downstairs in a kitchen drawer—but remembered that it was still in the possession of the Secret Service. My nine-millimeter Beretta was upstairs, but the knock came again and in that particular moment, I was tired of being afraid. So I left my weapons where they were and went across the living room.

I opened the door to a burst of swirling snow and a young man and woman wearing Clive Wallace campaign buttons on their damp coats. "Good evening, sir," the young man said. "Can we have just a few minutes to talk to you about Congressman Clive Wallace?"

Any other time, I would have politely said no and would have closed the door. But this wasn't any other time. The snow was quite heavy, and while the young man had spoken to me, energy and confidence in his voice, his companion had stood there, a brave smile on her face, but from the light from the living room, it looked like her lips were turning blue, and she was shivering.

"Sure," I said. "Come on in."

They came in, snow coming off their arms and shoulders, and they politely stomped their feet on the doormat. I closed the door. They were in their early twenties, energy just radiating from them, and they wore what I guess was called "protest chic," cargo pants and heavy boots and tweed coats, and those popular wool caps from South America with earflaps and long strings. He had a thin, stringy brown beard and she had long black hair that had mostly escaped her hat.

In their thin-gloved hands, they held pamphlets, and the young woman passed one over to me. "My First Sixty Days, by Congressman Clive Wallace," and on the back was a photo of the congressman, who looked to be about the same age as his volunteers.

"The name's James," he said, "and she's Julia. We're campaigning for Congressman Wallace, and I hope we can count on your support."

"I'm Lewis," I said, getting a brief handshake from the both of them. "And before we start talking politics, let's talk practical for a moment. How did you two get down here to my house?"

"We walked," Julia said, her voice a bit reproachful. "We were dropped off at the beach at ten this morning by our Tyler coordinator to canvass the neighborhoods, but nobody knew that most of the places here are closed for the winter. So many empty cottages and buildings...it was spooky as hell."

"Where are you from?"

James said, "I'm from Pennsylvania, and Julia's from Florida. We're taking a year off from Amherst to campaign for the congressman. Sir, if you'd take a moment to look at the pamphlet and understand where—"

But I was still paying attention to his friend, who had unbuttoned her coat and was looking around my house, and I thought I saw a furtive sniff. I thought of what she had said, and I asked, "When did you last eat?"

James, a bit defiant, said, "We had lunch, some sandwiches and—"

Julia looked right at me and said, "We're starved."

He turned to her and said, "We still have some canvassing to do and—"

I opened the door for his benefit. "Look out there," I said. "See that snow? You try to walk back up my driveway, there's a good chance you'll wander off and fall into some rocks or boulders. Maybe even get drenched by a wave. And this time of night, there's not many locals out there who are going to want to talk to you."

"Sir," Julia said, "if we could stay for just a bit, we'd be very grateful."

About two minutes earlier I had known where this was going, but it still didn't make me feel particularly happy. I was doing the right thing, but as I closed the door, I also knew the Lafayette House was not in my plans tonight. We spent a while in the kitchen, as I went through what I had in the pantry, freezer, and refrigerator, and as James took charge and vetoed almost everything and anything that was meat-related, dairy-related, or was processed in some way. Finally, Julia said, "Oh, for God's sake, just shut up and let the man feed us. If you can make us a veggie omelet or something, that would be great."

James started to ask me whether the eggs were free-range or not, when I heard a thumping noise, and turned to hide a smile, knowing Julia had kicked her companion from underneath the countertop.

As my omelet pan made its second appearance of the day, James kept up a running conversation about his life, about volunteering for the Congressman Wallace campaign, and about his goals for his life and that of the congressman. From his talk I knew he was an intense young man, with a passion for what he was doing, for not once did he mention Julia or inquire about my own political beliefs.

Even while they were eating, the fairly one-sided conversation continued, and once, while James was swallowing part of his meal, I caught Julia's attention and winked at her. That earned me a smile, a fair exchange.

But James had missed it all.

"The way I see it," he said, wiping up his plate with a piece of toast, "once the congressman gets to the White House, he's going to need us volunteers to move down there and keep the pressure up. That's the only way things will change. It will be a permanent campaign, day after day, week after week. We volunteers will move to D.C. and keep visiting the offices of the senators, and the congressmen, and the lobbyists, and we'll tell them that enough is enough. That change is coming, whether they like it or not."

"That sounds like a good idea," I said carefully. "But you're going to need to win a primary or two before you get there."

James smiled. "Don't you worry. We're going to win here next Tuesday, and win big, and that'll be the story of the year."

"The polls seem to say otherwise."

"The polls," James said. "Ha. First of all, they call people based on whether they've voted in the past. They don't count new voters. That's a good chunk right there, because Congressman Wallace has inspired hundreds and thousands of people who've never voted before. The pollsters also ignore those people who have cell phones, who are off the regular phone grid. Those people never get counted. And third, most polls are owned and operated by the big news media corporations. It's in their best interest to underestimate the support of Congressman Wallace."

"Why is that?" I asked, picking up the dishes.

"Because they know if the word gets out that Congressman Wallace's campaign is catching fire, is gaining support from the real people in this country, then the secret powers in this country, the corporations and their bought-and-paid-for politicians, will realize their time is over. That there's going to be big changes, real big changes, after the election. Read the pamphlet, Lewis, it's all in there. Sixty days. That's all he'll need to change this country."

Julia was keeping quiet, and I had the sense she had listened to this earnest screed about a half million times before. I started washing the dishes and James, taking my silence for encouragement, went on. "Sixty days after the inauguration. Two months, and at the end of two months, we're going to eliminate all forms of racism and sexism and ageism and ableism in government. We're also going to bring all the troops home, have free health care for everyone, free education right up to college and graduate school, a new energy policy that considers people before profits, and a revised welfare program for the young and the old, and everyone else in between."

"That sounds great," I said. "How do you think it'll get paid for?"

"Taxes," he said. "That's the way all societies take care of their people."

"I see," I said. "And do you pay taxes?"

James said, "Ha! To this oppressive regime? The hell I do. Besides, there's other ways to pay for what the people need. If we bring all our troops home, then we won't be instigating other peoples to hate us. Then you don't need a military. There's billions of dollars right there. And then there's the space program."

I paused in my dishwashing. "What about the space program?"

He made a dismissive noise. "Billions and billions...spent for what? To send military pilots in space? To get pretty pictures? To find out what kind of rocks are on Mars or the moons of Jupiter?"

I guess it's a tribute to the way I was brought up by my parents that the young man continued to sit at the counter and wasn't trying to breathe snow while having been tossed headfirst into a nearby snowbank. Julia looked at me and I could tell that she knew her companion had hit home with that last remark, and she said, "There's other causes Congressman Wallace is fighting for that don't mean money being spent."

"Sure!" James said, still charged up. "There's laws that need to be passed as well. Lots of different laws, like a law to eliminate heteronorminism, for example."

While this new recitation was going on, Julia came around the counter, wordlessly picked up a dish towel, and started drying the plates and silverware.

"I'm sorry," I said, also picking up a dishcloth. "I didn't recognize the last word you used. Heteronorminism."

"Sure," he said, as if eager to teach an oldster like myself something new. "You see, society and the way it projects itself in the media and advertising promotes the lifestyle of heterosexuality as the only acceptable sexual lifestyle there is. Heteronorminism. That leads to oppression and hate crimes and discrimination. What the congressman and others propose to do is to ensure that advertising and other media outlets do their part in recognizing other sexual identities, through a quota system. That way, by educating people as to what's really out there, you remove the fear. Remove the fear, you remove discrimination and the possibility of hate crimes."

I opened the cabinet, started putting the dry dishes away as Julia handed them over to me. "So...if gays make up five percent or ten percent of the population, you'd require that five or ten percent of advertising depict gay people in the commercials?"

He laughed at me. "See! Right there, that's a perfect example of heteronorminism. You automatically assume that sexuality is divided into two classes: heterosexuality and homosexuality. But there's so many others...transgender, preop transgender, transvestism, gender-neutral, and of course, the different classes within the leather community. It's a very diverse subject."

"Of course," I said, fighting hard to keep my face straight. "And your role is to educate the voters in New Hampshire as to the congressman's position regarding advertising and the different classes within the leather community."

"Among other things," James said. "No offense, Lewis, and really, I hope you don't take offense, but it's amazing that such a small, overwhelmingly white and reactionary state like this one has such an enormous influence in choosing our next president. It really is outrageous, once you think about it. And it makes our job so much harder."

I dried my hands and Julia went back around to the counter, and I said, "Well, lucky for us white reactionaries that you and so many others have volunteered their time to educate us correctly."

Julia raised a hand, to hide a smile, I'm sure, and James nodded and said without a trace of irony, "You are so right, Lewis. So right."

By now the snow was really coming down, and the wind off the ocean was making the windows rattle. I went to the door and managed to open it a bit, and the cold wind was sharp on my face and hands. Visibility was about three feet, if that. "No offense, guys, but I really think you need to spend the night here."

James said, "Don't you have a car or SUV that can get us up that driveway?"

Julia said, her voice tinged with sarcasm, "You're being silly, James. Would you really ride in that? What about your core beliefs?"

"All I'm saying is that—"

"James."

I closed the door and said, "Look. I'll build a fire in the fireplace, unfold the couch into a sleeper, and in the morning, after the storm breaks and the plows have gone out, I'll give you a ride to your Tyler canvassing coordinator, or anyplace else you'd like."

Julia smiled. She had faint dimples, and if I had been James, I would have ditched the Congressman Wallace for President campaign in a second for the opportunity to see that smile again.

"Thank you," she said. "That'll be wonderful."

But James didn't seem that happy. "Well...if I can use your phone, I guess that'll be all right."

So a fire was built and I folded out the couch, and brought down blankets and sheets and pillows, and Julia was quiet again, and I offered to turn on the television and James proudly said, "Haven't watched television in sixteen months and don't plan to start up again tonight," and I left them to figure out sleeping and other arrangements.

Upstairs, I washed up and went to my own bed, and looked out the window for a moment. I supposed I could wait until they fell asleep and then sneak out of my own house, to make my way in the storm to the Lafayette House.

But there were now too many variables. How to explain to these two volunteers why their host was trudging out in the middle of a storm? And how to explain my sudden presence at the Lafayette House, when every other sane person was sticking close to home? And I hadn't been exaggerating when I'd told the two how dangerous it could be, to try to walk out at night so close to the ocean and the shoreline. Two winters before, during the Super Bowl, a drunk football enthusiast, not wanting to stand in line at the Lafayette House to use the men's room, had stumbled outside to do his duty. He was found about a month later, wedged in some boulders a half mile up the coast, no doubt still legally drunk but also quite dead.

So another day would have to pass. I got undressed and slipped into bed, and picked up my trusty biography of Winston Churchill, and wondered if I had ever been that dense or idealistic when I had been James's and Julia's age.

Idealistic, perhaps, but I hoped never that dense. I read for about a half hour, listening to whispers and once a loud giggle from downstairs, before switching off the light and going to sleep, quickly wondering how Barbara and I must have sounded to our professors and older acquaintances, way back then in college.

The voice woke me up. "Lewis?"

I rolled over, sat up in bed. In the dim illumination of the clock and small night-light in the bathroom, I made out the form of someone at the foot of my bed.

"Julia?"

"Can...can I come over for a sec?"

"Sure."

Julia came over and sat down on the edge of the bed. I rubbed my face and said, "What's wrong?"

"It's...it's...oh, I'm sorry," and she started sobbing.

"Hey," I said, touching her shoulder. "Hold on, hold on, what's wrong?"

She wiped her eyes and said, "I'm sorry to dump this on you. Really. But can you help me?"

"What do you need?"

She sobbed. "Oh, Lewis, I want to go home!"

"Shhh, it's okay," I said. "Campaigning not working out for you?"

"Oh God, you don't know what it's like," she said, almost blubbering. "We sleep on floors or chairs...the food is awful...and I've never been so cold in all my life, and we spend so much time outside. The staff work us so hard and so many people hang up the phones or slam the doors in our faces or throw our pamphlets on the ground...and there's always more to do and I should be home, getting ready for second semester and I...want to go back home. I don't want to do this anymore."

"So why did you come here in the first place?"

"James," she said, practically hissing the word. "He made it sound so special, so romantic, so idealistic. Be part of an awakening movement, a community to change the world. He didn't say anything about cold pizza and no hot showers and dirty bathrooms. And he's...well, you saw how he is. So full of himself. So righteous. I mean"—and she giggled, a welcome change—"educating the average New Hampshire voter about Congressman Wallace and the leather community...he didn't even know you were making fun of him."

I looked at the time: one a.m. "I shouldn't have done that, but the temptation was too great. So. Why not go home? What's stopping you?"

In the faint light I saw her fold her arms, and she seemed to shrink into the frame of a twelve-year-old girl. "I told you he was idealistic...he can also get very angry if he doesn't think you believe in anything. That you're willing to compromise. And I get scared when he gets angry. I...I really get scared, and I don't know what he might do. Once I was upset that we went a whole day without eating and I told him that I wouldn't do that anymore, and he tugged my arm something awful. It hurt for two days. Do...do you think you can help me?"

I scratched the back of my head. "Across the way is a hotel called the Lafayette House. There's a shuttle service that'll take you into town tomorrow, to a newspaper store that's the local Greyhound stop. You can even buy the bus ticket at the hotel so there's no waiting at the store. And in an hour's time you'll be in Boston. From there I'm sure you can catch a flight or a bus ride home. That good enough?"

"Yes, yes, it is...but what about James?"

"You let me worry about James. You just worry about getting home. Got enough money?"

"Yes, that's not a problem."

"How about belongings? Luggage?"

"Everything important is in my bag. Other than that, it's just a bunch of smelly clothes I can do without."

"Then you'll be all set. I promise."

The sniffles came back. "Oh, Lewis, thank you, thank you so much."

"Not a problem. Look. It's late...why don't you get back to sleep."

She leaned over and kissed my forehead, and I guess I was a bit stunned at the unexpected attention.

And if I was just a bit stunned, then, a moment later, I became fully stunned.

Julia said, with a touch of shy hesitation, "Would...would you like me to spend some time here with you?"

I touched her shoulder again. "Any other night, any other time, I'd be honored. But go back downstairs, Julia. It'll be all right. I promise."

Another whispered "thank you" and she got up, and at my bedroom door she said, "You know. I haven't gotten a good night's sleep since I've been to New Hampshire. He snores and sounds like a washing machine...and he denies it! Can you believe that? He thinks I'm imagining it, night after night."

"Nights like these," I said, "I can believe almost everything."

12

In the morning I let them loose in my kitchen to fix whatever kind of breakfast suited them, and I shoveled a bit from the front door, and from the sliding door to the shed that served as a garage for my Ford Explorer. The snow wasn't as deep as I had expected, and I knew my Ford would plow us right up and out into the parking lot and Atlantic Avenue with ease.

I went back into the house, warm from my exertions. James was standing there with Julia, dressed, munching on a piece of toast. It wasn't whole wheat or whole grain or harvested from a cooperative in Baja, California, but I guess hunger trumped politics, at least this morning. I also figured that since James hadn't come out to help me shovel the way clear, he was saving his energies for something more important. Julia looked quiet, shy, and I said, "Ready to leave?"

"Sure," James said. "Our campaign guy, he's staying at the Redbird Motel, on Cromwell Street. I just called him and he's waiting for us. Can you drop us there?"

"No problem."

They joined me outside and in the open garage, James went ahead of Julia and climbed into the front passenger seat. I started up the Explorer and backed out into the snow-covered driveway and started going up the slight incline. James was talking to Julia about what they were going to do that day, how they would probably have to skip lunch because of the time lost due to last night's snowstorm, and how they would really have to redouble their efforts because the corporate-controlled media and rival campaigns would—

"Excuse me for a sec," I said, driving across the street to the Lafayette House, a quick and easy task due to the lack of early morning traffic. "I need to run an errand and then we'll be on our way."

I parked in an area marked for guest drop-off and I put the Explorer in park, shut the engine off, and said, "Julia? Care to come with me for a moment?"

"Oh, thanks, I will," she said quickly, and before James could say or do anything, she was outside in the parking lot, and fell in step with me as I went up to the front entrance of the hotel. We went into the lobby, and I made a left to the gift shop. Julia leaned into me as we went into the gift shop and said, "Thanks. Thank you very much."

"You're quite welcome. You have a good ride home, and a good semester."

Inside the gift shop, Stephanie was behind the counter and looked up from a sheaf of invoices that she had been examining.

"Morning, Lewis. What can I do for you?"

I said, "This is my friend Julia. She'd like a Greyhound ticket to Boston, and a ticket to the shuttle uptown."

"Oh, I think we can do that," she said, pulling a ledger and ticket book from underneath the counter. "You're in luck. The next shuttle leaves in about five minutes."

Julia started going through her purse and she and Stephanie started with their business arrangement, and I waited, looking out the gift shop window, as the women worked and information was recorded and currency was exchanged. My Explorer was in view and then James, probably realizing at last that something was amiss, got out of my Ford and started up the short walkway. I moved around and as Julia and Stephanie finished their transaction, James strode in.

"Hey, what's up?" he said.

I smiled at him. "Julia's heading home."

"You're joking."

"Nope."

He tried to get past me, and I moved in front of him. "Tell you what," I said. "We'll stay here for a minute or two, and then I'll give you a ride to the Redbird Motel to meet up with your campaign guy. How's that?"

He said something with lots of syllables that probably wouldn't endear him to the League of Women Voters, and he called out, "Julia! What the hell is going on here? C'mon, don't you care anymore?"

She kept quiet and grabbed her tickets, and walked by, heading toward the lobby and the outdoors, and James stuck a hand out to stop her and I moved it back, saying, "Let's be polite, all right?"

Two words, one being "you," and the other not being "you," and he tried to follow Julia out of the gift shop. He said, "Julia, don't you leave me! Damn it, don't you leave me! I'm not going to let you—"

Then he shut up, real quick, since as he went by, I grabbed his right hand, tightening my grip on his thumb, and then pulled it around and tucked his arm up toward his back. My friend Detective Sergeant Diane Woods had taught me this move—called a come-along—some years ago, and rarely have I ever felt such pain.

"Oooh," James said, stopping, his legs getting weak. I leaned in, whispering in his ear, "Don't move, don't say a word, or your thumb gets shattered. If I have your attention, say yes."

"Yes," he whispered back.

"Good," I said. "Now. You and I are going to stay in this lovely little gift shop, and we're going to admire their sweatshirt collection, and you're going to be a good boy. All right? Say yes again if you understand."

"Yes," he murmured.

"Nicely done," I said. Stephanie stood behind the gift counter, taking it all in, and her face had no expression. She was letting me be, which made me quite happy, for I wasn't sure what she would do about what was going on here, despite our casual friendship. And the lack of customers to see what was happening made me even happier.

Outside I saw Julia, standing by herself, and she stood there and I stood in the gift shop, holding the hand of a male college student from Massachusetts, and I thought that was a pretty odd way to start one's morning, no matter how you looked at it.

Then a white passenger van pulled up, and Julia quickly walked through an open door. I waited for a moment, to see if she was going to wave goodbye or look back or somehow acknowledge that I was there, which would have been sweet, but no, the door to the van was shut by the driver and it drove away. So much for sweetness.

I let James go. "There. Feel better?"

He turned, rubbing his hand, face red, and he said, "You son of a bitch, I'll have you arrested! Right now! See how that makes your day!"

I shrugged. "Give it a go. You're young, a college student, and a college student from Massachusetts. I live here, I know all the cops and most of the lawyers. We'll see who'll have the better day."

Another rub of his hand and another string of curses, and I felt disappointed in the caliber of today's college youth, since I had known all of those curses years ago when I was his age.

When he was finished with his latest outburst, I said, "Come on, let's go."

"What the hell do you mean, let's go?"

"You need a ride to the Redbird Motel. I said I'd give you a ride. Ready?"

Another two-word exclamation and he said, "No way in hell I'm getting a ride from you! Asshole. I'd rather walk!"

"Fine," I said. "Have a good day canvassing."

"Sure! And another thing...I made a half dozen phone calls last night from your phone. Long distance. Take that, sucker!"

He charged out of the gift shop, and I called after him—though I doubted he heard me—"Not to worry, I've got unlimited long distance. For just thirty bucks a month."

Stephanie finally said something, but started off with a loud laugh. "Oh, that's a good one."

I turned to face her. "Enjoy the show?"

"In a way, yes," she said, pulling together my morning newspapers. "You did well."

"Glad I could provide you with entertainment."

"Better than none. Here's your papers."

"Thanks," I said, pulling out my wallet, but Stephanie laughed. "Nope. On the house. You go along and read your papers, Lewis. Have a good one."

I put the papers under my arm. "I'm going to try, if the gods let me."

But the gods must have been otherwise occupied, for once again, in the lobby of the Lafayette House, I met up with Chuck Bittner, the rep from the Tucker Grayson campaign, who stood there, arms crossed, his pudgy face glowing.

"Mr. Cole," he said.

"Mr. Bittner," I said. "What, you live here?"

"As a matter of fact, I do. For the duration of the campaign."

"I hope the Lafayette House is charging you full freight."

"I'm sure they are," he said. "Last time, you gave me three hundred seconds. May I request half of that this morning?"

I shifted the papers from one arm to another. "All right. One hundred fifty seconds. Go ahead."

He looked at his watch. "At this time tomorrow, if you haven't agreed to make a statement on behalf of the Grayson campaign, we're going to publicize your Pentagon background and something new as well, something that has just come to our attention."

"And what's that? My unpaid parking tickets from the city of Boston?"

"No," he said, his voice triumphant. "A revelation about your background with Barbara Hale. Your choice. Either the word comes out and it comes from you, or it comes from us. And you get some very nasty news media attention. You come out in support of General Grayson, and you don't have to say anything about Mrs. Hale. Just your support of the Grayson campaign would be enough."

I thought about that, thought about what it might do to the Hale campaign, how Barbara would feel. God, how Annie would feel.

Remembered Annie's plea. No more bad news, please, she had said. No more bad news about you and Hale.

"No," I said.

"No, what?"

"No, I'm not going to say anything tomorrow, and no, neither will you."

He laughed, unfolded his arms. "Or what?"

"Or you'll regret it."

A smile was still on his face, and he reached over and grabbed my upper arm, squeezing it hard. "Mr. Cole, I may be retired navy, but I'm still in shape. Much better shape than you, I would guess. If anyone's going to be hurt, it's going to be you. And if you think you can threaten me, prevent me, stop me from doing what's right for General Grayson's campaign, then I just have three words for you. Bring it on."

I pulled my arm free, nodded, and walked past him. "Consider it brought."

Outside the sun was still shining and it looked like the day might improve, when I got to my Ford Explorer and saw that some thoughtful person had keyed both sides of my vehicle. On the passenger's side it was just a series of scratches, but on the driver's side, inspiration must have set in, for scratched in the paint was PIG.

Not very imaginative, but the point had been made. I got in and went home.

At home I went through the papers and made two phone calls to Felix Tinios, but he wasn't home or reachable through his cell phone. I got his to-the-point message twice: "Leave your name and number," which I did. An attempt to reach Annie was also equally unsuccessful.

Usually I like to take my time going through the morning papers, contrasting and comparing the different coverage and editorials, but this morning, well, there was too much going on. I had a late breakfast and even later shower, and as I was putting on a pair of socks, the phone rang.

"Lewis?"

"Hey, it's the soon-to-be-famous Paula Quinn," I replied. The expected laugh didn't come from the *Tyler Chronicle*'s best reporter, but what she said next made me close my eyes in embarrassment. "Not famous enough, if you forgot our lunch date today. I'm all by myself at the Harborview Restaurant."

I said something that James had said just that morning, and then said, "Ten minutes," and I finished dressing and got the hell out.

BY THE TIME the check arrived and I had passed along my credit card to the waitress, overruling Paula's earlier promise to pay, Paula's mood had improved. Some time ago we had shared a brief romance that hadn't panned out, and after some rough patches, we were doing well. Odd, but I didn't have that vaguely uncomfortable and queasy feeling with her that I had with Barbara Scott Hale. Maybe it was because Barbara was married and Paula wasn't, or that there was still a sense of unfinished business with Barbara and me and none with Paula, but I didn't want to think too much about it. Instead, I just sat and enjoyed lunch with her, admiring her little upturned nose, her smile, and the cute way her ears would sometimes poke through her blond hair.

Despite its name, the Harborview was in the center of Tyler proper, and only by standing on the roof and holding on to the fake cupola could anyone see a view of Tyler Harbor. Still, it's a popular place with the locals and tourists, and today, even in January, it was fairly busy. We sat in a booth that overlooked a mound of plowed, dirty snow in the parking lot, the cars and SUVs out there lightened by a faint white sheen that comes from the salt dumped on the roads to keep them clear.

I looked around and said, "I get the feeling most of these people won't be here come the day after Primary Day."

"So true," she said, sipping at her second iced tea. "You know the musical and movie Brigadoon?"

"Sure. About a mythical Scottish village that only appears to the rest of the world every hundred years or so."

"That's right. And this little state of ours is like Brigadoon. For three years in a row, we're just a little backwater, the prickly state north of Massachusetts that is mostly ignored by the rest of the world. Then, in that fourth year, something magical happens. This little state of just over a million people becomes power central. Pretty funny, isn't it? This little state of tax avoiders and sensible-shoe wearers and independent cusses plays a prominent role in who the quote leader of the free world unquote is going to be. If anyone had a question of whether God had a sense of humor, our little state and how we pick the president should settle it."

"And how are you doing?"

She smiled. "I love it. Honest to God I do. You know why?"

"Access," I said.

She stuck her tongue out at me. "Show-off. Yes, absolutely, access. The candidates need to get their message out to the locals, and the locals don't trust the big media, even the not-so-big media from Boston. So us little folks get all the attention from the candidates and their campaigns. When most times some local police chiefs enjoy their power trips by not calling us back in a day or so, it's wonderful to have media reps calling from Washington or Manhattan, wanting to know if we'd like to have a private, one-on-one lunch with the candidate that day. It's delightful."

The waitress came back with the check, and when she left I said, "So. Primary Day next Tuesday. Who's going to win?"

Paula said, "Well, of course, that depends on who you talk to, or who's going to spin what. The easiest prediction is that the junior senator from our southern neighbor, Nash Pomeroy, should win it in a walk. Favorite son and all that. And that's what his campaign is pumping...then there's Senator Hale. A Southern boy who one wouldn't think would do well in New Hampshire, but he just won in Iowa, and people love a winner. So it depends on whether, one, the voters want to vote for a winner, or two, vote for somebody else to shake things up so that New Hampshire isn't taken for granted."

"You hear anything about the Hale campaign?"

She made a face. "Considering who you're spending time with, I'd think you'd have an inside track on that."

"Maybe yes, maybe no. What do you hear?"

"Me? Usual stuff. Campaign in chaos, moving forward on momentum, need a win here in New Hampshire to bring in more big bucks for the Southern primaries. But even if he comes in second—or third, which I doubt—he'll stay in it for a while. He's from the South. Lots of primaries coming up in the South."

"That's it? No other gossip or dark tales or rumors?"

"If there is, I haven't heard it."

"How about General Grayson? Or Congressman Wallace? How are they going to do next Tuesday?"

She finished off her iced tea. "In a purely logical, mathematical sense, they will lose. But I'll predict here and now, my friend, each will declare himself a winner, no matter the outcome. They'll play the expectations game. Each side will tell pollsters and columnists and reporters that their internal polls only have them winning five percent of the vote, so when they actually win ten percent of the vote, all these sober-minded reporters can write inspiring stories of how they did better than expected, and how this has breathed new life in the struggling campaign of blah, blah, blah."

I reached behind me for my coat. "So. Who do you think's going to win?"

Paula made me laugh by lowering her voice, pretending to be some sort of television anchorman, and announcing, "Well, Lewis, the American people will win next Tuesday, of course..."

Outside there was no breeze and the thin January sunlight felt good on my face. I walked Paula to her car, and she said, "You and Annie...how's it going?"

"Goes well, between campaign meetings and appearances."

She grabbed my hand. "Good. You make it work, or I'll hurt you. Understand? She's good people, and I like what she's done to your mood."

"Thanks for the advice. And how's the town counsel, Mr. Spencer, treating you?"

She looked embarrassed and suddenly ten years younger.

"He's...he's fine...and you know what?"

"What?"

She touched her left ear, just for a moment. "He...thinks I should get my ears done. Flatten them so they don't poke out like they do. What do you think?"

I kissed her cheek. "I think he's a bonehead, that's what I think."

AT HOME I tried to spend some productive time in front of the computer, to come up again with a snappy column idea for June, and after a half hour or so of false starts, it just wasn't happening. Then I logged on to the Internet, to see what nonsense was being written about the primary and my home state, and after some time slogging through stories written by reporters who think it's charming as all hell that most of the small towns here still have white clapboard churches around grassy town commons, I spent some time searching for something about Barbara Hale and her famous husband.

I didn't find much. Through the magical powers of the Internet, I found some old file stories written when Hale was first elected senator, and a nice profile in the *Washington Post's* Style section, written after Hale had announced his candidacy, but not much else. It was odd to call up a search system on the Internet, and see dozens and dozens of photos of a woman who you once were intimate with, knowing that your mind's eye had clearer and better photos than what existed in the digital universe.

I also viewed some video clips as well, Barbara appearing with her husband, almost stuck to his side, as he appeared at campaign rallies in Iowa and Michigan and, yes, of course, New Hampshire. And in those clips, I saw her smile, saw her enthusiasm, and saw her devotion to her spouse, and something just didn't seem right.

Why would anyone want to kill her? What would be the point? Was she overreacting, and the real attempt had been against her husband, like everyone else thought?

And for God's sake, what in hell was Spenser Harris's role in all of this, and who had killed him and dumped him in my yard?

I looked at the clips, again and again, and there was a little tickling at the back of my skull, just the barest hint that something was wrong, and whatever it was, it was gone, the minute the phone rang.

"Yes?" I answered.

"You rang?"

It was Felix Tinios, and I spun around in my chair and put my feet up on the nearest windowsill and said, "Thanks for calling me back. Sounds like you're at a hog-calling festival or something equally charming."

He sighed. "I wish. Days like this, you get a better class of people at a hog-calling festival. Nope, I'm at O'Hare, ready to come home in an hour."

"Chicago? What in hell are you doing there?"

"My new job, son. Oppo for the Pomeroy campaign."

"A Massachusetts senator, and you're in Illinois?"

"The world of the oppo researcher travels far and wide. Especially when your subject has some interesting hobbies, none of which I'm going to mention over an open line. What's up with you?"

"You going to be tired when you get home?"

"Probably."

"Feel like a job?"

"A job? From you?"

"Yep."

Felix said cautiously, "It's...it's not a moving job, is it?"

"God, no," I said. "I've had enough of those to last a lifetime. Nope, something else. Tell me, ever see the movie *All the President's Men*?"

"Sure. Dustin Hoffman and Robert Redford. You got a newspaper job lined up for me?"

"Nope. Something else."

"Oh...okay, I got it. What time suits you?"

"Flying into Boston or Manchester?"

"Manchester. Just after eleven."

"How about if I pick you up and we go on from there?"

"Fine." And then he laughed. "Looking forward to it, if you can believe it. It'll be a nice change after digging up dirt all these days."

And after another minute or two of receiving flight and arrival information, I hung up and made another phone call.

It took some maneuvering, but I got through to the Hale for President campaign headquarters in Manchester, and actually got somebody on the line who knew Annie Wynn. "Hold on, I'll see if I can get her," and I could hear the phone clunk on a tabletop, and in the background, there was the noise of voices and keyboards being slapped and a television program, and then there was a clatter, and the phone was picked up.

"Annie Wynn."

"It's Lewis. How are you?"

A sigh. "It's been one of those days...look, I can't talk much. Did you ride out the storm all right?"

"I did, and when I see you next, I've got a funny story to tell you."

"My friend...it won't be tonight, I'm sorry. Maybe tomorrow." It seemed like the noise in the background grew louder.

"Well, how about dinner? I could drive out to Manchester."

Another sigh. "Cold pizza is what's ahead of me, Lewis. A wonderful thought, but I can't leave here tonight. There's too much going on. Look, I've got to run. I'll talk to you tomorrow. Deal?"

"Deal," I said, and that was that.

I put the phone down, stared at it for a bit, and then picked it up and did some additional calling.

TWO HOURS LATER, I was in Manchester, wearing my best suit and best wool overcoat, and even shoes that matched. I parked about a block away from my destination and walked gingerly along the slippery sidewalks. Snow piles were still on the sides of the street, and they were sprinkled with campaign signs from all the campaigns, like candles on a soggy slice of ice cream cake, melting on a plate.

Over my shoulder I carried a wide leather bag that bumped against my hip, and which was warm to the touch. I tried not to think too much of what I had in there as I made my way to the well-lit storefront that announced HALE FOR PRESIDENT. Inside I wiped my feet and took in the scenery. There were rows and rows of battered metal desks manned by men and women, mostly young and intense-looking. Phones were ringing, photocopying machines were humming, and hardly anybody was paying attention to the four television sets in one corner, all of them turned to a different cable news channel. Posters of Senator Hale were taped to the walls, and there was the constant movement and hum of people at work.

I stood there, just taking it all in, when a woman spotted me and came over, her sweater festooned with Hale buttons, and carrying a clipboard. She was about ten years younger than me, pudgy, with a no-nonsense attitude about her.

"Can I help you?" she asked, looking past me, as if counting down the seconds as to when she could pass me off to somebody else lower on the food chain.

"You certainly can," I said, removing a thin leather wallet from inside my coat. I flashed it open and quickly closed it. "The name's Cole. I'm from the FEC. I need two things, and I need them now."

Well, that got her attention. She was no longer staring over my shoulder. "What's the problem?"

"There is no problem," I said. "And it'll remain that way if I get what I need right away."

"What's that?"

"A private office, with a door, and a campaign worker you have here. One Miss Annie Wynn."

She seemed to hold her clipboard tighter. "Can you tell me what this is about?"

I stared at her. "Are you Miss Annie Wynn?"

"No, I'm not."

"Then that's all you need to know. Now. Am I getting that office and Miss Wynn?"

She seemed to struggle for a moment, but maybe the exhaustion and the looming deadline of the upcoming primary, and the fear of anything bad, overtook whatever common sense the poor dear had, for she nodded and said, "Follow me, then."

13

I don't know who the office belonged to, but it had a nice round wooden table adjacent to the desk, the door that I required, and I carefully removed the piles of files and papers from the table and placed them on the floor. My leather case was now open on one of the chairs, and I was about to get to work when there was a soft knock on the door and Annie came in, carrying the no-doubt required clipboard.

She started by saying, "What can I do for...Lewis, what the hell are you doing here?"

From the open leather case, I took out a small white tablecloth, which I spread over the table. "Feeding you dinner."

"Dinner? You're...damn it, Myra said there was somebody from the FEC here to see me, the goddamn Federal Elections Commission!"

I started taking out plates and wineglasses. "I never said I was from the Federal Elections Commission. I said I was from the FEC. Many, many years ago—unless my memory is wrong, which

is distinctly possible—I joined an organization called the Federation of Employed Consultants. Or something like that. They never sent me a renewal notice, so I guess I'm still a member in good standing."

Annie said, "Myra said you showed her a badge!"

Plates, silverware, wineglasses, and a little vase with a rose, made from plastic, unfortunately. I smiled. "Yes, I did. It was a junior detective badge I once got from Diane Woods at the Tyler Police Department. I'm quite proud of it, and love showing it off. I hope she didn't mistake it for something else."

Annie was trying to be angry and not laugh at the same time, and I wasn't sure which would succeed. "Lewis, I told you I didn't have—

"Annie."

"It's a madhouse here, and it's going to be—"

"Annie."

She looked at me, tired and quiet. "What?"

"You said you couldn't leave. So you're not leaving. You need to have dinner, and why not a good one? And why not a dinner where you can talk about something else besides the campaign? You can have some quiet time, a fine meal, and go back to work on the Hale campaign, full of vim and vigor."

She wrinkled her nose as she smelled what was coming from the open leather bag. "I know what vigor is, but what the hell is vim?"

"Beats me. What do you say we eat before it gets cold?"

I could sense the struggle going on inside her campaign volunteer mind, and finally she smiled and dropped the clipboard on the floor. "Wonderful. I'm starved."

So I dumped my coat and brought everything out, and dinner was chateaubriand for two, already sliced in generous portions, with garlic mashed potatoes, small salads, and asparagus spears in a cheese sauce for Annie. There was also a half bottle of a Margaux wine from France, which I poured for the two of us. As I spread everything out, she practically clapped her hands in glee at the spread of food.

"How in hell did you manage this?"

"I managed it by not cooking it," I said. "There's a new restaurant here in Manchester. Called Soundings North."

She picked up a fork. "Yeah, I've heard of it. But I didn't know they did takeout."

"They don't."

"So how did you get this?"

I picked up my own fork. "By a charitable contribution."

"A bribe?"

"Quiet, woman. Eat before you start drooling."

And she took a bite, and then another, and gave a soft sigh of pleasure, and that was dinner.

I made sure we didn't talk much about politics, but I also didn't press my luck. We ate, and ate well, and for dessert I had some sliced strawberries with heavy cream and some brown sugar, and hot coffee from a thermos bottle. She ate quickly and as I cleaned up, she said, "The best I've eaten in a very long time, Lewis. Thank you."

"You're quite welcome."

She looked up at the wall, noted the time, and said, "I hate to eat and run, but..."

"You've got to eat and run."

"Wait...you said something earlier about a funny story."

"It can wait," I said.

"You sure?" she asked.

"Unless you want to start telling me about Senator Hale's position on the various members of the leather community, yes, it can wait."

"I'm glad it can wait," she said, "Though it does sound like a hell of a story."

"You can't imagine."

Annie stood up, retrieved her clipboard from the floor, and I admired the view and how she filled out her tight black slacks. She turned to me and said, "Next Wednesday."

"I know. It comes after Tuesday."

"Smart-ass. No, what I mean is this...next Wednesday, it changes for the better. The primary will be done. I promise. After the primary I'm going to move in with you for a day or two and...catch up with things. If you don't mind."

"Best offer I've had all year."

She laughed. "And the year has just begun! No, Lewis, I need to tell you something. I've been asked to join the campaign in South Carolina when this is over...and I've been thinking about it. I believe in Senator Hale and what he wants to do when he gets in the White House. I truly believe in that...but I also don't want to stop seeing you. You mean a lot to me."

"Likewise from here, dear one."

"So, when Tom next talks to me, I'm going to tell him that South Carolina is off the table. New Hampshire still needs more work."

"As a resident of New Hampshire, I thank you."

"And I thank you for dinner. And delightful conversation. And the lovely dessert. And coffee."

I went forward and said, "How about one more helping of dessert?" and I pulled her toward me.

That brought a giggle and a few minutes of kissing and caressing, as we stood before the closed door, and she whispered in my ear, "You better stop now, or I'm going to do you right on the floor of Tom's office."

"And why's that a problem?"

"Tom is sort of my boss, and I want to be able to see him in the future without blushing about what the two of us did in his office."

I reluctantly let her go and gathered up my belongings, placing them back into the leather case. "Thanks," I said.

"For what?"

"For going along with dinner. For not tossing me out on my ear when you first saw me. For the smiles and good times."

She opened the door. "Come along, FEC-man, while I try to come up with an explanation of what we've been doing the past twenty minutes."

Outside it was the usual chaos of ringing phones and raised conversations, and there were some curious glances tossed our way. Annie leaned into me and said, "This. This is what I believe in. What do you believe in, Lewis?"

"I believe I must be going," I said. "That's what."

"Thanks," she said. "I'll call you tomorrow."

"That'd be great."

She walked away and was quickly corralled by some workers, and I went to the front door, where I slipped on my coat and grabbed my now lighter leather carrying case. I was about to open the door when a loud woman's voice got my attention. I and about thirty other people turned to look at a closed office door, about ten feet away from me, when it slammed open and the woman's voice now said, "Keep on ignoring me, you'll see what'll happen, you'll be goddamned lucky to come in third place next week!"

A well-dressed and well-coiffed woman stormed out of the now open door, and she blew by me like I was a piece of garden statuary, something to be ignored and perhaps defiled by small birds or dogs, but not anything that counted.

Which sort of disappointed me, since I had enjoyed talking with her the other night at her home.

The door outside flew open, cold air rushed in, and I caught one more glimpse of Audrey Whittaker, wealthy woman from Wallis—how's that for alliteration?—who seemed pretty angry at the Hale campaign.

I followed her out, perhaps just to say hello or to find out what had gone on, but the cold January sidewalks were empty by the time I made it out there.

So I trudged my way through the darkness and got to my Ford Explorer —still marked with PIG, visible from a nearby streetlight—and got in and started her up.

ABOUT TWENTY MINUTES later I was at the Manchester airport. Not so long ago, according to Felix and others, the airport had been a sleepy little regional facility that had about a dozen or so flights a day, with a parking lot next to the terminal building that charged two dollars a day for parking, and which trusted people to pay on the honor system by putting their money in a little brown envelope and mailing it in. Some place. I wish I had gotten to know it before it so drastically changed, after fliers—fed up with the continuous horror show that is Boston's Logan Airport—started streaming out to Manchester and Hartford and Warwick, Rhode Island.

Now the airport is bigger and there's a three-story parking garage, but any airport that has a stuffed moose in its arrival area still has some of its old New Hampshire charm. I put the Explorer in short term parking and made a ninety-second walk to the sole terminal building. Arrivals were on the second floor, and I did a quick check of the status board and saw that Felix's flight was on time.

So I sat down and people-watched for a while. I thought about the campaigns and the upcoming primary and other things, and I still thought about Barbara and our little make-out session in her hotel room, and I thought about the videos I had seen with her and her husband, and now I felt guilty, thinking about kissing a married woman, even one I had been intimate with all those years ago, and then, thankfully, the status board said Felix's flight had landed, so I could stop thinking so damn much.

I stood up. I would be so glad when next Tuesday would be here and over. Barbara would be gone from my state, to be with her husband, where she belonged, and I would stay here, and, delightfully, so would Annie.

From the arrival gate, people started to stream through, and I liked seeing the happy reunions among them as the plane emptied. Landing alone at night in a strange airport can be such a soul deadening experience, seeing other people's laughs and smiles and hugs. I waited and I waited, and pretty soon, the departing stream of people dwindled down to a trickle.

No Felix.

I double-checked the status board. It was the right gate, and it was the right flight. I then had that niggling feeling at the back of my skull, the one when you think you either made a dumb mistake or, worse, that something bad has happened to the one you are waiting for, and—

There, strolling along like he owned the damn place, was Felix, wearing black slacks and a dark gray woolen coat that went down to his knees, carrying a soft black leather briefcase, and keeping up an animated conversation with two flight attendants, one on each side. The women were laughing at something that Felix said, and he garnered a quick kiss on the cheek from both of them as he stopped before me. The women went on, their wheeled cases being pulled behind them, and the one on the left, a brunette, gave a quick wave to Felix when she was sure that her companion wasn't looking.

"Hi there," I said. Whenever I come back from a trip, I always feel like taking a long shower and brushing my teeth and changing clothes and dumping them in the washer, but Felix looked so fresh and relaxed, it was like he'd had a private cabin, all to himself, on the flight from Chicago.

"Hi, yourself," Felix said, looking at the slim forms of the departing flight attendants. "Need to know something real quick. You still with Annie?"

"As of a few hours ago, yes."

"Ah. And this little job you have for me...is that still on?"

"Yes, again."

Felix tore his glance away from the women. "Ah, a pity. If both questions had been in the negative, I would have quickly followed those fine airline employees, and such a night you and I would have had. Such a night."

I started walking toward the stairs that led down to the main floor. "And what kind of night would that be?"

"Sorry, I don't want to tease you with what you might have had."

"Really?"

Felix laughed. "One of these nights—not any time soon, but one of these nights—you're going to wake up at 2:00 a.m. with a snoring wife next to you, and maybe a squalling baby in the room next door, and a heavy-ass mortgage dragging you down, and you're going to wake up and say, 'Damn, I should have dumped everything and gone out with Felix that time in Manchester.' And that night will come."

We were now on the main floor, heading to the exit doors. "If and when that night ever comes, I'll make sure to call you."

"That doesn't sound fair."

"What the hell does fair have to do with it?"

We went through the doors and out into the frigid night air, and in the parking lot I said, "How in hell do you look so refreshed?"

"Clean living?"

"I sure as hell doubt that."

Felix said, "Then it must have been the first-class accommodations, out there and back again."

"First class? I'm not sure if I were a contributor to the Nash Pomeroy campaign that I'd be thrilled knowing they were paying for first-class airfare."

He shook his head as we approached my Explorer. "Lewis, I will make a prediction, here and now. Sometime in the next several weeks, Senator Nash Pomeroy of Massachusetts is going to drop out of the race due to health reasons, and if some enterprising reporter or blogger starts digging, stuff will be found about Senator Pomeroy that will make my first-class tickets look as scandalous as stolen pens from somebody's desk. I made an oral report to some of his campaign staff and that's the feeling I'm getting. You know, it's a queasy thing, to listen to a grown man cry, a man who's pinned all his hopes and dreams on a candidate that has such a back-ground—Now, what's this?"

Felix pointed to the PIG scratched on the driver's side door.

"Local outreach from the Clive Wallace campaign," I said, unlocking the doors.

He shrugged as he went around the front of the Ford. "Well, that's one way of getting a voter's attention, but I sure as hell don't recommend it."

Short-term parking was a whopping two dollars, but Felix insisted on paying for it and getting a receipt. "It's so rare that I'm doing something this legitimate, it's pretty much a new experience for me. Expense reports. Can you believe that?"

"Sure, I can," I said, and in a matter of minutes, we were heading east, on Route 101, about an hour out from Tyler. Felix stretched his legs and stretched his arms and said, "Okay, kid. What's the job? Based on your movie reference, I'd guess it's going to be a Watergate-type activity."

"I think so, but without the publicity and the book deals."

"God, now that's a hope. Who's the target?"

"There's an oppo researcher for the General Grayson campaign. His name is Chuck Bittner. Ex-navy. He wants me to make an announcement tomorrow endorsing the general and criticizing Senator Hale and his family."

Felix said, "No offense, my friend, but for a day or so, you were the lead suspect in the shooting involving the senator. Does this Bittner character really think having your endorsement is going to be a good thing?"

I checked the speedometer. Seventy miles an hour, just five miles an hour above the limit. Traffic was very light. We would make good time. "It's not the endorsement part they're excited about. It's the criticism aspect they're more interested in."

"Wait a second. You said something about the senator and his family. What do you know about the senator's family?"

I gave him a quick glance. "Keep a secret?"

"Ha-ha," he said, his voice flat. "Very funny. What's the big secret?"

"Well, it's an open secret among the Secret Service and some members of the Hale campaign, and a few others. Luckily, so far, it hasn't reached the news media, though give them some more time, I'm sure they'll get it. The senator's wife, Barbara Hale?"

"Yes, the blonde. What about her?"

"I dated her in college."

That got his attention. "You're kidding me."

"Not for a moment."

Then he laughed. "Lewis, you...you are so full of surprises, and this one, this one really tops the list. Dated the future first lady of our great land. I never knew you had it in you."

"Not sure what kind of 'it' you mean, but that's the deal. Tomorrow I'm supposed to endorse Grayson, criticize Hale and his crazed, power-hungry wife, and all will be right in the world."

"Knowing you, I know that's not going to happen. So what else?"

"The 'what else' is that if I don't go out and make this all public, Grayson's campaign will do it without me. It's a win-win for them. I go out and endorse Grayson, the media buzz will hurt Hale. I don't go out and endorse Grayson, and Grayson's campaign makes a big deal about the alleged shooter being an ex-spook with a mysterious past, connected romantically to Hale's wife, and the media buzz hurts Hale. And with just a few days before the primary, there's not enough time for Hale to recover."

"Knowing you and how you feel about Miss Wynn, I think hurting the Hale campaign is definitely off the plate."

"Definitely," I said.

We stayed silent for a few minutes, as Route 101 made its way through Epping, the self-proclaimed center of the universe. "This Bittner character...where is he tonight?"

"At the Lafayette House."

"How convenient. What can you tell me about him?"

"Arrogant. Assured. True believer in Grayson's campaign."

"What else?"

"Seems strong, in shape. Threatened me."

"Threatened you how?"

"Just said he was in better shape than me and tried to break my upper arm to prove a point."

"Tsk, tsk," Felix said. "How childish. And what would you like me to do?"

We were now approaching Exonia, home to Phillips Exonia Academy and an obscenely high population of writers. I said, "Your usual and customary approach to making otherwise reluctant people see the error of their ways."

That brought a good laugh. "You've been with me so long, my friend, that I'd think you could do it yourself."

"I could, but I need you."

'Why, thank you. Always nice to be needed. But don't sell yourself short, Lewis. You can be a strong fellow when the circumstances require it."

I passed a lumbering semi going up a slight incline. "It's not strength I'm worried about. It's something else."

"What's that?"

"You'll do it right."

"Meaning you would do it wrong?"

I gave the top of the steering well a small slap. "Yes, I'd do it wrong. I'd go at it wrong, take it to wrong places, and probably go too far. You won't."

"Why do you think that?"

"Because for you, it's professional. For me, it's personal. He wants to use me to hurt the Hale campaign, hurt someone I had fond feelings for and someone I currently have fond feelings for, and he brought up my past service and tried to use that against me. Ticked me off big-time. So, yeah, Felix, for me, it's quite personal. I know you'll do what has to be done, and I'll be there as well. But I trust you and your abilities. Which is why I need you. And why I thank you in advance."

"And you're welcome, too. In advance."

There was another moment of silence as we went over I-95, fairly busy at this late hour, and Route 101 had shrunk to two lanes, and the marshlands and frozen sands of Tyler Beach were now beckoning us.

Felix said, "Need to ask you something else."

"Go ahead."

"The fake Secret Service agent. The one...the one dumped in your front lawn."

I sighed. "Yeah, I was thinking the same thing."

"If this Bittner character is desperate to use you to stop the Hale campaign, then there's a good chance this isn't their latest try. Maybe Bittner—or somebody connected with him—was behind the whole deal. Getting this Spenser Harris character to talk to you. Lifting your .357 Ruger. Hoping and planning that you'd be at the Hale rally that day. Makes a rugged sort of sense, you know."

"I know. If we have time, maybe we'll chat that point up with Mr. Bittner."

I could see Felix's grin from the glow of the dashboard lights.

"Then that's a plan."

"Just curious, is our fake Secret Service agent still where we left him?"

Felix chastised me. "He's your fake Secret Service agent, and yes, he's still where we left him. And I know I said I would try to find out something about him, but in my spare time I've come up with squat."

"I suppose getting his fingerprints and trying to have Diane Woods do something with them is out of the question."

"Please," he said. "Detective Sergeant Woods already has a very low opinion of me. Why should we reinforce that?"

"All right."

Now we were racing along the clear asphalt of Route 101, approaching the few lights of the low buildings before us that were the heart of Tyler Beach. From the marshland the road then tightened up, narrowed on both sides by rental cottages closed up for the season, and there was not a single lit home or cottage about us as the road rose up to intersect with Atlantic Avenue.

I certainly hoped my new friend James from the Clive Wallace campaign was out there on this dark street tonight, trying to talk to whatever voters were huddled by themselves in the cold and dark.

We stopped at the intersection, crept forward through some parking areas. The Ashburnham House hotel and restaurant was to our right, and it was the only open place within view. I made a left and we went up Atlantic Avenue, heading north, about eight minutes or so from the Lafayette House.

Felix looked at the shuttered homes and businesses, the empty parking lots, the deserted side streets, and he said, "This time of year, and this little slice of paradise, looking like this, could make almost anybody slit their throat. How bloody depressing."

"Buck up. In six months this place will be packed with cars and tourists, and the primary will be a distant memory."

"Yeah, but it'll come back again, in winter. The great desolation. Empty streets, empty buildings. Like we suffered through a plague year or something. Blah. Enough to turn most guys to religion or legitimacy."

"Most guys?" I asked, trying to keep my voice innocent. "Like you, Felix?"

"That's why I said most guys. Keep quiet or you'll miss our turn."

Which was doubtful, since the Lafayette House was now before us, in its white Victorian splendor, but I guess Felix was tired of showing his metrosexual side, and that was fine with me. I turned left and was able to find a space, which pleased me. We got out and I left the doors unlocked— if we had to leave quickly, fumbling to unlock said doors could cause problems—and then Felix asked for a moment to go through his bag.

"Of course," I said, as he rummaged through his leather carrying case, and then he said, "Ah," and placed something in his coat pocket. I caught up with him as we went toward the entrance, and said, "As a matter of record, sir, are you carrying?"

"Yep."

"And what kind of weapon do you have?"

"This," he said, and he showed me what he had just placed in his coat. I looked at him and looked at the object, which quickly went back into his coat.

"Tape?" I asked. "Duct tape?"

"Absolutely."

"And why duct tape?"

Felix said, "Ever tell you the tale of my uncle Julius?"

"Nope, but I have a feeling you're going to."

"That's right. Uncle Julius was a disappointment to some family members, since he ran a small, legitimate hardware store in the North End, down in Boston. A little of this, a little of that. Everything from pipes to tools to small appliances. Was proud of showing people how to make small repairs around their homes and apartments. He told me once that most people could get away with two things in their home repair kit."

"And what's that?"

"WD-40 lubricant to make things go, and duct tape to make things stop."

I had to laugh. "Good for Uncle Julius. And you have the tape because..."

"Because someone's being a pain in the ass to you, and I'm going to make it stop. That all right?"

"That's perfect."

"Good."

We went into the lobby of the Lafayette House and I saw that the gift shop, the site of my earlier triumph that day, was now closed. There were just a few people in the lobby, but the lounge looked pretty well attended, with someone playing the piano, and a few drunken souls were trying to sing along in such a manner that I couldn't even identify the tune. I found a house phone and after a moment or two with the hotel operator, got the room of Chuck Bittner.

"Yeah?" came the foggy reply.

"Chuck, it's Lewis Cole."

"Lewis Cole...Jesus, man, do you know what time it is?"

"No, I don't, and that's not the reason I called you. I'm...I'm ready to make an announcement. I just need to run something by you."

Now he didn't seem so asleep. "Good. Where are you?"

"In the lobby."

"Room 312," he said, and that was that.

I hung up the room phone and Felix fell in step with me as we headed to the bank of elevators. As we waited for an elevator, Felix said, "All right with you, I'll take the lead here. Okay?"

"Sounds fine."

"Way I see it, you want a promise from him to leave you alone, not to bring you into the campaign. Correct?"

"One hundred percent. But Felix..."

The indicator light dinged, and the door slid open. We went in and he said, "Yes?"

"He's going to be a tough one," I said. "Ex-navy. Full-time campaign worker for General Grayson. True believer in the general's cause. He might not roll over for you like other guys you've...encountered."

Felix gently pushed the button for the third floor. "Don't fret, son. Don't fret. You forget how I do love a challenge."

"So you do consider this a challenge?"

Felix had a faint smile on his face and then the door opened up, and he said, "Hush. Just let your uncle Felix make it all right."

We went down the soft-lit hallway, found Room 312 with no difficulty, and Felix said quietly, "Okay, you stand in front of the door, so he can see you through the peephole. Make sure you're standing there, nice and still, and when the door opens up, you take two steps to the right, wait, and then follow me in. Once you're in—and this is important—don't touch a damn thing. Got it?"

"Yeah. Stand in front of the door. Nice and still. Two steps to the left and—"

"To the right, moron, to the right, didn't you hear what I just said?"

I gave him a smirk to let him know he wasn't the only one playing games here tonight, and he shook his head, and I stood before the door to Room 312 and gave it a sharp knock. From inside I could make out the low murmur of a television set and then the sound of someone approaching the door. I stood still and quiet, but out of the corner of my eye, I made out Felix to my left, standing flat against the wall, and now he was wearing thin black leather gloves. Damn Felix. I hadn't even seen him do that.

The sound of the door unlocking almost startled me, and then I took two steps to the right and—

Felix moved whip-snap fast, going right into the room, one hand on the shoulder of a very surprised Chuck Bittner, wearing a white terry-cloth robe and—

A heavy, meaty sound as Felix punched him square in the nose, and—

I followed in, the door shutting behind me. Chuck was on the ground, and Felix quickly tore off a strip of duct tape, slapped it over Chuck's mouth, and Chuck scrambled to move away from the pain and the attention, and Felix got up and rolled Chuck over on his side. Chuck then tried to take advantage of that, by clambering up on his hands and knees, but like some damn wrestling move from TV, Felix slammed into him with his whole body weight, falling onto the man's back with his knees, and that must have hurt like hell.

Chuck collapsed with an "oomph" and a groan, and in the fast mess that followed, Felix worked quickly again, binding Chuck's wrists together with duct tape. Felix got up, breathing just a bit hard, and then he grabbed Chuck by his upper arms and maneuvered him onto an unmade bed. Chuck hit the bed on his side, another moan following, and he looked at me and I looked at him. Blood was streaming from his nose, trickling down the shiny gray duct tape. Felix looked to me and said, "Glass of water, if I may? And don't forget what I said about touching things."

I went into the open bathroom, got a small drinking glass, holding it with a white washcloth, and filled it with water using another washcloth on the tap. I came back out into the room and the television was just a bit louder. Felix took the glass and drank it all, and then put the glass in his pocket—no use leaving DNA evidence behind—and came back over to the bed. Chuck looked at me and looked at Felix and started making grunting noises from behind the tape.

14

Felix shook his head, took a chair and sat across from Chuck.

Felix said, "Before we begin, my apologies. I have the utmost respect for men and women in and out of uniform who've volunteered to serve. I might have been in the service as well, except for a juvenile record that made even the most aggressive recruiter turn gray with dismay. So. Having said that, my apologies for breaking into your room, sir, and causing you pain and discomfort."

I stood there, waiting, and Felix leaned over and said, "But apologies aside, sir, I have loyalty to that gentleman standing by the wall, a loyalty I take quite seriously, and before the two of us leave here tonight, we're going to reach an understanding. If I make myself clear, just nod your head."

There was no nod, just a vigorous shaking of the head, and violent grunting noises that, if they had been decipherable, were no doubt laced with a host of obscenities. If this bothered Felix, he didn't show it. He didn't have to. There were other ways.

Another strip of tape appeared in his hands, and this time, it was shoved against his bleeding nose. There was a muffled howl as Felix worked the tape, blocking both nostrils, and Chuck's chest started heaving. Felix leaned in again and said, "Nothing works one hundred percent, so I'm sure you're getting some oxygen into your system...but is it enough? We'll see. In the meantime, stop flailing around and give me a nod that you understand what I'm saying, and the tape comes off your nose."

Chuck's fleshy face started changing colors, and then, movement stopped and I thought he had passed out, but no, he nodded. Briefly and quickly, but he nodded. And true to his word, Felix removed the tape from his nose, and there was a hoarse, rasping sound as Chuck started panting through his nose.

Felix, his voice now soothing, said, "Ah, now, that wasn't hard, was it? Just a little nod and you started breathing again. A wonderful thing. We're very proud of you, sir."

The breathing became more normal, but there was anger behind those eyes, a deep and abiding anger that made me want to look away, but Felix would not move, would not flinch, and he stayed right there, right in the man's face.

Felix said "I don't think I need to tell you, but I'm going to remind you of what's next. I can take the tape off your mouth and you can start in on how my friend and I broke in here, assaulted you, and how you're going to have us arrested and ruin us and sue us and take all our money and our homes. It's what I'd expect from a man in your position. I've heard it before. And you know what? It doesn't mean a damn thing. So let's not waste each other's time with such nonsense. We came in here for a specific reason, one specific goal, and once that goal's been achieved, we'll all move on. Do you understand what I'm saying? If so, do favor me with another nod."

I waited, wondering how far Chuck would go in fighting Felix, but there was just the faintest of head movements. Felix took it and there was such pleasure in his voice, I almost expected him to start clapping.

"Very good again, sir," Felix said. "So. Let us begin. Here's the agreement we're going to reach. You and the Grayson campaign are going to leave Lewis Cole alone. You're not to contact him or bother him in any way. You're not going to even mention his name in your staff meetings. You're not to leak information about him to any friendly press or Internet blogger. In other words, you are going to forget his name, his appearance, his life, his background, his very existence. Now. Have you understood everything I've said? Have you? How about a little nod for the home team?"

The eyes were still burning with hate and anger, but there was that faint nod. "Good. Now, having gotten that out of the way, I'm sure you're wondering, what's in it for you? What possible benefit do you gain from having agreed to all that?"

Felix carefully crossed his legs, clasped his hands over his knees. "A smart and legitimate question. And here's the answer. We depart. At once. Never to bother you again, never to cross paths again, never even to breathe the same air in the same room. We depart, you depart, and after the primary next Tuesday, you and the general move on to South Carolina and all is right with the world. Do we have an agreement?"

The air seemed heavy in the room as we waited. I suppose I should have felt guilty or embarrassed or upset at what Felix was doing to this man, but I remembered Bittner's touch upon my arm, and the words he spoke about my service in the Department of Defense. I had lost dear ones many years ago that were close enough to be family, especially one woman (ah, Cissy, came the quick and sharp memory), and having this man before me try to use that service and those memories for political purposes...it was like someone urinating on the altar at Notre Dame at the height of a sacred Mass.

Not to mention the threats that would have impacted both Barbara and Annie.

So I felt fine. But still, I waited.

Chuck looked at me and then looked at Felix, and there was the nod.

Felix unfolded his legs. "Ah, good. Now that we have this agreement, I guess I can take the tape off, and we'll be on our way."

Was that it? I wondered. Was that going to be it? But I guess I knew Felix better than I thought, for when he leaned forward to remove the tape, he suddenly stopped and sat back down in the chair.

Another few moments of waiting, and Felix quickly shook his head. "No. It's not going to work. I mean...we're all men here, men of the world, worldly men. How can any agreement we reach last when you're under such duress? What would stop you from calling the police after we leave? I mean, Lewis here would probably skate, being such good friends with the local gendarmes, but not me. As you could probably deduce, I've had my share of police attention over the years. No, I'm afraid this isn't going to work. I'm going to have to come up with something else. Lewis?"

"Yes?"

"Any ideas?"

"Fresh out," I said. "But give me a few minutes or thereabouts. I'm sure I'll come up with something."

Felix turned back to the former navy man and said, "So, that's the quandary we're in. You see, if you were anybody else, I wouldn't have any problem. Pain and the threat of pain are wonderful motivating factors. A few minutes with an exposed light bulb and some tweezers, you'd be ready to sign over the title property to your home to make me leave. But once we start down that path, well, there're no good choices available to us. You can still go back on your promise to us...even more, if pain is involved, because no matter what pull Lewis might have with the police, it won't go very far if pain is involved. So it has to be something else. Something else that matters to you, something that will ensure that whatever promise you made here to leave Lewis alone actually sticks."

Felix then got up and walked around the room, looked at the television set—which was broadcasting a C-SPAN program about the day's speeches from the different primary candidates—and then grabbing the remote, he sat on the bed with Chuck. Felix patted him on the shoulder and then started flipping through the channels, and then he toggled a switch on the remote that brought up a menu selection guide on the television.

"Time for a little contemporary history lesson," Felix said, stretching himself out as Chuck kept his hateful stare on me. "Do you know what the single largest entertainment source—in terms of money made—is on cable and satellite television nowadays? Do you? Oh, I'm sorry, you can't reply. Well, it's not much of a challenging quiz. The answer is, of course, pornography. Hard to believe, but it's true. All these large hotel and motel corporations, and legitimate cable and satellite television networks, they all have a hand in promoting and trafficking hard-core pornography. Oh, this type of investment doesn't get much play in the news media—especially since some of the very same news media have a hefty stake in porn—and some conservative groups try to embarrass them to keep them from doing such kinds of business, but you know what? Even in the most conservative states, there's a healthy demand for it. And when there's demand, business will follow. Such that even in a quaint New Hampshire resort like Tyler Beach, the most high-grade hotel, the Lafayette House, will offer to its adult consumers a wide range of pornographic delights that even thirty years ago might have gotten you some serious jail time in any major city across the nation."

I tried not to smile. I had an idea where Felix was going. Felix went through the menu choices and said, "Each man to his own poison, I say, and to each man his taste in porn. Lord knows I have no halo over my head...so let's take a look at some of these titles. Hmmm...Locker Room Studfest, Saturday Night Cruising Delight, Buns and Rods of Steel—not really Casablanca, but they sure do offer a varied sort of entertainment. Don't you think?"

Felix rolled off the bed and his voice got sharp. "So this is how it's going to be. I'm going to remove the tape. You're going to say in a nice, clear voice that nothing is required of Lewis, that nothing is going to happen to Lewis. And if I remove the tape and I don't hear those words, then the tape goes back on, and your television starts displaying the latest and greatest in gay male pornography. Lewis and I stay here for a while. Order lots of room service. Play the television really, really loud, so when management comes and kicks us out...well, the story the next day, just a few days from the Tuesday primary, is that a campaign adviser to General Tucker Grayson entertained two men in his hotel room while watching well-muscled men have their way with each other on the television. All programming, of course, recorded on the room bill. Do we have an understanding now, Mr. Bittner?"

A quick nod this time. No hesitation. "Good," Felix said. "I'm going to remove the tape and wait for those magic words."

Chuck winced as the tape came off—some skin was probably caught in the adhesive—and he breathed in some and said, "You have my word."

"Glad to hear that," Felix said. "But let's put some more meat into that."

Chuck closed his eyes and said, "What you said...nothing is going to happen to Lewis Cole. No news story, no news leak. Nothing. You have my word on it."

Felix turned to me and said, "Satisfied?"

"Almost," I said. "One other thing."

Chuck cursed and said, "Changing the rules of the game already, are we?"

"No," I said. "Just being political for a moment. I'm sure you know the drill."

"Fine, asshole," he spat out. "What else?"

"Spenser Harris," I said.

"Spenser who?"

"Spenser Harris. Is he an operative of yours?"

He shook his head, licked his dry lips. "Never heard of him."

"Perhaps under another name. He's in his late thirties. Trim. Black hair, a few streaks of white on the sides. Tanned skin. Fit. Likes to dress well. Occasionally he pretends to be a Secret Service agent."

Another shake of the head. "Look, I don't know the name, don't know the description. You can blackmail me all you want, do whatever you want, but I don't know Spenser Harris, and I don't know anybody like him."

Felix was still looking at me, raised an eyebrow, and I shrugged. Felix rolled Chuck over on his side and like magic, a folding knife appeared in Felix's gloved hand, and after a moment or two of sawing, the tape at Chuck's arms was cut free. Felix stepped back and I got up. Chuck rolled over and looked at me, the hate still in his eyes.

I said, "We'll be on our way, but I'll leave you with one more thought, Chuck. This is our turf. Our field of battle. Even if you check out of here tomorrow and think of doing something funny with me, we have friends with the management here, friends that owe us favors. So don't think that coming up with an invoice showing your porn movie rental can't be arranged in a very short period of time. Enough to impact this primary, or any other future primary we choose. Got it?"

"Asshole," Chuck said, sitting up in bed, tearing at the strips of tape around his wrists, fingers fumbling some.

"Probably, but you invited me to bring it on. Which is what I did."

He rubbed his face and said, "Pussy boy. You had to come in here with muscle to do your dirty work. What kind of fucking wimp are you?"

I was going to say something, but Felix was quicker. He said, "Truth be told, sir, I'm the wimp."

"What?"

Felix put the knife away. "Lewis told me about his past encounters with you and your threats. He told me what he had planned for you. Trust me on this, I'm the wimp in this equation. I managed to calm him down, for if he had come up here by himself, you'd now be in that bathtub, bleeding, still bound with duct tape but missing a few inches of flesh that I'm sure you're awfully fond of."

He said, "Get the fuck out. Now."

Felix said, "Ready?"

"You got it."

So we got up and we left.

Once we went down in an elevator and made our way through the lobby, outside the cold air was refreshing and it felt good to be out of that room. We paused in the parking lot and Felix said, "You okay?"

"I'm fine. And you?"

Felix brought his hands together, up to his face, blew warm air into them. "Always nice to practice one's skills, to see that you still got it. And tonight, I still got it. Makes me feel good about myself. You sure you're okay?"

"I'm all right...though I have to admit I feel guilty."

"Guilty? About what?"

I started walking to my Ford. "Guilty about lying to Chuck."

"When did you lie to Chuck?"

"When I said we were friends with management. Maybe you are but I'm not. I think the management here is a jerk. But it made sense to tell Chuck otherwise."

I'm not sure Felix realized the joking nature of my comment, for he took it seriously. He said, "Well, we all have compromises we have to live with. I'm sure you'll get over it."

"Yeah."

At my Ford I turned and looked back at the Lafayette Hotel.

I had Felix here at my side, and with his skills and talents, I'm sure we could have returned back to the hotel and have gotten to work and might have been quickly successful breaking in and finding that surveillance tape.

Yet...

We had been lucky tonight, getting in and doing our business and getting out with an agreement that pleased me, for not only protecting my sorry butt but also removing a potential embarrassment for a political candidate I didn't have particular allegiance to, but who was important to someone very dear to me. So, all in all, it had been a productive night. I didn't want to push it.

"Lewis?"

"Yeah?"

Felix looked over at me from the passenger's side of my Ford.

"You okay?"

"Sure," I said, opening the door. "Just daydreaming for a second."

"That's fine," he said. "But how about daydreaming your way to getting my tired ass to home and to bed."

"No problem," I said, and in a matter of moments, we were on our way north, back on Atlantic Avenue.

Felix lives in North Tyler, on Rosemount Lane, a street that juts off to the right and which has fairly nice views of the ocean. There are six homes on Rosemount Lane, and five of them are clustered together near the road's entrance. Felix's stands alone, on a slight rise at the end of the road, and though he has never come right out and said it, I know he likes the location of the house. Homes like his are easy to defend.

I drove into his driveway, and he said, "Coffee? Drink? Further conversation?"

"I thought you wanted to get to bed."

"Hell, Lewis, I may be getting old, but I'm not ready to be buried."

"Neither am I, but I've had a long day. Thanks for your help. I owe you one."

He grinned. "We've gone beyond determining who owes whom anymore, Lewis. You just take care of yourself."

"I will. And are you finished with the Nash Pomeroy campaign?"

"Oh, probably," he said, retrieving his leather bag and putting it on his lap. "Let's be honest. When you're sent out on a research trip like this, to find out oppo stuff on your candidate, the people who hire you are hoping for the best. They've heard the rumors, they've looked for the facts, and now they want to know the truth. It's like the guy who hires a private investigator to see if his wife is cheating on him. Deep in his heart he knows, but he wants to grasp at the straw and hope that it's all a mistake. Well, the guys who hired me...tomorrow they're going to fire me, no doubt about it, once I submit my written report. But I've already been paid in advance, my job is done, and there you go."

"A nice, professional attitude, Felix. You'll go far."

"I'm sure. And speaking of going places...you do well by that Annie girl, okay?"

"What makes you say that?"

"Just a thought. You back her up. I know she's working long hours and doesn't have much time for you and all that happy crap, but she's doing something important. And it can't last too much longer. So you don't screw this one up. She's...she's made you a better person, my friend. You smile more, you talk more, and you don't walk around anymore like the weight of the goddamn world is on your shoulders. So. Got it?"

"Got it, Dr. Felix," I said. "You go on and let me sleep."

"That I will," he said, opening the door. "You just have fun not sleeping alone, all right?"

"Good night, Felix. You want I should walk you to the door?"

"Damn it, like I said, I'm not dead yet."

He slammed the door shut and maybe it was just the way the night had gone, but I did wait until he got up to the door and went inside, and the lights came on. He didn't need my protection or my backup, but still, I wanted to make sure everything was all right.

A hell of a goal.

I backed out and went home. At home there were four messages on my answering machine, three from groups reminding me that in the event I had been living in my cellar for the past six months, that next Tuesday was indeed Primary Day, and that my vote was sorely needed so that the forces of darkness and Satan would not emerge to march upon the land, sowing war and pestilence in their path, or something like that. I deleted them all.

The fourth message was from Annie, and was to the point:

"Lewis, you wouldn't believe how much grief I got from my bosses about your little dinner stunt tonight. In fact, Tom wanted to punish me by sending me up to Colebrook, right then and there, until cooler heads prevailed. So, yeah, your little dinner idea really caused some heartburn tonight."

Her voice dribbled off some and I waited, not breathing, just listening, when she laughed and said, "And you know what? It was worth it, worth it very much. Thanks again. You're the best, my dear, the very best. Sleep well and I'll talk to you tomorrow."

I smiled at that and went into the living room, watched some of the late-night cable news, and interspersed among all the talking heads, I saw a fresh clip of Senator Hale and his lovely wife, Barbara, at a campaign event way up north, in a mill city called Berlin. At the rally I saw the confident look of the senator, and the loving look of his wife, who was at his side throughout his remarks, and when that bit of political news was over, I shut the television off and went to bed.

THE NEXT MORNING I hesitated at the door before embarking on my usual routine of getting my morning newspapers from Stephanie at the gift shop across the way. It had been my routine for months, and save for those times when the weather was really rotten, or I was ill, I had never skipped it, not once. But this morning was different. I wasn't sure if I wanted to be there, on the off chance of running into Chuck Bittner after our little adventure from last night. I was not sure how an encounter like that would be, but I had a feeling it wouldn't be a particularly cheerful one.

So maybe I wouldn't go today. Maybe.

I thought about it some more and then grabbed my coat. The hell with it. I was going to keep to my routine and not let anything bother me. That was my decision, and shortly thereafter, I was trudging my way up the packed snow to the place where my newspapers awaited me.

Funny thing about decisions. The simplest ones sometimes can have the most deadly and far-reaching consequences, for if I had skipped getting the papers that morning, my, how things would have turned out differently.

So differently.

The gift shop was crowded, and Stephanie had to wait on a practically UN General Assembly of guests—I heard German, French, and something that might have been Korean—before she came to me. She looked around the store and smiled and said, "Tell you something, if you've got time."

"Sure, I've got time."

"Ever tell you where I grew up?"

I thought for a moment. "Someplace in Pennsylvania, I believe."

"That's one way of putting it. Yes, someplace in Pennsylvania. Foley's Corners. Tiny little place that shouldn't have existed, except there was coal in the hills, coal that was easy to get to. But by the time I came around, the coal was gone, the coal company was gone, and there wasn't much left for the people there."

Truth is, I didn't have that much time to talk to her—I hadn't called Annie yet and there was still that damn magazine column to finish, along with other pressing issues—but this was the most Stephanie had ever said about her past, so I stood there, polite, and nodded in all the right places.

She went on. "Those people included my dad, whose own father and grandfather had managed to support a pretty big family on a coal company's salary. But by the time he got married and had me and two other daughters, well, jobs were mostly part time work, stitched together here and there. Some fathers adjusted, some fathers rolled with the punches. My dad wasn't one of them."

She took a breath and I saw that her hands were trembling.

"My dad...well, I don't know if it would have been different, if the coal were still there...but all I remember are the shouts, the slaps, the broken dishes and the empty beer bottles piled up in the rear yard by the toolshed. Lots and lots of empty beer bottles."

"Must have been rough," I said. "I'm sorry."

She nodded, bit her lip. "I'm sorry, too. Sorry that I'm going on so long, telling you this. But there's a point, Lewis, if you just give me a few more seconds."

"Absolutely."

"Point being...Dad was a bully. And when he wasn't hitting my mom, he was hitting me, or hitting my sisters. The hitting went on right up until I joined the air force, and when I came back from Texas, after basic training, that night...it stopped. I dragged him out to the rear yard and I...well, I made it stop. I know it sounds pathetic, a daughter beating up on her old, drunken father in the family's backyard, but I don't care. He never hit my mom or my sisters again. Not ever."

With that, she reached under the counter, pulled out my morning newspapers. This morning, unlike any other morning, they were folded over and held together by a rubber band. I left the money on the counter. She handed them over to me and I almost dropped them, from the unexpected weight.

I looked into her face, now content, now relaxed. "Lewis, I've always hated bullies, especially bullies who pick on women. And what you did yesterday for that college girl...it was special. And I had to pay you back for it. Just so you know."

I hefted the weighted newspaper, my hand tingling with anticipation, knowing exactly what was in there. "Stephanie...thanks. Thank you very much."

She shook her head quickly. "It's nothing. I should have done it for you earlier. I really should have...but I was scared. Scared like I was when I was a girl, before leaving home. And I don't like being scared like that."

I started out of the gift shop. "I'll get it back to you, soon as I can."

Stephanie smiled. "I know you will."

15

If it wasn't for the snow and ice still on the ground, I would have trotted back to my house, but cracking my skull or losing the videotape in a snow-drift wouldn't have been too bright. So I took my time and I got into my home safely, dumped my coat on the floor, and was unsnapping the rubber band from the newspapers as I entered the living room. The newspapers fell away and there it was, a standard black VHS tape. I turned it over and there was a white label with neat printing—PARKING LOT SURVEILLANCE—followed by beginning and end dates. I turned on my television and VCR and got to work.

I was surprised at how easy it was. The view was of the parking lot, all right, in shiny black and white. There was a fishbowl effect with the lens, skewing the view at the edge of the screen. At the lower right-hand side of the screen was a time and date stamp, which was helpful since it wasn't a continuous video. It was more like a series of snapshots, one every few seconds. But after a few minutes of rewinding and playing, I got it down to the moment that morning when Spenser Harris had made his last visit to my home.

I leaned forward on the couch, to get a better view, I suppose, and I let the tape play through that special morning. Everything looked quiet. Two sedans and an SUV were parked at the south end of the lot. Very normal. Very quiet.

There. Movement to the left of the screen, the north end of the lot, near my driveway, and I froze the tape. And shivered.

Sure. I recognized that figure, all right.

It was me, heading up to the Lafayette House to get my morning newspapers.

I don't know why, but seeing myself on the television screen, in not-so-living black and white, creeped me out. The little form there, in electrons and bits and bytes, that was me. Innocently going up to a hotel to get reading material, not knowing, not even imagining what was ahead of me. It was like a time machine, glimpsing back into the past. Almost as weird as seeing that tape of myself the other day, vomiting so magnificently in the parking lot of the Tyler Conference Center.

I shivered again, let the tape play through.

The electronic Lewis Cole left the screen. Another car parked. Then a white panel truck came in, parked at an angle at the north end of the lot, where my driveway was. A guy came out carrying a large leather bag. I remembered the truck. An electrician's truck, if I was right. Yeah. Some guy named Jimmy. Could Spenser and his killer have gotten to my house that way?

A few more frames clicked through. Nope.

A black car appeared, maneuvered its way to the north end of the lot. The car had black tinted windows. The way it was parked, the driver's side was obscured by the panel truck, but the passenger's side was clear enough. The door opened up.

And a living, breathing, talking Spenser Harris got out.

"I'll be damned," I whispered, leaning even closer to the television. I reversed and played the tape again. A black luxury car, and Spenser Harris, stepping out.

So far, so good.

I let the tape play on.

Spenser leaned into the open passenger door, talking to the driver, it looked like, and then he stood up. The door was slammed shut. Spenser moved off to the left, disappeared from view.

I waited.

The phone rang, making me jump. I let it ring and ring and went back to the television, my own little time machine.

Even though it was partially blocked by the panel truck, the driver's side door then opened up. Somebody got out. A figure in a coat. That's all I saw. Couldn't tell if it was male or female. But the driver went to the left, too, following Spenser.

I waited.

Then the figure came back, opened the driver's door, leaned in and got in, closed the door.

But there was something there. I stopped, rewound, played. Stopped, rewound, played. And again.

The driver and no-doubt shooter was wearing a white trench coat of some sorts, the belt tied at the waist, and black gloves.

I rubbed my chin.

Couldn't see a face, couldn't see a head. Was there anything else?

I let the tape play again.

Oh yes, there was something else. Stopped, rewound, played.

And saw the car maneuver its way out of the spot by backing up, going forward, backing up, and then leaving the lot.

The car was now recognizable. It was a black luxury car, made in Great Britain, the latest model of the Jaguar XJ8, and I could see that the front license plate was New Hampshire, that it was vanity, and though I couldn't make out all of the letters, I was positive what the front plate said.

WHTKER.

I shut off the television, ejected the tape, and got the hell out.

WITH TAPES IN HAND, I drove south about ten minutes to the Tyler post office, where I mailed something out and then checked my incoming mail. My box was chock-full when I pulled it out, and I went over to one of the counters and sorted through everything. I had fourteen pieces of mail.

One was my checking account statement from the Tyler Cooperative Bank, and another was a mailing from the National Space Society. The rest of the mail was brightly colored flyers divided as so: pro-Hale, pro-Grayson, pro-Hale, anti-Hale, anti-Nash, anti-tax, pro-tax, anti-gun, pro-Grayson, pro-Wallace, pro-gay marriage, and anti-Grayson.

I gathered them up and tossed them in an overflowing trash can, also filled with similar messages of democracy.

Just another day in the land of the first-in-the-nation primary.

NORTH of the center of Tyler, Route 1 widens some, allowing a depressing series of mini-malls and strip stores to fester and take growth. Paula Quinn of the *Chronicle* once told me that it was like the malignancy that had grasped so many of Massachusetts's North Shore communities had infected Tyler, and who was I to disagree?

Stuck between an auto parts supply store and a sub shop was a tiny place called Mert's Electronics, about a hundred yards north of Tyler center. Parking wasn't a problem so early in the morning and so early in the year, and inside the store, I breathed in for a moment, taking in the view and the scent. The scent was of burned wire and dusty radio tubes and old ways of communicating, and the view...old television sets piled up next to CB radio gear next to cardboard boxes of circuit boards and radio tubes, and shelves and shelves of dusty gear that looked old when Marconi had retired.

At the rear of the store was a waist-high counter, and an older man was sitting back there, eyeing some papers as they came out of a computer printer, and he nodded at me as I approached.

"Lewis," he said.

"Mert."

Mert Hinderline was retired navy after thirty years in the service, with mermaids tattooed on his forearms as a constant reminder, and a ready smile and dapper little mustache that wouldn't look out of place on a 1940s film star. He was smart and affable and knew electronics, and his store wouldn't last anywhere else, I guess, except for Tyler and its collection of eccentrics. Like me.

"What can I do for you?" he said, putting another piece of paper down.

I held up the tape. "Need something duped. Two copies, if that's all right."

"The whole tape?"

"Just ten minutes' worth. Got it cued up right where I want it to start."

He held out a beefy hand. "Pass it over. Can do it right now and you can stick around as it dupes, if you'd like."

"Sure," I said, dragging over a metal stool. "I can wait."

He went to the rear of the store and out of view, and I heard movement and switches being thrown, and I looked to the printer, to see what he was doing. Next to the printer was an old Apple computer, and displayed on its monitor was a page of a Website dedicated to a political action committee opposed to the current administration that used the words "storm trooper" and "fascist" and "book burner" a lot. The printer still ground along, and I saw what Mert was doing: He was printing off screen shots of the Web page.

Seemed like a waste of time and paper, and when Mert came back and said, "All right, ten minutes and we'll be through," I asked him about the printing.

"Looks interesting," I said, pointing to the stack, "but I never thought of you being interested in politics that much. Especially fringe politics."

"Oh. That." He scratched his ear and said, "I'll tell you, but you've got to promise that you're not going to laugh at me."

"That's not a problem, Mert," I said. "Last summer, when my VCR croaked, the manufacturer said dump it and buy a new one. You got it up and running again in fifteen minutes with a fifty-cent part. So, no, I'm not going to laugh at you."

Mert grinned and picked up another sheet from the printer tray and put it in a separate pile. "I'm a volunteer. Belong to something called the Gutenberg Society. We're preserving our historical record for future generations."

"Oh."

Mert said, "I know what you mean by that. What does that have to do with printing off Website pages and e-mails and other electronic stuff? Quick answer is, everything. You see, in this wonderful and wild electronic age we're in, it's actually easier to do research on the Eisenhower adminis- tration than this administration and its immediate predecessors. Too many documents are now in an electronic format. The older presidents, they did everything on paper. Stored properly, paper can last hundreds of years.

Electronic files? Who knows? There are gigabytes of information stored on electronic files that can no longer be read, because computers and their operating systems have surged ahead, leaving older files useless."

From beneath the counter he pulled out a framed photograph, a black-and-white picture of a young man in a sailor's uniform standing on a ship. He said, "My dad. Was a quartermaster aboard the USS Converse in World War II. A hundred years from now, this photo will still look like this. Same thing with my wedding day picture of me and Cathy. But there's color pictures of me, taken in the 1980s aboard my own ships, that have already faded and will be blank in fifty years. And don't get me going on digital cameras. All these wonderful photos, and who knows if they can still be viewed in ten or twenty years when new operating systems are being introduced."

I nodded. "Read something similar to that about authors and their books. Used to be, researchers could look in the papers of a writer from fifty or a hundred years ago. Could look at the various drafts, see the hand-written notes, the sections that were crossed out, the inserts that were made, and could see the process of how a writer reached the final version of a novel. But now...so many authors edit on-screen, and make changes right up to when the book is finished, so all that's in the records are the final versions. There's no record of how the author got there."

"Exactly," Mert said, and he gestured to the computer screen. "So that's what we do in our little volunteer group. Digital information can be manip-ulated, can be changed, can disappear. So what we do, we make hard copies, as much as we can, so that future generations can have an idea of who we were and what we did. And not have to worry about the final record being cleaned up and edited."

From the back room came a ding as a kitchen timer sounded, and Mert got off his stool and went to the rear of the store and came back with three tapes. He handed them to me, and I thanked him and said, "How much?"

"Oh, let's say five bucks for the cost of the tapes. Sound fair?"

"More than fair. Sounds pretty damn generous."

I handed him a five-dollar bill and he said, "Well, there was a discount. For two things."

"What's that?"

"For not laughing at me, and for listening to me."

I picked up the tapes. "My pleasure."

Mert smiled and sat down next to his busy printer. "Just remember what I said, Lewis. Digital information is wonderful. But it can be manipulated."

"Just like people," I said.

He nodded in agreement. "Just like people."

A QUICK STOP back at the Lafayette House, and I walked quickly up into the lobby and to the gift shop. Stephanie was using a label gun to put price labels on Tyler Beach sweatshirts, and I went over to her and handed back a copy of that day's *New York Times*, wrapped around the original surveillance tape and held again by a rubber band.

"Sorry," I said. "You must have given me an extra paper this morning, Steph."

Her smile looked relieved. "Thanks for taking the time to bring it back."

I looked at her, a smile on my face as well. "I owe you one." She put the paper and surveillance tape under the counter.

"No, no debt, Lewis. It's all taken care of. I hope it helped."

"More than you know," I said, and I got out of there as quickly as I got in.

A PHONE CALL later and I was in the office of Detective Sergeant Diane Woods, south of the Lafayette House, and I said to her, "Well, I'm pleased that I can get you on a Saturday, but I'm not sure how pleased you are."

She shook her head, leaned back in her chair. "Not very, and neither is my sweetie Kara, but primary season will be over in three short days, and that will be just fine. I love making detail money but

you know what? It's a nice little bundle that's going to pay for a vacation to Cozumel next winter for the both of us, but I'm getting sick of all the candidates and their precious little staffs. 'Why can't the traffic go there instead of here?' 'Can't you do something about the news helicopter over-head?' 'Can't you put the protesters over there behind a fence?' Bah. Four years from now, let Vermont have this little circus."

Diane's office is in the rear of the one-story concrete cube that is the

Tyler Police Station, and her desk was reasonably clear. I always told her that a live camera feed depicting her desktop could tell an alien species what season it was in New Hampshire: a clean desk meant it was winter, and an overflowing desk of papers and files meant it was summer. Diane had told me at the time that any aliens that existed no doubt spent their summer at Tyler Beach, and they could all go to hell, and that was that.

She was dressed in civvies today, heavy brown turtleneck sweater and well-worn blue jeans, and as she leaned back she had her hands behind her head, like a prisoner giving up, except I don't think Diane has ever given up anything for anybody.

"What's going on with you?" she asked. "The Secret Service treating you well?"

"I don't think they're treating me like anything, and for that I'm thankful."

Her face looked a bit somber, and she said, "I hope you don't have bad feelings about that day I took you in to meet Agent Reynolds. I was doing you a favor, Lewis, though I'm sure as hell it didn't seem like it at the time. I wanted to bring you in nice and quiet, without them charging into your house and knocking things over and slapping your wrists in handcuffs or something like that. What I did seemed to be the best alternative."

I smiled to show her there were no hard feelings, and I said, "If one has to be arrested by the Secret Service, getting there through the actions of a friend is as good a way as any."

"Why, thank you, Mr. Cole. Nicest thing anybody's said to me today. And besides the Secret Service, how are the chattering classes of the fourth estate doing? Leaving your ass alone?"

"Ass is very much alone and belonging to me."

"Good. So. Now that we're all caught up and everything, what's going on?"

I took a breath. "Audrey Whittaker."

She tilted her head a bit. "Audrey Whittaker. Socialite lady for whatever passes as society on the New Hampshire seacoast. Very wealthy, working on her second husband, quite active in political affairs. Believe she's supporting Senator Hale from Georgia. Why the curiosity?"

"What else can you tell me about her?"

Diane dropped her hands and let the chair move forward some. "What else do you want to know?"

"Has she...has she ever been the subject of interest from law enforcement circles?"

Diane now stared at me for long seconds, and I knew exactly then how she got suspects to talk, with that firm gaze and clear eyes. "That's a hell of a question, Lewis. Especially the way you just put it. Mind telling me what's gotten your attention?"

"Something involving a column I'm working on," I said.

"Oh, That makes it clear then. One of your famous columns that never seems to make its way into print. All right. I can tell you from my own personal experience that Audrey Whittaker, to the best of my knowledge, has never been—-as you so delicately put it—the subject of interest from law enforcement circles. But..."

My ears got quite sensitive at that last word. "Yes?"

She said, "Like I said, from my own personal experience, nothing. But it doesn't mean that something hasn't gone on that I don't know about. Which means a records check could reveal something. But there's something you've got to know before you ask me to do that."

"Which is what?"

Diane carefully picked up a pen and moved it from one side of the desk to the other. "It's like this. Used to be, in the wild and woolly days when I first became detective, you could do a records search for no other reason than to satisfy your curiosity. Those days are gone. Records of inquiries are kept, and questions can be asked. Like, why are you so interested in so-and-so, Detective Woods? Is there an official reason for this inquiry? If not, why? And what prompted you to make such an inquiry if there's no official reason?"

"I see."

"Good. Because I'll do a records search for you, Lewis, if it means something important for you. But you should know that if something about Audrey Whittaker becomes public knowledge in the next week or month or something like that, some people might want to know why I was doing a records search on her, and for what reason. So, having wasted about half your Saturday morning, I just want to know this: Lewis, do you want me to do a records search on Audrey Whittaker?"

I looked back at her and thinking of our friendship and our past and favors done and favors expected, I took a breath.

"No," I said. "I don't want you to do a records search on Audrey Whittaker."

Her mood instantly changed, and the atmosphere in the room seemed to lighten right up. "Fine. I'm very glad to hear that. And here's a bit of advice from an old detective who's seen an awful lot. Ready?"

"Go ahead, ma'am."

"Leave Audrey Whittaker alone. She's old, she's rich, and she has a lot of time on her hands. A very dangerous combination. Focus on Annie Wynn. She's good for you, Lewis. Very good for you. And take it from someone who's an admirer of the female form and function."

"Glad we have something in common."

"More than you know. Now, if you'll excuse me, I've got some case folders to go through, and my better half is promising me dinner and entertainment, and since I've been lacking in the home-cooked meal and home-made entertainment departments lately, get the hell out."

I wished my old friend the best and did as I was told.

IT TOOK some tracking on my part but by the time late Saturday afternoon rolled around, I had finally found Paula Quinn. She was at a campaign rally for Senator Nash Pomeroy of Massachusetts, and after promising at a volunteer desk that I would work my local polling station on Tuesday, bring five friends to the polls, wear a Pomeroy button on my coat and a Pomeroy bumper sticker on my car, and commit ritual suicide if he didn't win on Tuesday, I was allowed in.

The rally was at the MitchSun electronics plant in Tyler Falls, owned by an eccentric entrepreneur called Eddie Mitchell. Eddie was a firm believer in the electoral process and took a major hit in his productivity every fourth January by inviting candidates to stop by and talk to his employees. For the employees, it meant an extra-long meal break—especially for those doing time-and-a-half work on Saturday—and for the candidates, it meant a captive audience of about a hundred potential voters.

Inside the plant's cafeteria, I found Paula at the rear, hiding a yawn with one hand, typing away on a laptop with the other. The light green tables were occupied by workers in white coats and slacks, not bothering much to hide their bored expressions, while on the far side of the room, Senator Pomeroy—a product of prep schools, Harvard, and district attorney work in Massachusetts—gave a talk in which he left no doubt that he'd rather be back in Washington than talking to his lessers here in—horror of horrors— New Hampshire. He was standing behind a portable lectern that had a POMEROY FOR PRESIDENT sign taped to its front, and even the gaggle of cameramen and reporters off to one side looked almost as dispirited as the candidate and his audience.

I sat next to Paula and she looked over at me, and then looked over at me again with surprise and said, "What are you doing here?"

"Looking for you."

"Well, that's flattering. You need something, is that it?" There was a not-so-nice edge to her voice and I said, "Well, I was going to trade you something. Information for information. How does that sound?"

"Newsworthy?"

"Quite."

"Very newsworthy?"

"Oh, you know it."

"Newsworthy in a presidential primary sense?"

"Wouldn't waste your time otherwise."

She grinned and turned away from her laptop. "Oh, you better not be teasing me."

"Haven't teased you in months, and you know it."

"Lucky me. Okay, you go first. What do you need?"

"I need a quickie bio on Audrey Whittaker, and I already know she's rich, she's married twice, and that she's active in political events. What else can you tell me?"

Paula said, "Knowing how you operate, I'm sure you don't care much about her charitable activities."

"I'm looking for something a bit more edgy."

"Hmmm," she said. "Edgy. How come she's gotten your attention?"

"You know my methods, Paula."

That earned me another smile. "Another quest from the mysterious Mr. Cole...how can I deny you that?"

"You've denied me before."

"On other things, my friend. All right. Audrey Whittaker and edgy. Here's the story I've been told, and you can't tell anybody else where you heard this story, because I'll deny having told you. Lord knows, I wouldn't touch it with a ten-foot pole. Or even a twenty-foot pole. Nasty stuff, it was."

I touched her hand. "I knew I could count on you."

"Ha, How sweet. Look, here's the deal. Word is, this particular event happened two, maybe three years ago. She lives in one of those so-called summer homes up in Wallis whose construction costs can support a school for a year. Nice place, of course, and across the street, there's a tiny little strip of beach. I mean really, really tiny. Most of the shoreline up there is nothing but rocks and boulders, but from what I've found out, over the years, she and her minions—God, I wish I had a minion on days like these—would secretly and quite illegally improve that tiny section of beach. Nothing blatant, just a few boulders removed, year after year, and a little sand dumped in the right places. Pretty soon, Audrey had the only private beach on the oceanfront in New Hampshire."

I said, "No such thing as a private beach in New Hampshire. State law."

Paula laughed. "Look who's talking, the gentleman with his illegal No Trespassing signs outside his house."

"The signs are a suggestion, not an order. Besides, we're talking about Audrey Whittaker."

Up forward, Senator Pomeroy seemed to pause in that part of his speech that said, *Pause, wait for applause*, and when no applause came forth, he pressed on.

"Yes, we are, aren't we. Anyway, Audrey—from what I was told—loved to bundle up a picnic lunch, chair, umbrella, and thermos full of martinis, and walk out her front door, down the majestic front lawn, across Atlantic Avenue to her private little beach, and spend the better part of a day there. Pure delight, for a woman like her. Her own private beach, her little stretch of paradise, which she didn't have to share with members of the working class."

"What happened then? Someone from the state tried to kick her off?"

Paula shook her head. "Nothing so official. One day she went there and found some people on her private beach. Three families, up from Mass-achusetts—Lawrence or Lowell, still a bit murky—and they were having a grand old time partying and playing loud music, little barbecue grills, the usual stuff. Audrey told them to leave. The families told her no, in so many words. I guess they had gotten the word that there are no private beaches in New Hampshire. More words were exchanged, Audrey left, and when the families left...well, they and their friends never came back. Not ever."

"Why?"

Paula tried to laugh, to lighten her mood, but it didn't seem to work. "Lewis, from what I hear, she went back to her house and got to work—with her minions lending a hand, I'm sure—and soon enough, she found out who those three families were and where they had come from. She picked one family, randomly, probably, and she destroyed them."

"Destroyed them? How?"

"From what I hear, the father worked in maintenance for the Lawrence school system. His wife worked in the system as well, as a secretary. Within a week, both of them were out of work. Then they were evicted from their apartment. Their children got into trouble at school and were suspended. No matter what they did, no matter who they talked to, their lives were ruined. They even packed up from Lawrence and moved to New York. And like some curse or something, she followed them there as well. Last I heard, the parents got divorced, Dad is serving time at Concord-MCI, Mom is on welfare, and who knows what kind of future the children will have. All because they were on her beach. And didn't leave when they were asked."

Above us, Senator Pomeroy's face was turning a light shade of red, as he did his best to work the crowd into a frenzy. Near me, a woman of about thirty was looking up at the senator while she worked on her nails.

I said, "Appreciate the history lesson."

"That was the lengthy lesson," Paula said. "Here's the short lesson. Don't piss her off. She's a wealthy woman with time on her hands who can afford to see her whims, no matter how nasty they are, be fulfilled. I'd hate to see you become one of her whims."

"Point taken," I said.

The young lady next to me started working on her other hand. Paula said, "So, that's what I've got for you. What's your side of the deal, my friend?"

I thought for a moment and leaned into her and said, "Take in this scene well."

"What scene is that?"

"Of Senator Pomeroy, running for president."

She turned to me, face now serious and inquisitive. "Say that again."

"Senator Pomeroy. He won't be a candidate in a few weeks."

"He's dropping out?"

"That's what I hear."

Now her tone matched the look on her face. "Lewis...this is Paula from the *Chronicle* now talking to you. This isn't Paula your bud...got it?"

"Got it."

"All right then," she said. "What do you have for me?"

I chose my words carefully. "An informed source connected with the Nash Pomeroy campaign has confirmed that due to personal reasons, Senator Nash Pomeroy will withdraw from the presidential primary race within the next few weeks."

Her hands seemed to fly across the keyboard. "How good is this source? Not some volunteer who's upset that they've run out of bumper stickers."

"Nope, a well-paid consultant."

"Okay," she said. "The personal reasons. What do they involve?"

"Something involving the senator and events in Illinois."

"Illinois? Far from home."

"Away from your fellow scribblers and other prying eyes."

"Can you tell me what happened in Illinois?"

"No, I'm afraid I can't," I said.

"And this is good information?"

"Solid," I said.

"Real solid? I mean to put this out in the Monday paper...and it's going to cause a hell of a crapstorm with the Pomeroy campaign and the other news media, my little paper breaking a story like this."

"Solid as a rock."

Paula finished typing and then gently scratched one of her delightfully protruding ears. "You know, this is the kind of story that's going to need another source before going to press. No offense to you and your mysterious informant."

"No offense taken. Who?"

She grinned. "My dear Mr. Spencer, that's who."

"The Tyler town counsel? Your better half?"

"The same," she said. "He has connections to the Nash Pomeroy campaign. Once I get out of this wake, I'll give him a call. Man, that's going to tick him off something awful."

"Think he'll talk?"

The smile got wider. "If he wants to continue to be lucky with me, he'd better talk, and better give it all up."

"If he's smart, he'll do just that."

Senator Pomeroy then wrapped things up by saying, "...and I look forward to your support next Tuesday. Thank you, thank you so very much!"

Some steady applause that dribbled out after a number of seconds, and she put her mouth up to my ear and said, "Thanks, Lewis. A scoop like this...well, it'll make all this weekend and night work this past month worth it."

"Glad to hear it," I said, standing up.

She stood up as well, gathered her laptop, and looked at Senator Pomeroy, gamely shaking the hands of those few voters who came up to him.

Paula shook her head and said, "You know, there are times, like I told you back at lunch, when I think this primary season is so special. And then I look at what we have here. The endless cattle show. The endless droning recitation of canned speeches. Candidates who hate what they're doing, and hate being here. Makes you wonder how this fair little country of ours stumbles along. Lord knows candidates like Lincoln or FDR or JFK or even Ike couldn't survive what goes on now, with the cable networks and all the background investigations. So what do we end up with? Bland candidates with bland backgrounds who try to be everything to everybody...that's what we get."

"You know what Churchill said," I told her.

"What? About fighting on the landing fields and beaches?"

"No," I said. "Something about democracy being the worst political system ever devised, except for the rest."

"Sounds right," she said. "I just hope the people, God bless 'em, never decide to put that statement to the test and try something else. Thanks again for the tip, Lewis. Gotta get going."

"Me, too," I said,

I went out of the cafeteria and spared a quick glance back.

Senator Nash Pomeroy was navigating a crowd of reporters and news photographers, the harsh light from the television cameras making his face look puffy and red. Paula was right. It was a hell of a process.

But so far, the only one we've got.

16

At home I built a fire and checked my messages. Another baker's dozen, of which I deleted twelve. It got to the point where I knew to delete the message when I heard nothing for the first few seconds; it usually took that long for the automated message to begin its spiel, allowing me to avoid yet another heartfelt automatic plea to either vote for somebody or vote against somebody. There was also one live message, from a very real person —Annie—which I returned, and I was pleased that it went right through.

"Oh, Lewis, it's you," she said, and I sensed the exhaustion in her voice.

"Sounds like you're running on caffeine and energy," I said.

"Lots of caffeine, not much energy. Oh, we're getting close, my dear, so very close."

"What's going on?"

"Latest round of polling shows the damn race is still fluid," she said. "Hale still holds on to a lead, but that hold is damn slippery. All it'd take is one bit of bad news, one bit of controversy, and it could sink us...but if we hang on till Tuesday morning, then we can make it. And then it's on to South Carolina."

"South Carolina...with or without Annie Wynn?"

She laughed. "South Carolina...here's your answer about that. All right if I move in with you Wednesday morning? Take a vacation?"

"Where do you want to go?"

"Mmm," she murmured. "No goddamn where, that's where. I want you to unplug the phone and your computer, and I want a fire in the fireplace all day and night, and I want all of my meals served on a tray on my lap. And the only thing I want to see on television are old movies. Cary Grant. Gregory Peck. Audrey Hepburn. Katharine Hepburn. Spencer Tracy. Think you can arrange that for me?"

"Consider it done."

Another sigh. "But I have something for you, if you'd like."

"What's that?"

"Monday night," she said. "You free?"

"Of course."

"Good. We're having an old-fashioned wingding of a political rally for Senator Hale, at the Center of New Hampshire. Free food and drinks, music, lights, camera, and action. One last big-ass rally before voting begins the next day. I'd love to have you there, right with me, holding hands, as the campaign wraps up in New Hampshire. Tell me you'll say yes."

I looked at the dancing flames, thinking, just a couple more days, that's all, just a couple more days. Then this damn primary and its problems would be over.

"Yes," I said. "Of course, yes."

"Thank you, dear," she said, and I made out voices in the background, and she said, "The campaign calls. See you Monday night, 5:00 P.M. The Center of New Hampshire."

"5:00 P.M., Monday night. It's a date."

She chuckled. "It seems like ages since I've heard you say that. A date it is. Bye, now."

"Bye."

After I hung up, I looked at the flames again for a while, before getting up and making a simple dinner of corn beef hash, fried up in a big black cast iron skillet. Feeling particularly bachelorish, I ate from the pan to save some cleaning up. Annie would have been horrified to see me and that made me smile, to think of her face. After I ate, I made a speed clean of the kitchen and decided it was time to go to bed. Tomorrow was going to be a long day, and I know it was arrogant of me to say so, but I had no doubt what I was going to do on Sunday would have an impact on who the next president of the United States would be.

Despite all that, I slept fairly well.

SUNDAY MORNING I went over to the Lafayette House for my daily dose of newspapers, and Stephanie wasn't working that day, so I got out with my heavy load of reading without any serious conversation. I was also pleasantly surprised at seeing a familiar face while leaving the lobby; Chuck Bittner, campaign operative for General Grayson, who looked at me and pretended he didn't know who I was. The pleasant surprise, of course, was not in seeing him; it was in his ignoring me. I guess our little visit was already working. I returned the favor and walked back home.

It was a brisk morning, a faint breeze coming off the ocean, the salt smell good to notice. Out on the horizon were the lumps of rock and soil marking the Isles of Shoals, and I made out a freighter, heading north to the state's only major port, in Porter. There was a nice winter contrast to the snow and ice on the ground, the sharp darkness of the boulders, and heavy blue of the water that reminded me again of how nice it was to live here, even in the dark times of winter. Even when the quadrennial circus was in town, bringing with it all sorts of problems and headaches.

Like a dead man in my yard. And a former college lover, probably destined to become the next first lady, and my poor Annie, working so hard, working so diligently, for something she believed in. I shifted the papers from one arm to the other, glanced at all the big headlines predicting what might happen here come this Tuesday.

At home I made a big breakfast of scrambled eggs, sausage, toast, tea, and orange juice, and plowed through most of *The New York Times* before I decided it was time to get on with the business of the day. I washed the dishes, went upstairs and showered and checked my skin, as always, and got dressed. Usually getting dressed means finding whatever's clean in my closet and bureau, but this time, I decided to do it right. I put on a clean dress shirt, white with light blue pinstripes, a new pair of heavy khaki slacks, and a red necktie. Sensible winter footwear, of course, and a dark blue cardigan. I looked at myself in the mirror before heading back downstairs and said, "Dahlink, you look marvelous."

Downstairs I grabbed my coat and a duped copy of the Lafayette House surveillance tape, and in addition to my cell phone, I thought about bringing something else. I hesitated, and then shrugged and went back upstairs. Better to be safe, and I thought Felix would approve, though I'm not sure about Diane. From my bedroom I grabbed my nine-millimeter Beretta and shoulder holster and slid it on underneath my cardigan. The heavy weight on my shoulder felt almost comforting. I then went downstairs and outside to the crisp January morning. Freshly showered, fed, dressed, and armed, I felt like I was ready to take on the day and win.

My Ford Explorer started right up and in a matter of moments, I was heading north. My plan was a simple one. I was to see Audrey Whittaker and see her I would, for there was no doubt—with the primary just two days away—that she should be either home or somewhere reachable. Then, I would show her the tape, and tell her my demands: layoff. Just layoff whatever the hell she was doing. For I was doing this for two women in my life, one past, one present, each of whom was hoping for the very same thing. For Barbara, and for Annie, I would ensure that things would be quiet, at least, for this upcoming primary, so their man would have a clear shot at the White House.

After Tuesday...well, I'm not sure but I thought I would probably be an accessory to covering up a crime. I had no doubt about the circumstances of Spenser Harris's death, or whoever he was. I just wasn't too upset about it, since he had been part of something that was going to put my butt in jail, and if his body was to be dumped on the side of a road in rural Massachusetts sometime this spring, well, I'd let the professionals sort it out.

In the meantime, it was a glorious Sunday and the road was clear on my drive to Wallis and the home of Audrey Whittaker, and I was going to take care of everything. And tomorrow night I'd be at that party with Annie and wish good luck to Mrs. Barbara Hale and her husband, and after Tuesday, everything would be back to where it should be.

In any event, that was my plan.

And as the old joke goes, if you want to make God laugh, make plans.

I looked quickly to the right before I turned into Audrey Whittaker's house, to see that little stretch of beach that had caused such heartache to a Massachusetts family that didn't like being bossed around by an old New Hampshire lady. I wasn't too worried about what she might do to me—even if she did shoot Spenser Harris—for I was fairly independent and relied on almost no one else for my health and livelihood. And I was also sure that we would reach some sort of understanding, for it was in her interests, as well, to keep up her appearance as the grand dame of New Hampshire politics. And if it was going to take a bit of time to reach an agreement, the Beretta within easy reach would ensure that I wouldn't end up like Spenser Harris.

There was no checkpoint at the driveway entrance, so I sped right up and noted a couple of SUVs in addition to the Jaguar with the WHTKR vanity plate. I parked my Explorer and got out and shook my head again at the PIG scraped into the paint. I would really have to get that fixed, one of these days.

Up at the massive oak door, I pressed the doorbell but didn't hear a thing. Maybe it's a sign of being rich and powerful, that you can't hear your doorbells from outside, so I pressed it again.

This time, the door opened up.

I waited, duped tape in my hand.

"Yes?" came the woman's voice, and I hesitated, disappointed, for it wasn't the right woman.

Instead of Audrey Whittaker, there was a young, strong looking woman, wearing black slacks and a black turtleneck shirt, and her blond hair was cut quite short, and seemed to be a dye job.

"I'm looking for Audrey Whittaker," I said.

"Is she expecting you?" she replied, and her voice had a slight Hispanic accent. I thought I had seen her before, perhaps the last time I had been here.

"No, but it's urgent that I see her. My name is Lewis Cole." She smiled and shook her head. Now I was sure. She had been with that catering crew that night, no doubt one of Mrs. Whittaker's employees. "She's not here, but if you come in, I'm sure I can get somebody to help you."

"Thanks," I said, walking in and letting the door slam shut behind me.

I was in the large reception area, and it looked so different from the last time I was here, with the people milling about, the HALE FOR PRESI-DENT signs, the check-in table and the coat area. Now, the place looked like it really did, wide and open and almost sterile. My house was old and small and was cold in the winter and too warm in the summer, and beach sand sometimes got into the sheets and the sugar container, but at least it was a home. This was an estate, and I decided I didn't like it.

Voices, out in the large hallway that led into the house, and I turned at the sound of a male voice, a male Southern voice, as the man said, "I was just leaving, but maybe I can help you. Mr. Cole, you said you wanted to see Mrs. Whittaker?"

I turned and saw a man with a red beard there, a man I had seen a couple of times before, here and at the Tyler Conference Center, what was his name, it was...Harmon. Harmon Jewett, that was it. Longtime loyal Jackson Hale supporter, a man who wanted to see Hale elected president no matter what, a man who, as Annie said, had a temper that could curl paint off the side of the house.

And a man who was walking toward me, carrying his coat and gloves in his hands.

A belted white trench coat. And black gloves.

Like the driver and shooter in the videotape I was carrying in my hand.

I looked at his clothing and looked at him, and said, "No, I'm all set. I'll come back later."

Harmon shrugged. "Suit yourself."

I turned and before me was the door leading out of this large and empty and cold house, and as I went to the door, to safety, something powerful struck me at the back and brought me down.

I think I screamed. Or yelled. Not sure. But one thing was for sure:

I bit my tongue and struck my head when I fell. My body was out of control, was moving on its own, my legs trembling and flailing, my arms and hands spasming. The floor was cold and harsh against my skin. I tried to roll over and step back up, but it was impossible, my body had suddenly short-circuited, had failed me, and I managed to look up and Harmon was standing there, looking satisfied but grim.

"So glad you came by," he said. "Saved me and Carla here from having to fetch you, you dumb fuck."

Something in his hand crackled and there was a black plastic object, blue lightning flowing between two electrodes, and he knelt down and shoved it in my back, and I screamed again, flailing.

He pulled his hand back, smiling. "Amazing how ten thousand volts can get somebody's attention. Carla, c'mon, we don't have much time, what do you have to tie 'im up with?"

Carla replied in Spanish and Harmon said, "Fuck it, we'll make do with what we got here. Damn jerk threw us off schedule. I'll take care of him, you see what the hell's on that tape he brought. Must be something important if he was holdin' it like that."

Hands worked at my necktie and my belt, and my hands and ankles were tied together, and I tried to talk but my tongue had swollen up and it didn't seem like everything was working well. Carla left my field of vision and Harmon patted me down and pulled out my Beretta and laughed in my face.

"What the hell were you going to do with that, boy?" he asked, waving it in front of my nose. "Threaten that shriveled old bitch with it, make her wet her adult diapers? Christ on a crutch, boy, she lets me and others in the campaign use her home and her food and her car to further the career of one Jackson Hale, you think you were going to do anything with this to change her mind? Or scare her? Stupid bitch thinks she's gonna get a slow dance next January twentieth with Jackson, and nothing you can do about it."

Carla appeared, a bit breathless. "Saw the tape, *jefe*. Looks like you're on it, the day Spennie got whacked."

Harmon laughed and said, "Okay, destroy it, and when I say destroy it, melt the little fucker so nothin' can get salvaged off it. The way they can reconstruct tapes nowadays, there's no way I'd take a chance on that. I'll take care of our friend here. Lord knows, we're gonna need him tomorrow."

Carla left my view again, and then Harmon grabbed my legs, started dragging. My mind was foggy, my legs and arms still twitched, and there was a metallic taste in my mouth, from where I had bit myself.

As he dragged me, he kept up a little chat, like he was happy to hear his own voice. "We had you set up months ago, pal, to do what had to be done. All that hard work, plottin' and plannin' in the shadows. Thought we had every angle figured out. But how the fuck was I gonna plan on you tossin' your cookies so you didn't get arrested at the shooting and get us all those lovely headlines? Fool. But good plans always have Plan Bs, and you're gonna be nice and set for Plan B."

My head hurt, from having fallen and from having been dragged across the cold tile. Somewhere a door opened, the creaking hinges sounding so loud it made my head hurt even that much more, and Harmon knelt down again. "Here's the set. Old bitch Whittaker, her first husband drank so much she didn't want a sloppy drunk living with her again, so she cleaned out first hubbies wine cellar, so it's empty now, and I hope you're not thirsty, 'cause that's where you're gonna be kept for a while...oh, and one more thing. You be a good boy or I'll come back down there to visit you. Understand?"

Again, I moved my mouth, but nothing came out, not even a whisper.

Crackle, crackle, came the noise, and I screamed once more, quite loud, arching my back, as the stun gun was shoved into me again. Harmon got up, breathing hard. "Didn't hear a word from you, so wanted to make sure I made my point. Okay, pal, here you go. Watch that first step."

Some first step. He dragged me through the door and shoved me down some stone steps, and my head struck the stone again, and my jaw, and the back of my head, and I yelled or screamed again, and there was the slam of the door, and then, darkness.

Darkness, where everything seemed to hurt.

I was out of it for a while, not sure of the length of time. I think it was for a long while. But eventually I became aware of some things, like my arms and wrists aching, and my feet falling asleep, but most of all, the taste of copper in my mouth and the deep, throbbing, aching pain along the side of my face. I gingerly moved my jaw, and though it didn't seem broken, it sure as hell had been dinged up some.

I then was aware that I was on my side, on a stone floor. I breathed some and exerted and breathed and managed to sit up. That seemed to have been a mistake. My head spun and nausea rippled through my stomach and saliva gurgled up in my mouth, and it took some long minutes of deep breathing before I didn't feel like throwing up.

I blinked my eyes a few times. At first, I thought the room was pitch black and as dark as the interior of a tomb, but there was light coming in from somewhere. I moved my head about and made out two tiny windows, about ten or twelve feet off the ground, off to the right. I looked around a bit more and took in the small wine cellar. It looked like there were empty wooden shelves along the stone walls, fit for hundreds and hundreds of wine bottles, and not much else. Behind me was the stone staircase that Harmon had so thoughtfully tossed me down some time ago.

I tried to straighten my legs out, but I didn't have much success. I took a deep breath, tried to propel myself up, and my feet slipped, and I fell back and struck my head on the stones, and all was darkness again.

WHEN I CAME around the light was even dimmer. I looked to the tiny windows and saw that whatever light was coming through had to be from an outside spotlight or something. Which meant it was evening, though I didn't know how late it was. But New Hampshire winters produce pitch darkness after 4:00 p.m.. or thereabouts, so who really knew. All I knew was that I was in one serious world of hurt.

I moved around some and this time, I got my legs straightened out. Took a breath. Took stock. Arms and wrists still aching, feet and hands tingling from lack of circulation. Jaw and head one big throbbing mess of a headache, but still, no apparent broken bones. Took another breath. Started to think.

Harmon Jewett. Annie had told me how he was utterly devoted to Jackson Hale, would do anything and everything to further Hale's career. And I remembered what Barbara had told me, the last time I had seen her, in Manchester. About how some crazed people in a campaign would do anything to see their man elected, even up to and including the attempted shooting and killing of the candidate's wife.

Harmon Jewett. Looked pretty damn crazed to me. Had set me up for the shooting at the Tyler Conference Center, and from his talk about Plan

B, I was going to be set up for something on Monday, the day before the primary.

I didn't know the how and where, but I was sure of the why: to get his man elected.

And maybe he would get elected. I don't know. But I did know that I hadn't volunteered to be part of anybody's damn plan, and I was going to do something about it.

I moved. Ouch, damn it, and I whispered, "Pretty bold talk for a man all bound up."

So. Time to get unbound.

By now my eyes had adjusted even better in the darkness, and I saw that except for the shelves, the place was pretty damn empty. It was about fifteen feet square and cool, and I started to move out in the center of the room, by folding and unfolding my bound legs like some overgrown centipede. I had moved about halfway out into the room when I had to stop. I was breathing so hard it made my jaw and head ache even more, and I was afraid the pain would make me pass out again. So I stopped, looked at where I had come from.

Just a plain stone staircase, hugging the far wall, heading upstairs. No banister. Just plain cut stone. Not much to work with there. There was also no handy-dandy workbench, with saws, files, or other sharp tools hanging down for easy access. Nothing. I moved my head. Three walls, all with the framed shelves for holding pricey bottles of wine. And from what I could tell, each shelf was empty. Just me and the stone and the dirt and the staircase and the shelves, and the two tiny windows.

My heart rate eased some, as did my breathing. Time to get back to moving.

Stretch, constrict, stretch, constrict, and as I moved, I saw the pieces of what had happened slide into place. The shooting at the Tyler Conference Center. I was to have been the patsy, the nutty former lover, trying to kill the senator's wife. But the bullets missed and I'd got sick, and that story didn't pan out. Then there was Spenser Harris, the faux Secret Service agent. Killed and dumped in my yard to do what...make me lash out? Make me run to Barbara Hale for another setup?

Who knew.

But I did know one thing. I had to move faster.

Stretch, constrict, stretch, constrict. Something in my coat pocket was pushing against the small of my back, hurting it like hell, but it wasn't going to stop me.

More movement. Now I was hungry, too, and thirsty. Stretch, constrict, stretch, constrict.

And I still hurt like hell.

STOPPED FOR A MOMENT. Almost there. Looked up at the windows. There was light now coming in, strong light, fresh light.

It was Monday morning, a day before the fine citizens of this state would help choose the next president.

I shook my head and kept moving, and then, when my bound hands touched the smooth wood of the wine shelves, I stopped and took another long break, breathing hard, head throbbing and aching. A long, hard slog. A very long, hard slog.

And not over yet. Not by a long shot.

I MOVED MY FINGERS ABOUT, searching for a piece of sharp wood, a protruding nail, or even a bit of metal framework, anything that could cut through the necktie holding my arms still.

Nothing.

Just smooth wood and stone.

I moved to the left, my bound hands still underneath the bottom shelf of the empty wine rack. Moved along, moved along, still feeling nothing but smooth rock and stone. From overhead, there were heavy footsteps up on the foyer floor. Up there, movement, up there, people at work, planning and plotting, waiting for me to fulfill my role.

The hell I would.

Now I was at the end of the shelves. Nothing. I looked back to where I had started. About halfway back across the room. Another section of the shelves remained. I took a breath, started inching back like one bruised and tired inchworm. Back to the shelves, moving along, my hands searching and poking, probing, feeling along and—

Something sharp.

Something sharp bit at my hand. I froze.

Didn't dare move, just waited.

Moved my hand again. Whatever was there had moved. Closed my eyes. Took a breath. Moved my hand again.

Nothing.

Upstairs, more footsteps, the murmur of conversation. I moved my hand. Still nothing.

I wiggled around, shoved my hand under the shelf, grunting in the process, scraped some skin off my wrist and—

Sharpness again.

My fingers were numb, tingling with lack of circulation, but I held on to whatever was there.

I moved forward, my hand tight against the sharpness, and I felt it and I thought I smiled, there in the darkness.

A piece of glass. Part of a broken wine bottle.

For this had been a wine cellar for quite a number of years, and I had a thought, a prayer, really, that somewhere along the line, a bottle would have been dropped, would have broken, and a piece of glass would have been overlooked as whoever had done the dropping would have had done a sloppy job in cleaning up.

I felt along the piece of glass. A sharp edge. I moved back against the shelf, lodged the glass against the wood, and started moving my bound wrists against the glass. Up and down, up and down, and—

The glass slipped.

Cut against my right wrist.

"Shit," I said, feeling the glass drop, feeling my wrist burn with the cut, now replaced with warmness as the blood started trickling down.

Reached and groped and got the glass.

Back again, cut and cut, and I felt the fabric of my necktie start to fray and break away. More cutting, more cutting, and I started moving my wrists and—

Everything tore away.

My wrists were free. Freedom.

I was free.

I rubbed and rubbed my wrists, the blood roaring back into my fingers, tingling and tingling, more rubbing.

I leaned forward, started working on the leather belt around my ankles, my fingers numb and my wrist bleeding, and I tore a fingernail or two getting it off, but off it was, and I stretched my legs and rubbed out the cramps, rubbed some more, and yes, I was free...

I looked up at the staircase, the locked door, the two tiny windows.

Some freedom.

17

I went through my pockets, wanting to find out what in hell had been poking at me, and I felt a small square of plastic and metal, and I pulled it out, and almost shouted with glee at what was there.

My hardly used cell phone, tiny and overlooked.

I pulled up the tiny antenna, switched it on, and started punching in the number of the Tyler Police Department. Diane would help me, Diane would know what to do, and—

Nothing.

Nothing at all.

Looked at the tiny display screen.

In tiny little letters that felt twelve feet tall. NO SERVICE.

Of course. Why should anything be easy?

I stood up, swaying, almost fell down again. Stretched and gasped as cramps rippled through my legs, and then I moved, rubbed again. I went up to the stone staircase, gently moved up along the steps, trying to keep the noise down, until I reached the top. Just for the hell of it, I moved my hands along the wall. No light switch. And I tried the doorknob. Locked, of course.

Cell phone in hand, I tried again.

The phone flickered into life, swinging between SERVICE and NO SERVICE. Close...so very close.

I looked around the cellar, saw the light streaming in through the two small windows.

Maybe...just maybe.

I quietly went down the stone steps, almost fell as another series of cramps went running through my legs, and I went over to the shelves, looked up. About eleven, twelve feet. A hell of a thing. Blood was still trickling down my right wrist and I made a sloppy bandage with my handkerchief.

And then I started climbing.

The wood had sharp edges against my hands, and I winced as I made my way up, the shelves groaning under my weight. About halfway, my foot broke through one of the slats, making a loud crack that I was sure could be heard as far away as Porter, and I murmured another series of expletives when the cell phone dropped from my hand. I looked down in the dim light and almost passed out when I saw the piece of metal and plastic split apart when it hit the stone floor.

I made my way slowly down to the floor, went and gathered up the pieces, and went to the center of the cellar, where the light was best. I put it back together as best as I could, and then went back to the wine rack, putting the cell phone back into my coat. Something must have loosened from my previous attempt, for the wood groaned and I felt the shelves move away from the wall.

"Close," I whispered. "So damn close."

I moved back up the shelving, taking it slow, knowing that by going slow, I wouldn't slip but was leaving open the chance of the damn thing collapsing under my weight, and I let that cheery debate run itself out as I got higher and higher, right up to the top, right by one of the two windows. The window was built into the stone foundation and couldn't be opened, and in any event, it was too small to crawl through, but what I wanted to get through the window wasn't made of proteins. It was made of protons. Or something similar. My grasp on science right at that moment was pretty damn fuzzy.

Hanging on with one hand, I got the phone out of my coat, pulled the antenna out with my teeth, and held it up to the window, pressed the keypad.

There. I'll be damned.

SERVICE.

But another message was blinking at me. LOW BATTERY.

I guess my phone was one of those newfangled ones, for there was a digital countdown letting me know exactly how many seconds of usable power I had left, and I saw the number thirty become the number twenty-nine, become the number twenty-eight...

Who to call?

Back in my coat pocket again, looking and finding...a slip of paper in my hand, up to the window and the light, and there, the one call I would make. A call to warn her, a call to let her know, to go into hiding, to prevent her husband's defeat tomorrow, to call the Secret Service and do what had to be done...

I punched in the numbers and waited, imagining the little digits running their way back to zero, and from upstairs, I heard a phone ringing. What a coincidence.

An odd counterpoint, this phone ringing, the upstairs phone ringing—

A *click*. It was answered. A hesitant voice. "Hello?"

"Barbara?"

And everything got quite cold, as I realized the phone upstairs had, had...

Had stopped ringing. "Lewis? Is that you?"

And in the background, a very familiar voice, one I had heard the day before, as he was thumping me with a stun gun.

"Here? The sumbitch phoned you here?"

She hung up. I looked at my phone, now dead, and let it gently fall out of my hand and drop to the floor.

I slowly and carefully made my way back down to the stone floor, and feeling like the floor itself was being carried on my shoulders, I went over to the bottom of the stairs and looked up at the closed door.

And waited.

I didn't have to wait long.

. . .

THE DOOR OPENED and the lights came on, blinding me for a moment. I raised up a sore and bloody hand to my eyes to shield them. Harmon Jewett yelled down, "You wanna come up here, boy?"

"Do I have a choice?"

He laughed and a woman murmured behind him, and then he came down the stone steps, smiling widely, holding out the stun gun in his hand. Behind him was someone dear and familiar, and with each step she took downstairs, she broke my heart again and again. For a moment I was that college-aged boy, wondering and wondering why she had left me and had never called or written.

"Barbara," I said.

"Lewis."

She came down to the bottom of the steps and was now standing close to Harmon, standing right close to him, and with her arm through his, her head lowered. I flashed back to what I had seen, what I had remembered, about her and Jackson Hale. Over the past several days I had seen numerous videos of Barbara with her husband-candidate, and in each video—save one—she had been the devoted spouse, standing right next to the senator, smiling with him, laughing with him, applauding at each appropriate applause line. In each and every video, save one.

The one from the Tyler Conference Center.

And in that snippet of history, I remembered seeing Barbara with her husband, standing apart from her husband, standing very far apart from her husband...because she knew.

She knew gunshots were going to be fired. She knew.

She always knew.

Harmon said, "Hands where I can see 'em, boy."

I held my hands out, and Harmon chuckled. "Glad to see you're bleeding. Helps everything else as well."

I ignored him, stared at the woman I had once loved so long ago, and before me...before me was a stranger.

I said, "I guess first lady wasn't that attractive to you, was it."

Her head snapped right up, and the sharpness of her eyes and her tone chilled me. "When did I ever have a choice? When did I ever have the right to say no? When did I ever have a voice in what was going on? When? It was all assumed. It was all planned. And if I hated being a senator's wife, being first lady to this nation of clowns was going to kill me. Was going to absolutely kill me..."

"And killing your husband was going to change things?"

Harmon said, "Not kill 'em. Just wound him. Except that damn Spenny couldn't hit the broad side of a barn...and our planned patsy was busy pukin' his guts instead of being inside the building and takin' the fall. So instead of a wounded candidate and a scandal over his wife's former lover, we got a bump in the fuckin' polls, if you can believe it."

Now I looked to Harmon. "This is what you do when you're marginalized, when Jackson Hale won't fire you? When he keeps you on his payroll?"

Harmon spat something on the ground, his voice as sharp as Barbara's. "His payroll. His gratitude. Damn him, if it weren't for me, he'd still be some little state senator cutting ribbons at Piggly Wiggly openings. I made him, and now I'm gonna unmake him, and steal his woman in the process."

He leered at me and squeezed Barbara tight, and in looking at her and looking at him, I could not imagine what had brought them together, what they hoped to do, and then I gave it up. Trying to fathom who they were and what they were doing was like trying to understand quantum theory with a third-grade math education. It just made my head hurt.

And the time for thinking was over. "Barbara..."

She didn't say anything. My throat thickened and I said, "Just the other day, some smart man warned me of the danger of manipulation. I just wish I had appreciated how smart he really was."

Still no answer.

With a touch of impatience, Harmon said, "Upstairs, friend. Now."

"Or what? Plan to shoot me and dump my body with a rifle in my hand in front of Hale campaign headquarters?"

"Nope. Or I take my stun gun and shoot ten thousand volts into your private parts, then drag you upstairs. Either way, you're going upstairs."

Barbara's head was lowered again, as if that earlier outburst had tired her. "So...is that it? That's all it's been since you've been here? Me as a tool so you can spend your days with...with this creature?"

Her voice soft, she said, "He loves me, Lewis. He will do anything for me. Anything. And he will save me from going back to D.C. anymore so I can stop wearing that damn happy wifey mask."

She turned and went up the stairs. Harmon grinned at me, like a good ole boy sharing a joke with another equally good ole boy. I started up the stairs and Harmon gave me a wide berth, and as I got to the top of the stairs, Barbara was there and I had a quick thought of making a break for it, but the other woman—Carla—stood there with a wary expression on her face, a nine-millimeter automatic pistol pointed in my direction.

Harmon joined us and said, "Permit me to introduce my companion, one Carla Conchita Lopez. Carla was once a member of the Guatemalan People's Army...or the People's Army of Guatemala...or some damn thing, until she got a taste for capitalism and headed north. She got caught up in an immigration sweep in Atlanta couple of years back...and long story short, my cousin from INS dumped her in my care. Old Spenny. Old stupid Spenny, couldn't hit a target to save his life, and he sure as hell didn't. Jesus, you were supposed to call the cops when you found his body in your yard. Why the hell didn't you do that, boy?"

"Guess I forgot."

"Where is he now?"

I said, "In a safe place. You want to trade? His body for my freedom?"

He grinned. "Not much of a trade. Sorry."

Harmon went to a pile of clothing by the door and said, "The cuffs, babe. Toss him the cuffs."

With her free hand, Carla reached into a pocket in her slacks and pulled out a set of handcuffs, which she tossed to me. I caught the jangling pieces of metal and looked over to Harmon.

"Put them on," he said, "or I tell Carla to shoot you in your kneecap. Either way, it don't matter to me, 'cause the cuffs will be where they belong. Carla's one tough bitch, buddy, and some of the stories she told me about down south would make your balls ache. So do what you're told and don't fuck with her."

I was still looking at Barbara, still trying to remember those magical days in Indiana, at the university, and then giving up. No more time for the past. None. I had to focus on the here and now, as hard as it was. Barbara stood by Harmon, and she was still not looking at me.

"The handcuffs, Lewis. Now."

I slowly put one cuff on one wrist, and then the other on the second wrist. The clicking sounded as sharp as a sliding saw hitting a bone. "All right," I said. "Your patsy is ready. So? Shoot me now, or shoot me later? And do you trust me with a gun?"

Harmon walked over to the small pile of clothing on the floor. "Who said anything about a gun? Carla, keep an eye on 'im."

He bent down, picked up what looked to be a cloth vest, and my aches and pains and cramps went right away as I saw the wires leading up from tubes of material, fastened to the outside of the vest. He held it up like a fisherman proud of the trophy he had just captured and was about to bring home.

"Carla here, when she was active in her little revolutionary movement, developed some nice skills, including bomb making. And what's gonna happen here, Lewis, is that you're puttin' this vest on...and in about twenty minutes, ol' Senator Hale is coming here for what he thinks is goin' to be a quick campaign stop to say thanks to that ol' bitch Audrey Whittaker, who is over in Concord expectin' the senator to have a drink with her...and when he comes up that driveway, why, you're gonna run out to meet him. You see, for the past half day, you've been holdin' the three of us hostage, which we're gonna swear to the investigatin' authorities. Plus, in that vest is some love letters you've written to Barbara...love letters that come from your computer that we didn't have a chance to use the first time around...and that little scandal will defeat that little bastard tomorrow."

The cuffs were cold and made my bleeding wrist sting even that much more.

"If stopping him is so important, why not put the word out about me? If that's the scandal you're looking for."

Harmon said, "Who humped who twenty years ago—so what?—but a crazed stalker, tryin' to kill the senator over a long ago love affair...so much juicier, so much juicier that you dumb Yankees up here, who hate scandal so much, will give the nomination to somebody else...and give me and Barbara a good laugh when we're done, just to see what we managed to pull over that numb Jackson."

I said, "Just so you know, Harmon, there's another copy of that surveillance tape. A copy I mailed to a trusted friend. Let me go and we can settle this ... settle it so nothing else happens, nobody gets hurt."

Harmon said, "Carla? The tape?"

She shook her head. "Can't make out your face. Can make out the license plate of the car. That's it."

Harmon turned to me, triumphant. "That ol' biddy lends her car, her house, and sometimes what's left between her legs to people she wants to help. So by the time investigators try to figure out what's what—especially with no body for Spenny—whoever's president will be working on his second term."

Barbara had moved next to Harmon like an obedient puppet.

She was by the door, Harmon standing next to her, and Carla, in turn, standing next to him. All three of them standing in a row, looking at me.

I said quietly, "Barbara...you know what's going to happen. If I go out there wearing that vest, he's going to trigger it by remote control. Barbara, he's going to kill me. He's going to kill me in the next few minutes. Barbara."

She said nothing. Just reached out and sought Harmon's hand, which he gave her. He was holding the vest with one hand, squeezing her hand with the other.

"Now, Lewis. Put the vest on now."

I lowered my head and moved forward, gauging my steps, and when I got close to Harmon and Barbara, the vest now held out to me, I tried to catch her eyes, tried to look at her, tried to make her see the man who was in front of her.

But she was studiously ignoring me.

And so I went up to Harmon and Barbara and slugged her in the chin with my left elbow as hard as I could.

18

Barbara yelped and fell to the ground, still holding on to Harmon, and he stumbled and Carla shouted, and I grabbed the doorknob with my cuffed hands and opened the door and ran outside, almost tripping on the slippery steps, but I ran and ran and ran out onto the driveway. I was moving quick and thinking even quicker, and I knew the grounds would hold no shelter for me, not with the snowbanks of the driveway and the snow-covered lawn. I would slow down instantly in the thick snow and be a quick and easy target, so I stuck to the curving driveway, running and running, hoping that its gentle curves and the high snowbanks would hide me for a few seconds, for I was sure Carla was right behind me with a shoot-to-kill order, and somewhere back there, both she and Harmon and yes, damn it, Barbara, had a Plan C to take care of everything.

It was cold and windy, but I didn't mind. I was moving quick, the cramps and discomfort in my legs and arms now overlooked, the open entrance to the estate now before me, wide open, and as I ran toward the opening, I had a fearful thought that perhaps there was some automatic system back at the house to close the gates, but nothing happened as I approached the stone columns and the silent cast-iron gates.

There. Right through. Now I was at Atlantic Avenue. Look to the left, look to the right. The road here was fairly straight.

No traffic. None.

Ah, hell.

Then the sound of an engine.

Look, look, look, a voice inside me started screaming.

A dark blue pickup truck came around the corner, heading in my direction. I ran toward it, holding my arms up, yelling, pleading, and—

The truck sped up and passed me by, the older driver grimly staring ahead, pretending I didn't exist.

Of course.

Who in hell would stop for a crazed man with no coat, standing in the middle of the road, wearing handcuffs?

The sound of the gunshot spun me around, broke my stillness. Carla was running down the driveway, followed by Harmon, and I looked again at the roadway.

Nothing. Just an empty road, both sides with high snowbanks. Can't go back. Go down or up the road and be exposed like a fumbling ant on a kitchen counter.

Can't wait for another disinterested driver to intercede. Only one place to go.

19

So I ran across the two-lane road, hands still cuffed before me, and I scrambled up the snowbank and down the other side, feet digging into the crusty stuff, my legs and back now wet through from the snow. I now had cover, for a minute or two, and I was panting and shuddering, for it was still cold, still windy, and before me were snow-covered rocks and boulders, and the waves of the Atlantic Ocean, coming in, like they always do, nasty and gray looking.

Plans. I had very grand plans. To stay alive and maybe move south, move among the rocks and boulders, keep some cover between me and my pursuers, and if I was very, very lucky, I could make some good progress, until...

Until what? Saved? Rescued? No one knew I was here, and sure, maybe tomorrow or the next day, Felix would receive the Lafayette House videotape that I had mailed him, but I didn't have tomorrow or the next day.

All I had was right now, and right now was pretty damn grim. I went down the first set of rocks, looked at the place where there was a level snowbank, not much else, and I thought that must be where Audrey Whittaker's illegal—and to a certain Massachusetts family, dangerous—beach was hidden. Right now, it didn't look dangerous. Just looked empty. Audrey.

One of these days, maybe I'd offer an apology to her for having thought she had something to do with this mess.

I moved across the slippery rocks and boulders to the south, scrambling as best as I could, hands cuffed before me, lungs burning with heavy breathing, my back suddenly feeling itchy and exposed, not letting the thoughts of betrayal overcome me. There would be plenty of time for that later. Right now I had to move, had to hide, had to—

Another gunshot. I ducked, glanced behind me, saw a figure up on the snowbank, saw that it was Carla, and I slipped and fell, striking my right knee on an exposed piece of rock, making me snap my jaw in pain. I got up, my bare and handcuffed hands red and raw from being dunked into the snow, and I kept on moving, weaving, thinking that if only I could get more rocks and boulders between me and my pursuer, and if that campaign convoy from Senator Hale finally got up here, even Carla might not want to be running around with a weapon in the midst of all the Secret Service and news media and—

Good thoughts, great thoughts, right up to when I got up on a piece of New Hampshire granite, slippery cold with ice, and fell into the ocean.

THE COLD FELT like a telephone pole being swung against my chest, and I raised my head, coughing and sputtering, completely drenched, salt water in my mouth and nose, and my feet flailed about until I got traction and stood up, and I tried to slog my way back to shore, and I made one step and two—

The waves rolled in, banged me against a couple of rocks, and then dragged me out. The shock to my system made everything look gray, like some sort of veil had been pulled over my eyes. I moved my feet again, this time feeling nothing under me, and the weight of my wet clothes was starting to drag me down. The part of my mind that was still thinking rationally knew that in January in the Atlantic Ocean, I had just a handful of minutes left before hypothermia closed its cold fist around my heart and killed me. That's it. No appeal, no good nature, nothing. Just the cold facts.

I coughed and gasped and raised my head again. I hated being in the ocean even on the hottest days of the year, and in January...there was no coastline before me with open, inviting, sandy beaches and on-duty life-guards looking for swimmers in trouble, swimmers like me. No, except for that strip of land converted by Audrey Whittaker, this was rocks and boulders and fissures and—

A wave was coming in. I moved with it, hoping the momentum would carry me far enough, and it did. Maybe I was wave riding or something, letting the wave carry me, and if it carried me far enough, I could get traction and—

The wave petered out. I coughed and choked from the salt water. My legs moved again, scrambling, and there was nothing to stand on, and the waves dragged me back, even farther away from safety. I was shivering wildly now, teeth chattering, and I rolled over, tried to get on my back, maybe floating on my back would give me a better chance of getting to shore.

On my back, my handcuffed hands on my chest, the hands lobster-red, wondering if I could swim somehow, even with my fastened hands, or maybe kick my way to shore, if I was very, very lucky. But I was so cold, and my wet clothes were dragging me down and my teeth were chattering, and my legs and arms were numb, and I began to imagine things. Imagining I was warm, imagining I was in the desert, that's right, back in the Nevada desert so many years earlier, when I was younger and dumber and full of vim and vigor and energy, fighting the good fight from the Department of Defense.

Oh yes. The desert. When my intelligence section was accidentally exposed to something horrible and illegal, and the helicopters came, the helicopters came, and everyone died, everyone save for one poor fool, one poor fool named Lewis...

Now I was certain I was hallucinating, for I was quite warm, warm indeed, and the ocean felt as warm as it did in south Florida, and the sound of the helicopter was quite loud, chattering and overwhelming everything, and I closed my eyes and floated and things felt light indeed before there was nothing else there. Nothing at all.

THE VOICE SAID, "Are you all right? Can you wake up?"

I shifted my weight and winced from the pain in my right knee and—

The pain in my knee.

I opened my eyes and wiped them with my warm and dry hands.

I sat up. I was in a bed, and I looked around and it wasn't a hospital, but it was a hotel room. That was my very first big surprise. My second very big surprise was sitting next to me in a hotel chair.

Secret Service Agent Glen Reynolds.

"I'm awake now," I said, my voice just barely above a whisper. "And I don't know how all right I am. I hurt like hell, but I'm alive. I suppose I have the Secret Service to thank for that."

"You do."

"Very well. Thank you. Thank you very much."

I sat up in the bed, put a pillow behind my back, winced again from the pain in my leg, and said, "The senator?"

"He's fine. Just gave a hell of a campaign speech a while ago."

"His wife?"

"Standing right next to him like a good wife and the possible first lady she might become. All nice and normal."

I looked again at the room. A funny world. It seemed like we were in the Lafayette House. How bloody ironic.

"And Harmon Jewett? And his woman companion?"

Reynolds shrugged. "In custody, talking to us. And they'll probably be in custody for the foreseeable future."

"I see."

I moved again in the bed and the pain wasn't as sharp this time. Goody. I was making progress. I looked at Agent Reynolds and remembered the last time we met, and what he had told me about staying away from the senator's wife and bookstores. I said, "You've been following me, right?"

"Of course. Off and on, here and there. We would have been remiss if we hadn't. For a few days you were the chief suspect in the attempted assassination of a leading presidential candidate. You were subsequently cleared of that attack, but just because you were cleared for that doesn't mean you were cleared for doing anything stupid in the future."

"Thanks. I think."

"You're welcome, Mr. Cole. You see, you have an odd and dark background, which we couldn't get into, no matter how much we dug," Agent Reynolds said pointedly, as if it had always been my fault. "So yes, we kept an eye on you. Right up to the point when you went for a swim earlier today after your visit to Mrs. Whittaker's home. Lucky for you, we had an airborne asset in the area, and we were able to reel you in after you took that swim. Any longer...they would have reeled in a corpse."

"How in hell did you bring me here?"

He shrugged. "Through a service elevator. So things would be nice and quiet without all that nasty publicity."

I rubbed my wrists and saw that one was bandaged, the one I had cut on the glass shard back in the basement. I looked at him and his calm appearance, and I said, "You guys are up to something, aren't you."

"Define 'something.'"

"So far, you haven't threatened me with arrest. Or anything else. We're having an adult, intelligent conversation. No mention of Harmon and the senator's wife conspiring either to have him killed or to lose the election. All the while using me as their handy-dandy nut with a grudge."

Reynolds held his hands together in his lap. "That's sheer speculation and idle chitchat, Mr. Cole, and you know it. If Harmon and his friend do face the music, it will be on violating federal firearms and explosives statutes, and probably homicide, if we're lucky and we find the right evidence."

"Homicide?"

"Of course. Mr. Jewett's companion, Carla, claims that Mr. Jewett killed his cousin, one William Spenser Harrison, aka Spenser Harris, just a few days ago. Carla wants a deal before saying anything else about the circumstances or location of his death, and right now, it's in the lawyers' hands. Which is fine. We don't like people pretending to be Secret Service agents, and since it looks like this fake Secret Service agent met a demise that he so richly deserved, I'm quite content to let others take care of matters."

"I see."

Reynolds said, "You wouldn't happen to know where Mr. Harris is currently located, would you?"

I said carefully, "I've not spoken to him since that day before the attempted assassination."

"So you say."

I changed the subject and said, "What about Barbara Hale?"

"The senator's wife?" he said. "I imagine that she will be traveling apart from the senator during the rest of this campaign...and I also imagine that her movements, conversations, phone calls, and e-mails will be strictly observed just to make sure that any future unpleasantness doesn't occur."

"The senator...he knows?"

"Of course."

"And..."

"What do you think?" Reynolds asked. "At this moment, do you think he's going to dump everything to try to have her arrested? Be real, Mr. Cole. He's within a few months of getting his party's nomination. If that means believing that his wife is slightly unbalanced, and that she and her troubles can be kept under wraps and control...well, that's what's going to happen."

The room seemed to vibrate just a bit, as if something were about to spin free and shatter, and I guess it was just a reaction to my deep-January swim. I shivered suddenly and pulled the thick blankets closer to me.

"So it's a cover-up. Why's that?"

Now Reynolds smiled. "Cover-up is such a loaded phrase. We prefer...we prefer a reality check."

"A what?"

"Reality check. And the reality is, well, I know a bit about your background, Mr. Cole, which is why we're having this kind of conversation. In your previous life you had a very high security clearance. That's why I think I can trust you with what you said earlier, about having an adult conversation."

"Go on," I said.

"For the past several years and campaign cycles, the Secret Service has become a modern-day Praetorian Guard. We've been putting our elected officials in a safe, quiet bubble, where never is there a disquieting word to be heard. We've been on our way to losing our professionalism and becoming just another part of the political process. You know, the sane, non-corrupted, non-cynical political process that makes this country so great and admired."

"I see," I said.

He shook his head. "We got a new administrator two years ago. And he put the word down. We were going back to our roots, as a protective force. We weren't going to be adjuncts of an administration or a campaign. We were going to serve and protect. That's it. Mr. Cole, you served some time in government. What's the worst thing that any government agency fears?"

I thought about that for a moment, and was going to say budget cutbacks, when something else came to mind. "Public humiliation or embarrassment."

He gently clapped his hands together. "Exactly. Embarrassment, which leads to headlines and news stories and the death of a thousand cuts from the news media and the Internet."

I thought it over and said, "So, the public release of information from the Secret Service that the wife of a leading presidential candidate is having an affair with a political operative in the campaign, and who may have a role in the shooting attempt on the senator himself...that's not going to happen, is it?"

"Not from us," he said. "You're a bright fellow. Imagine the uproar that would cause. The day before the New Hampshire primary, having a story like that make the front pages of all the newspapers and every minute of every cable show. We'd be accused of trying to influence the election. Of favoring one candidate over another. Of being the power behind the throne of whoever might become the next president." Reynolds shook his head. "Not going to happen, not this time."

I said, "By keeping quiet, you can be accused of the same thing."

"Maybe so. But we keep quiet about a lot of things. About which presidential candidate's spouse has a drinking problem. Which presidential candidate has a fondness for bisexual pornography. Or which child of which candidate has a problem of assaulting women. Not our job to make that stuff public. So here we are."

I was feeling warmer, though my right knee was throbbing like the proverbial son of a bitch. "So here we are," I said. "Is this the point in time when you tell me to keep my mouth shut, or else?"

Reynolds smiled and said, "No. It isn't the time. Not sure if that moment will ever come, no matter how many bad movies you've seen or bad books you've read. But it is the time when I tell you it's your choice to do what you will about what happened to you. And that you should think carefully about the choice you make."

"How's that?"

He said, "In a manner of minutes, I'm going to leave this room, Mr. Cole. A doctor is going to come in to give you a final check-over. The room is yours for the night, if you'd like. And after I leave, you can do whatever you want. Stay here. Depart. Call up CNN and tell them everything you know. However..."

"Yes?"

"What you need to think about is this," Reynolds said. "You have it in your power to destroy or damage the candidacy of Senator Jackson Hale. You. And it's up to you to decide if it's worth it for some sense of justice or getting back at a woman who apparently used you and betrayed you. For what it's worth, a fair number of people want Hale in the White House. Do you want to keep that away from them?"

"I don't know," I said. "But if I do talk, it'll make things hell for you, won't it?"

"We've been through hell before. Like November 1963. We'd survive. Question for you—I know you like your privacy. Would you survive?"

I looked at that professional face, the face of a man sworn to throw his body in front of an assassin's bullet for a man or woman who might not even be worth it. Some sort of man, some sort of dedication.

I burrowed back into my blankets.

"Sure, I'd survive," I said. "But there's more to everything than survival."

Reynolds stood up. "Ain't that the truth." He reached inside his coat pocket, took out a business card and passed it over. "Here you go. My card. Business and cell phone and home phone numbers. Call me if I can do you a favor, or something."

I looked at the card and said, "How about now?"

He shrugged. "Sure. Go ahead."

"My friend Annie. She's involved with the Hale campaign. I want to make sure that...well, if Barbara Hale can't get at her husband, I want to make sure that nothing bad happens to Annie."

A quick nod. "Sure. I'll make sure it happens. Anything else?"

"Not at the moment."

He started for the door. "If that's the case, Mr. Cole, well, it's been a bit of an adventure getting to know you. Look forward to the adventure ending tonight."

"Back to Boston?"

"I wish. Off to South Carolina, for the next stop on this crazy trip we call choosing a president."

Damn. I turned and looked at a small digital clock on the nightstand and the coldness returned and I said, "Is that time right? Is it really that late?"

"Sure is," he said, now at the door, "and I've got to get going." So he left and I looked at the clock again. It was just past 9 P.M. I was supposed to have met Annie Wynn in Room 110, more than four hours earlier.

I picked up the phone at my side—and, by the way, confirmed that I was at the Lafayette House—and called her cell phone. Went directly into voice mail. I left a long and heartfelt message, and then I called home to check messages on my answering machine. Eight messages, all reminding me to vote tomorrow.

None from Annie.

I called her cell phone again.

And went straight to voice mail again.

Damn.

There was a knock on the door, and I called out, "Coming!" thinking that maybe some magic had been worked, that Annie was here to see me, but no, no such luck on this cursed day. I went to the door and opened it and a sour-looking man in an ill-fitting brown suit said, "Mr. Cole? Frank Higgins, on contract with the Secret Service. I'm here to see that you're breathing and all that."

He looked me up and down. "And I can tell that you're at least doing that."

I went back inside the room. "Nice diagnosis, so far."

"Yeah, well, the night's still young."

ABOUT A HALF HOUR LATER, I was hobbling my way through the lobby of the Lafayette House, my right knee in a brace, leaning on a metal cane, the metal cold and uncomfortable in my stiff fingers. The lobby was crowded with all sorts of campaign people, press types and the usual hangers-on, some passing out press kits or leaflets, grabbing almost everyone and anyone trying to get his or her message out before the big day tomorrow.

I went past the gift shop and then made my way in, looking for a familiar or friendly face, and found neither. There was a young woman I didn't recognize behind the counter, dressed in black and with a hoop through her left nostril, leafing through a copy of Rolling Stone magazine that had a nightmarish cover depicting all of the candidates currently traipsing through my home state.

I went up to her and said, "Is Stephanie off tonight?"

She looked at me and said, "Hunh?"

"Stephanie Sussex. The gift shop manager. Where is she?"

"Oh," the young woman said, flipping through another page. "She don't work here no more."

It was like I was back in the ocean again. "What?"

"She don't work here no more. I guess she got fired."

"Fired? Why?"

She shrugged. "Heard she pissed off the boss. Which isn't hard to do, if you know what I mean."

I said, "I do. I really do."

Damn. I turned around. What a perfect way to end a perfectly miserable day.

20

Getting home was challenging with my bum knee and the rubber-tipped metal cane slipping on the snow and ice. Usually, the sight of my home at night is welcoming. Seeing that small place of refuge and comfort by the water's edge after the past forty-eight hours I had just experienced should have cheered me up, but it didn't. It looked dark and brooding and I thought that if it wasn't for my hurting knee, I would have turned around and gone back up to the hotel to take Agent Reynolds up on his offer for the free stay.

But instead I made my way inside, checked again for messages—none —and turned up the heat. I poured myself a big glass of Bordeaux and stretched out on the couch, wincing at the pain, pulling a down comforter over myself. I called Annie three more times on her cell phone. The phone wasn't picked up, not once.

I drank my wine and if I had had the energy, I would have built a fire, but the energy just wasn't there. To torture myself, I guess, I turned on the television and went through the various cable channels, catching the head-lines of the evening, a few hours before the start of the New Hampshire primary. The campaigners were scrambling and the polls were in disarray —not one of them agreeing with another—and I saw just one thing that made me smile, a story that Senator Nash Pomeroy was trying hard to kill:

the junior senator from Massachusetts was about to drop out of the race over the next several weeks. The spokesmen and spokeswomen for Senator Pomeroy seemed halfhearted in their denials of the story, which had been first reported in a small newspaper based in Tyler, New Hampshire, and later broadcast across the world.

Good job, Paula, I thought, thinking that here at least was one place where I hadn't carpet-bombed to dust my relationship with someone dear to me.

I finished off the wine and pulled the comforter up and watched television until I fell asleep.

THE PHONE CALL from a woman came late that night, just before midnight.

I scrambled some in the darkness on the couch, reached the phone and put it on my chest and said, "Hello?"

"Lewis?"

A woman's voice, but one I didn't recognize. "Yeah. Who's this?"

"Lewis, my name is Angie Hawley. I'm an assistant for Barbara Hale, Senator Jackson Hale's wife."

I rubbed my eyes in the darkness. "Good for you. Must be a hell of a job."

She ignored my little editorial comment and said, "I have something I need to pass along to you."

"You do? What's that?"

"Mrs. Hale wants to—"

"Wait."

I sat up, rubbed my eyes again.

Sir?" she asked. "Are you there?"

"Yeah. Hold on. Are you telling me that you have a statement for me? From Barbara Hale?"

"Well, it's not really a statement, it's more like a—"

"Wait, just one more time. Is she there?"

"No, it's just me."

"So she doesn't want to talk to me one-on-one. She wants you to read a statement to me. Am I right?"

She stopped, like she was trying to figure out how to appease me, and she said, "Partially right, sir. But—"

I said, "Sorry, not interested," and I hung up.

And surprisingly enough, it didn't take too long to fall back to sleep.

THE RINGING PHONE woke me from a dream in which I was sinking into the ocean, icebergs around my feet, and a woman said, "Hello?" and I said, "Annie?"

"Um, no, sir, this is the campaign of Congressman Wallace calling, to see if you need a ride to the polls today, and—"

I hung up. Scratched my chin. Checked the time. Almost nine o'clock. Sweet God.

I picked up the phone again, dialed the number that was burned into me.

Nothing. Damn.

I switched on the television and made a light breakfast of tea and toast and ate while sitting on the couch. I had a bit of a smile in seeing that the thriving metropolises of Dixville Notch and Hart's Location, up in the northern regions of the state, had opened and closed their polls overnight, thereby casting the very first votes in the very first primary state, said votes totaling about a dozen. I suppose it was a testament to the depths that the news media and the campaigns had sunk that these few votes were interpreted and analyzed for most of the morning by people who should have known better.

I was washing my meager dishes when the phone rang again, and I hopped over and picked it up and sat down and said, "This better not be a solicitation of any sorts."

The man on the other end laughed. "Hell of a way to start Primary Day."

I sat on the couch. "Felix. What's up? Thought you'd be at Pomeroy headquarters."

He laughed again. "After what I found out for them, I took their cash and practically went into hiding. It's going to be a rough week or two for all concerned before the plug gets pulled on the campaign. What are you up to?"

"Sitting. Watching. Waiting."

"You vote yet?"

I looked out the window, at the cloudy sky. "Nope."

"You going to?"

I said, "Wasn't planning to."

"Why the hell not? Sure doesn't sound like you, not at all."

I looked at the brown brace holding my knee together. "Well, I banged up my knee yesterday."

"What happened?" Felix asked.

"I'll tell you later. Right now, it hurts like hell, and I don't feel like moving."

Felix said, "Man it up, nancy-boy. I'm coming over to get you to the polls."

"Hey," I said, but by then, I was talking to a dead phone.

TRUE TO HIS WORD, Felix rolled in about fifteen minutes later. He came through the front door without knocking and whistled when he looked at my knee brace and the metal cane that I was using.

"What does the other person look like?"

"A hell of a lot better than me," I said.

"Which was..."

A wide smile before he closed the door. "Teaching himself how to be left-handed for the next month or two, after growing up right-handed."

"Care to tell me the story?"

"Promise to keep quiet?"

His face fell a bit, like I had insulted him, and he said, "After all these years."

"Oh, for God's sake, put away that hurt puppy look and help me get out of here."

In a flash, his ready smile returned, and he said, "Point noted. Sometimes I like to practice the hurt puppy look. You wouldn't believe the places and the women it's gotten me."

"I can imagine."

He laughed. "No, you can't."

I grabbed a coat and made my way to the front door. Felix was driving a black Toyota Highlander with dealer plates, and as he helped me down the steps, I said, "What's going on here? You've been raiding a local dealership?"

"No, just partial payment for a favor done, that's all."

We went around to the passenger's side door, and Felix opened the door and helped boost me up, and I felt slightly ashamed, like I was suddenly old and needed help to get around. Before Felix closed the door, I said, "What kind of favor?"

He said, "There's a dealership in Porter where I get my Mercedes serviced. The service manager had a problem with his daughter. Or, more to the point, the daughter's boyfriend. The daughter was no longer interested in the boyfriend. The boyfriend had other ideas and was quite determined in his other ideas. The police did what they could, but the boyfriend...well, he was persistent. When I found out what was going on, I had a talk with said boyfriend and showed him a better way of living. Case closed."

"Really?"

He gave a slight shake of his head. "Young men like that, they really need to learn how to channel all that excessive negative energy, especially when it comes to relationships. So I gave the young man an opportunity to redirect his energies away from trying to win back his old girlfriend to something more productive."

ALONG THE WAY to the polling station, I said, "You know, I've never really seen this part of you, Felix."

"Which part is that?"

"The civic part, interested in voting and all that. Doesn't quite...fit."

Felix said, "Oh, my friend, it does fit, and fit very well."

"Really?"

"Oh yes."

We were on Atlantic Avenue, heading south, and then he turned north on Winnicut Road, one of the direct routes into Tyler proper. We passed through an area of homes and subdivisions, and a fair number of homes had campaign signs out in the snowbanks. The last day, I thought, the very last day. And then the signs would magically disappear overnight, and New Hampshire would once again return to its usual state of peace, harmony, and understanding among all peoples.

Yeah, right. In a month some of these signs would still be there, the paint faded, the sticks cracked, still waving in the breeze like the banners of a defeated army, stuck in the mud of some forgotten battlefield.

Felix said, "My grandfather's fault, I guess. Mikos Tinios. Grandpa Mikey is what we called him. A short guy, spoke passable English, had a thick white handlebar mustache and loved to play tricks on his grandkids. You know what I mean. Pulling nickels out of our ears, making cards disappear, stuff like that. Lots of laughs. Seemed like the happiest guy you could ever meet. And one day...oh, I don't know how old I was, I was maybe eleven or twelve, he was in his backyard—about five yards to a side, but he was so damn proud of that little plot of earth—sunning himself. I still remember what he was wearing, these old khaki shorts and beat-up sneakers, and he was under a beach umbrella, drinking ouzo or something, and I saw these old, old scars on his chest and belly. And, being the inquisitive little squirt that I was, I asked him about it."

"And what did Grandpa Mikey say?"

Felix's voice was quiet, almost somber, a tone I usually don't associate with him. "At first, he tried to make a joke about it, about being a circus performer and being mauled by lions and tigers, but I didn't believe him, not for a moment. I mean, the old boy used to tell me stories about gypsies and Greek gods and ghosts, so I didn't believe the circus crap."

"So suspicious at such a young age," I said.

"Yeah, well, blame my environment. Anyway, so I pressed him and pressed him, and finally, the story came out. Old happy Grandpa Mikey, he with the big booming laugh and love for his family, was a partisan in Greece during the 1940s. Some of the scars, he told me, came from the Nazis...and others came from the communists, during the civil war after World War II, and then he changed the subject. Even my dad didn't say anything to me about it, it was my mom who told me the rest. Grandpa Mikey was a famous partisan fighter, famous for going behind enemy lines —whether they be German lines or communist lines—and doing the killing that had to be done. With a knife. Never a firearm. Too noisy. With a knife...and when something approaching peace had finally come to Greece, Grandpa Mikey came to America. And you know what? I think he was happiest here, in the States. And not once did he ever forget to vote. Not once. When I got older and he got older, and getting him to vote meant bundling him in a wheelchair and carrying an oxygen tank along, he told me that it was a blessing to be in this land, where you settled your arguments at the ballot box, and not with a knife blade or a bomb."

Now we were at the polling station for the town, the uptown fire station for Tyler. Felix found a parking spot near the rear and said, "So I make it a point to vote, and I've not missed an election yet. All for Grandpa Mikey. In his memory."

"Good story," I said.

"Wasn't a story," he said back. "It's the real deal. So, go ahead and do your part, all right? I'll be waiting for you. And maybe later you'll tell me about that knee of yours."

"Okay," I said, stepping out, wincing as my right foot hit the ground and my banged-up knee flexed some. I walked across the plowed parking lot to the front of the fire station, where the town's uptown fire engine and ladder truck had been pulled out to make room in the equipment bay for the voting stations.

A mass of people were outside the door leading into the fire station, all of them holding signs or placards for their various candidates. There was nothing else on the ballot today save presidential candidates, and sample ballots were pasted up at the doors leading into the fire station. I spared them a quick glance as I hobbled up to the doorway.

On one ballot, there would be one name listed, that of the current president, who was running unopposed. And on the other ballot, besides a host of minor candidates, the list would include those names that I had become so familiar with these past months. Senator Jackson Hale, Senator Nash Pomeroy, Congressman Clive Wallace, and retired general Tucker Grayson. The volunteers were laughing and talking and were trying to make eye contact with us few voters as we trickled in, and they all stood behind orange tape, strung along some sawhorses on loan from the Tyler Highway Department.

Among the people were two Tyler police officers, making sure that the campaign workers kept their distance—New Hampshire is very strict on anyone hassling voters as they enter their polling station—and one of them turned and said, "Hey, Lewis. What in hell happened to your leg?"

It was Detective Sergeant Diane Woods, of course, and I went over to her and said, "A slip and a fall. Nothing too serious. How are you?"

She was smiling. "Great. Voters are fine, the campaign folks are minding us and keeping behind the barrier, and I'm making some good detail time. Man, the money I made off these people this year...Kara and I are going to have fun trying to spend it all."

"Glad to hear it," I said.

I was going to say something else, but she gently grasped my upper arm. "Would love to chat with you some more, friend, but I have to at least pretend I'm working."

"Understood."

She said, "Anyway, it's good to see you. Lunch next week?"

"Sure," I said, and as I went into the fire station, I think Diane called out, asking me how Annie was, but I pretended not to hear her.

Inside was the low murmur of people working, of democracy in action. On a table to the left was a large blowup of two sample ballots, and overhead were two cardboard signs. A-N, one said, O-Z, the other said, each with an arrow pointing in opposite directions. I got in the A-N line and moved forward, as the line went up to a table where three older women of a certain age sat, with large bound volumes before them. The supervisors of the checklist, making sure that only registered voters got to play at democracy today.

When I reached the table, one lady, wearing black-rimmed eyeglasses with a gold chain hanging from the stems, said, "Name?"

"Cole, Lewis Cole."

She opened up the book and with a ruler in hand went down the list of names. She stopped and looked up. "Address?"

"Mailing address is Box 919, Tyler. Physical address is Eight Atlantic Avenue, Tyler Beach."

She nodded and said, "Mr. Cole, you're listed here as an Independent. That means you can either have a Democrat or Republican ballot. Which do you want?"

I told her and she passed the ballot over and said, "Step over there, and one of the poll workers will assist you."

"Thanks," I said, and as I made my way out, she said, "By the way, I love your magazine columns."

I almost froze in my tracks. It had been many, many months since I had heard anything remotely like that.

"I'm glad you do," I said, and I meant every word of it.

In the equipment bay of the fire station, voting booths had been set up, made of a metal framework and covered with stiff canvas, the material being painted red, white, and blue. An older man of a certain age, wearing a VETERANS OF FOREIGN WARS cap, waved me along to an empty booth. I went in with my ballot. Before me was a metal counter that didn't seem too sturdy, and a pencil attached to the booth with a length of string and some tape.

I held the ballot on the counter, examined it, and in the space of five seconds made my mark.

I opened up the curtain and went down to the end of the equipment bay, where a large wooden box, almost the size of a steamer trunk, had been placed on yet another table. The hinged box was locked, and four or five sets of eyes watched me as I slipped my ballot inside an opening at the top.

There. I had voted. And in the simplicity that is Tyler, New Hampshire, the ballots would be hand-counted in front of election officials and representatives from all the campaigns, and the number of ballots would be matched against the registrar's tally of how many voters had come in. A simple arrangement, and one that didn't lead to conspiracy theories about manipulated electronic voting machines, or, God help us, hanging, pregnant, or swinging chads.

It was a method that had been used in Tyler for two hundred years—that same old wooden box—and I hoped it would still be in use two hundred years hence. I went back to the registrar's desk and ensured that my voter affiliation went back to Independent.

And then I took a last glance and listened to the soft murmurs of the people coming in and out of the fire station, the voters here in this small town, one of scores of small towns in my quirky home state, and it felt all right.

Even with the events of the past week, with what I had learned about Senator Hale and his wife, and what I had learned about me and Annie, and the oppo research guy for General Grayson and Felix's own work, and the signs and the phone calls and the mailings, it was all right. This is what counted. Free people coming in for a free election, in a small step to choose our next president. It was loud and unpredictable and vulgar in so many ways, but it ended up working, more often than not.

Near the exit at the rear of the fire station was Paula Quinn, reporter's notebook in hand, and I smiled at her as I approached.

"I thought all you nasty members of the fourth estate weren't allowed inside this sacred precinct," I said.

"Maybe so, but I have pull with the town counsel, as you know. And I'm being very polite, asking a handful of typical voters what they thought of today's primary."

I waited and said, "Well?"

"Well, what?"

"Aren't you going to ask me anything?"

She laughed. "Didn't you hear what I said? I'm looking for a typical voter. You are anything but typical."

"Maybe so, but look who's talking. How's the Nash Pomeroy campaign treating you?"

"The death threats have subsided just a bit, but my word, I owe you a big thanks for that tip, Lewis. It's really worked out for me."

"How's that?"

"You name it—CNN, NBC, Fox—I've been on most of the cable and news channels talking about my story. Millions of people saw me, Lewis. Millions! And just this morning, I got a phone call from a publishing house in New York wanting to know if I can do a quickie book about the primary and its history. Is that fun or what? My very first book."

"Sounds like lots of fun, Paula. I hope it works out for you."

Another smile, a touch on my arm. "I owe you. Big-time."

"Just make sure I get an autographed copy, and we're even."

"Deal."

So I left the fire station and went out in the cold, where an earnest young man who wouldn't take no for an answer claimed to be working for the Voter Resource Group, or something like that, and forced an exit poll questionnaire in my hand. I didn't feel like arguing or fighting, so I took a few minutes to fill out the form on a table set up in the parking lot, and put it in a box to be counted, tabulated, and presented as a story during tonight's evening newscasts on the primary and exit polls, where various pundits would try to decipher the results and explain the Meaning of It All.

As I put the survey form in the box, I hoped other Tyler voters and voters in the rest of the state took my lead, for I told the poll takers that I was a gay woman, between fifty and sixty years of age, making less than ten thousand dollars a year, and that my most pressing concern this election year was deep sea fishing rights. Oh, and to wrap things up, I told them that I had voted for a dead man: Gus Hall, head of the Communist party of the United States.

Democracy in action. Sometimes it ain't pretty, but it sure can be fun.

A FEW MINUTES LATER, I caught up with Felix, who was standing outside his borrowed Highlander. He was talking to two young women whose campaign signs were hanging by their sides, ignored and forgotten, while he chatted them up. They both had long hair—one blond, the other brunette—and he looked at me and said something to the young ladies, and they went back to their assigned tasks.

I got inside the Highlander and Felix joined me, and I said, "What is it with you?"

He laughed. "Just keeping my skills in shape. That's all."

He closed the door and started up the engine, and I said, "Hold on for a second, will you?"

"Sure,"

I looked at the voters coming out of the fire station, two or three at a time, and I thought about what it had been like inside. People voting, people coming together, people doing what was right, what had to be done...

There. There it was.

Something small in the grand scheme of things, but something, if I was lucky, could be accomplished before the end of the day.

I turned to Felix. "Feel like keeping other skills in shape?"

"Depends. What do you have in mind?"

"I need to make something right. I'll need you, and I'll need somebody else."

"Who's this somebody else?"

"Someone you've met before."

"Oh," Felix said. "Does he know he's being volunteered?"

"No, but I don't think he cares."

"Where does he live?"

"Right now, in a cooler in a storage facility in Massachusetts." Felix's face was impassive and stayed that way for a bit, and then he grinned. "See? Always told you that a body could come in handy. What do you have in mind?"

"Head south and I'll tell you," I said. "And another thing. You're going to get a videotape in the mail, either today or tomorrow."

"I am, am I," he said, pulling out of the parking lot. "And what's that about?"

"I'll tell you that, too," I said. "Plus how I got my leg dinged up."

Felix said, "Damn, you better speak fast. It doesn't take that long to get to Salisbury."

"I'll do my best," I said, and then I began talking.

SEVERAL HOURS later my hands were sore, and my knee was throbbing like a son of a bitch, but I was back in the Lafayette House, and back in the office of Paul Jeter. He didn't look too happy to see me, and I knew that his displeasure was going to deepen in the next few seconds or so.

"Well?" he said. "I agreed to see you because you said you had something to tell me, something of great importance to the Lafayette House. Get on with it."

"Sure, but first I need to know something from you. What's happened to Stephanie Sussex?"

"Who?"

Oh, so he was in the mood to play games. "You know who she is. Your gift store manager."

"Our former gift store manager."

"Why is she your former gift store manager?"

"I would imagine that's none of your business."

"Probably. But as a friend, I would really like to know."

"And I would really like to know why you're here. Mind telling me?"

"All right, I will," I said. I took a cell phone out of my pocket and flipped it open, manipulated a button or two, and passed it over to him. He held the cell phone with distaste, like I had pulled it out of a sack of dung, and then his expression really went south when he looked at the cell phone, and then looked at me.

"What's the meaning of this?"

"Recognize the room?" I asked.

"Of course. It's one of our suites. And who is this...man?"

I now held my cane in my hands, to have something to do with them, I guess, or to prevent my hands from shaking.

I said, "Who the man is doesn't really matter. What matters is the room that he's in. The room is registered to a Michael Marone. You and I both know that that name is a fake. The room actually belongs to a star Boston Celtics player. I don't have to say any more about that, now do I?"

Now his face was alternating between the paleness of shock and the redness of anger. It was an amazing thing to watch.

"You...you...who the hell is this man?"

I reached over and took the cell phone out of his hand. It belonged to Felix, and I had promised him I would bring it back to him, right after he had made some phone calls to contacts in Boston to find out certain bits of information that were turning out to be quite helpful.

"I don't know who this man is," I said. "But what I do know is this. He's dead. Quite dead. And he's in your hotel, and he's in the room of a star guest. All I need to do is to make a single phone call to a friend of mine in the Tyler Police Department, and a storm of publicity is going to descend upon this hotel like nothing you can imagine. Add in the fact that because of the primary, we have a large portion of national news media representatives in the area...you can just imagine what will happen. That Celtic's career will take a major hit. Any other prominent guests you have here will want to take their business elsewhere. And all this negative attention will no doubt mean the Lafayette House will be looking for a new manager before the end of the week."

I could see the emotions struggling underneath that expression, and it was vaguely repellent, like seeing two caged scorpions fight it out. Finally he seemed to catch his composure and he said, "How did you get that body up there without being seen?"

"Trade secret," I said.

He pondered that for a moment and said, "What do you want?"

"I want Stephanie Sussex to have her job back at the gift shop. I want her to get a nice little raise. And I want her job protected, so that in a month or six months or a year, she doesn't get laid off because of some sort of restructuring. You agree to that, and the body is out of here within a half hour, and nobody has to know anything. How does that sound?"

"How do I know I can trust you?"

"Because I'm such a quiet and considerate neighbor. Most of the time."

It looked like he wanted to spit at me but instead he said, "You have a deal, you bastard. Now get out of my office and get the hell out of my hotel."

I got up, leaning on my cane. "My pleasure."

I WAITED out in Felix's borrowed vehicle, in the rear service area of the Lafayette House, and eventually Felix came out with a laundry cart, whistling, it looked like. He maneuvered the cart to the rear of the Highlander and opened it up, and I stared straight ahead while Felix did his work back there. I wished I could have helped him, but I was still too damn sore. There was a thumping, and the sound of something being dragged across the carpeting of the vehicle, and then Felix climbed in and said, "What now?"

"Can you...can you place him somewhere?"

"Sure."

I handed over a business card. "Good. And when you're done, make a call from a pay phone...maybe in Maine or New York, if you're paranoid.

Just let the guy on the other end know what you've done and where Spenser can be found."

Felix took the card. "You sure?"

"Yes."

"This is the Secret Service agent who arrested you last week, right?"

"Right," I said. "But he's also the Secret Service agent who arranged to have me pulled from the ocean yesterday."

Felix pocketed the card. "Consider it done."

FELIX MADE the short drive to take me home, and riding in the rear, nice and quiet, was the mysterious Spenser Harris, ending up who knows where. I asked Felix just that question and he said, "Let me worry about that. All right? You'll see it in the newspapers soon enough, I'm sure. Just remember this. Uncle Felix knew best...never throw away a body unless you know you don't have a need for it."

"But at the time, I didn't know that."

"Which is why I know best," and he glanced back for a moment, adding, "though I sure as hell didn't think this poor son of a bitch would be traveling so much."

"I'm sure he's not complaining."

Felix said, "You think? Now. Here you go. Need a hand getting inside?"

"Nope," I said, opening the door to the cold air and the sound of the ocean and the sight of my home. "I can make do."

"Glad to see that. Now it's time to go home and see who the hell won today."

I turned and smiled before shutting the door. "Don't you know who won today?"

"No, I don't. Do you?"

"Sure," I said, and as I closed the door, I called out, "The American people."

When I got inside, I found that there were five messages on my answering machine, four of which were frantic calls from the various campaigns to make sure I had voted, and if I hadn't voted, a quick call would mean I could get a ride to the polls, right up to the last minute. Not a problem at all, Mr. Cole, so please do call us if you can, they all said. I deleted all four of those messages, and I took my time listening to the fifth one, the one that meant very much to me. The phone message had poor quality, like it had been made in a very loud and very empty space, and as it started, it turned out that my guess was right.

"Hey, Lewis, it's Annie," her tired voice began. "I'm at the Manchester airport. Things are closing down here at campaign headquarters, and you know what? I've changed my mind. I'm off to South Carolina after all."

I closed my eyes. Her voice had gotten a bit shaky at those last few words. Even amid the ambient noise of the airport terminal, I could hear the intake of breath as she went on with her message.

"Don't take offense...and please, believe me, it has nothing to do with you not being with me last night at the rally. I know something important must have happened, and I know you want to tell me all about it...but I don't want to talk things out. I'm tired of talking. I like doing things. I like accomplishing things. And I helped accomplish a lot here in the state these past few weeks. And to see everybody pack up and start preparing for the next battle...I didn't want to abandon them. Oh, hell, I do want to be with you, but these people...I'm part of something now, something I want to see through. And...well, it's like this, Lewis. I'm going to South Carolina because I believe in something, something very important to me. Something that I'm ready to give up my schooling and my career and other things for, to do what I have to do. As for you I don't know what you believe in, Lewis. I just don't know. Do you? Do you believe in something?"

She coughed and her voice quickened. "Well. They're calling my flight. You take care...and I'm sure we'll talk sometime. And I know I'll be back to see you soon. Just not now. Bye."

I held the phone for a bit, and hung it up, and just looked outside at the wide and unforgiving ocean.

What do you believe in? she had asked. What do you believe in.

And what I wanted to say was this: I believe in you, Annie, and I believe in your dedication to the man you want to become president, and because of that, I kept secret what happened to me and his wife and his wife's lover, so that I wouldn't destroy a campaign that was so important to you.

That's what I believe in.

I listened to the message one more time, erased it, and then spent the next few hours on the couch, watching the various campaign coverage. I didn't eat, didn't drink, just kept in view what was going on with all the pollsters, pundits, and talking heads.

I paid particular attention to the representatives from the different campaigns, for like Paula Quinn had predicted a few days earlier, each and every one of them had declared victory.

Nice to be so sure.

Oh, how I envied them that.

21

The day after the primary, freezing rain set in, and I almost slipped twice in my driveway, going up to get my newspapers, even while using my cane. The lobby of the Lafayette House was full of reporters, campaign staffers, and other various primary-related folk, all trying to get out of town to the next leg of this circus called democracy, and I ignored them all as I went into the gift shop. Stephanie Sussex was there, smiling at me, back at her old job, and for a bit I felt good. I had finally made some amends to someone.

I went to pay for my morning papers and Stephanie refused to take my bills. "Are you kidding?" she said. "Not after what you did for me so I could get my job back."

"How do you know I had anything to do with that?" I asked. Her eyes flashed at me. "Don't think I'm stupid," she said. "I got fired because Paul learned I had been through the surveillance tapes. The fact I got my job back in just over a day...I'm sure you had something to do with it. I'm positive."

I smiled as I put the papers under my arm. "Maybe so...but I have to keep a secret."

She looked about her and lowered her voice. "So. What did you do? Hurt him? Threaten him?"

I shook my head. "Nope. I just pointed out the error of his ways, and he was eager to cooperate."

That made her laugh. "Must have been a pointer made of steel, aimed at the little bit of flesh inside him called a heart. You go on home, now, and stay out of the rain. All right?"

"Sure," I said, and as I turned to make my way out of the gift shop, Stephanie murmured something and I said, "Did you say something?"

Her face looked like I had caught her at something, and she said, "Um...just a little saying, Lewis. Something I learned in catechism class, many years ago. A righteous man will get his rewards, both in heaven and on earth, and I was saying I was sure there were many rewards waiting for you. For what you did for me."

I nodded in appreciation. "Thanks, Stephanie. I appreciate that."

She waved a hand. "Go on. I'll see you tomorrow...and don't bother bringing any money, all right?"

"You've got it."

Outside in the lobby, I made my way to the doorway and then stopped. The freezing rain was coming down hard, sweeping across the parking lot, drenching those few guests coming in, holding up umbrellas or newspapers over their heads. The lobby was emptying out and even though I didn't feel any particular affection for the primary and what it had spawned, I could sense a taste of loneliness, of emptiness, as these driven people left my fair state and went somewhere else.

So I stood there, just watching the rain fall. I suppose I should have put the papers under my coat and worked my way down to my house to watch the news of the post-primary, to see the talking heads at work, to build a fire and hunker down and be safe and alone in my home.

Like before.

That's what I should have done.

To go home, be safe, be quiet, be alone. Like before.

But instead, I went to a nearby bank of phones, and made a phone call, and I was lucky for the very first time this day, as a familiar and friendly voice answered.

I said, "Felix?"

"Of course. Who else?"

I smiled at his teasing voice. "Just checking. I need a favor. Like, right now."

He said, "Yesterday wasn't enough, what we did with Paul Jeter and your fake Secret Service agent?"

"Oh, it was plenty, but I'd like to think you got some professional experience out of it, experience you can use down the road."

"Maybe so," he said, laughing. "Maybe so. What do you need?"

"Ride to the airport."

"Which one? Manchester or Logan?"

"Don't know yet. I'll figure it out by the time you get here."

"Where's here? Aren't you home?"

"Nope," I said. "I'm in the lobby of the Lafayette House, and that's where I want you to pick me up."

"Right now? Aren't you going to pack?"

"No, I'm not. I need to get to the airport, and I need to get to South Carolina. Today."

He laughed again. "All right, Lewis. I'll be there in just a bit. And if I can be so bold to ask, what the hell is in South Carolina?"

I looked at the cold, driving rain, and thought about a warmer place, a nicer place, and I said, "My reward. I need to get to my reward."

"Good for you," Felix said, and after hanging up the phone, I just waited, and no doubt the people coming in and out of the Lafayette House wondered about the smile on my face, but some secrets, I would always keep.

DEADLY COVE
Book #7 of the Lewis Cole Series

In the commotion of an anti-nuclear protest, a sudden eruption of gunfire pushes Lewis Cole into a race against time.

While covering an anti-nuclear protest, magazine columnist and former Department of Defense research analyst, Lewis Cole, is thrust into chaos as shots ring out among the crowd, leaving Lewis's friend injured and a charismatic activist dead.

Determined to seek justice for his friend and unsatisfied with leaving the investigation solely in the hands of the authorities, Lewis delves into the background of the murdered activist and the anti-nuclear protesters that have gathered on the picturesque New Hampshire seacoast. The protesters, willing to resort to violence, are determined to seize control of a nearby nuclear power plant and halt its production. As Lewis digs into the case, he uncovers hidden connections among those advocating for nuclear power and the passionate protestors opposing it.

But as Lewis closes in on the truth, he becomes the target of someone desperate to silence him, putting his life in constant peril. With his own future hanging in the balance, Lewis must expose the underlying conspiracy and put his resolve to the test.

Deadly Cove, the seventh novel in New York Times bestselling author Brendan DuBois' Lewis Cole series, is a captivating crime thriller perfect for fans of James Patterson and Michael Connelly.

Get your copy today at
severnriverbooks.com

AFTERWORD

This was a fun novel to work on—with research already having been done—but I faced a particular challenge in writing this one, and it's because of one of the subplots: romance. Yeah, romance, the lovey-dovey, birds & bees stuff, all that kissing...ack! Okay, maybe a bit over the top, but I was conscious in writing the sex scenes that not only would close friends and family be reading it, but my Mom as well. Yes, even at this stage of my career with lots of published novels and stories under my belt, I still worry about my Mom's response.

Part of the challenge in writing a detective novel with a subplot is dealing with the romantic partner. They can't be window dressing. They have to be part of the book, part of the story, and part of the action. I like to think in PRIMARY STORM, I pulled that off.

So. What happens next for Annie Wynn and Lewis Cole? Not for me to say, but it's for you to find out in the next book in the series, DEADLY COVE.

And as before, I'd like to make note of some little in-jokes and references in PRIMARY STORM. When Lewis goes to meet Barbara Hale at the local bookstore, there's a note of a certain bestselling book with the face of the Mona Lisa on the cover. That book, of course, is THE DA VINCI CODE, written by friend and fellow author Dan Brown. And speaking of bookstores...the one I described here does, exist, though not in my fictional Tyler, but in the very real town of Exeter, N.H.

The scene where Lewis is visited by campaign workers in the middle of a raging snowstorm actually happened to me in 1992. During a blinding snowstorm at my apartment, there was a knock one night. I answered the door and found a snow-covered volunteer for the Paul Tsongas campaign, eagerly handing out a campaign pamphlet written by the former Massachusetts senator. After he left, I looked out my apartment window, and saw him in the heavy and driving snow, going from one door to the next.

That brief encounter has always stayed with me, and I was glad to put it in PRIMARY STORM.

ACKNOWLEDGMENTS

The author wishes to express his thanks and appreciation to his wife, Mona Pinette, for her sure touch as an editor, to his St. Martin's Press editor Ruth Cavin, and her assistant, Toni Plummer, and to his agent, Liza Dawson. Special thanks as well to the dedicated staff at both the Stratham-Newfields Veterinary Hospital of Newfields, New Hampshire, and the Harvest Hills Animal Shelter of Fryeburg, Maine. And thanks, too, to those members of the news media and political campaigns who bring a special sort of madness to my home state every four years.

ABOUT THE AUTHOR

Brendan DuBois is the award-winning New York Times bestselling author of twenty-six novels, including the Lewis Cole series. He has also written *The First Lady* and *The Cornwalls Are Gone* (March 2019), coauthored with James Patterson, *The Summer House* (June 2020), and *Blowback*, September 2022. His next coauthored novel with Patterson, *Countdown*, will be released in March 2023. He has also published nearly two hundred short stories.

His stories have won three Shamus Awards from the Private Eye Writers of America, two Barry Awards, two Derringer Awards, and the Ellery Queen Readers Award. He has also been nominated for three Edgar Allan Poe awards from the Mystery Writers of America.

In 2021 he received the Edward D. Hoch Memorial Golden Derringer for Lifetime Achievement from the Short Mystery Fiction Society.

He is also a "Jeopardy!" gameshow champion.

Sign up for Brendan's reader list at
severnriverbooks.com

Printed in the United States
by Baker & Taylor Publisher Services